Hard to Handle

The Walkers of Coyote Ridge, 4

DEAD HEAT RANCH
Boots Optional
Betting on Grace
Overnight Love

DEVIL'S BEND
Chasing Dreams
Vanishing Dreams

MISPLACED HALOS
Protected in Darkness
Salvation in Darkness
Bound in Darkness

OFFICE INTRIGUE
Office Intrigue
Intrigued Out of the Office
Their Rebellious Submissive
Their Famous Dominant
Their Ruthless Sadist
Their Naughty Student
Their Fairy Princess

PIER 70
Reckless
Fearless
Speechless
Harmless
Clueless

SNIPER 1 SECURITY
Wait for Morning
Never Say Never
Tomorrow's Too Late

SOUTHERN BOY MAFIA/DEVIL'S PLAYGROUND
Beautifully Brutal
Without Regret
Beautifully Loyal
Without Restraint

STANDALONE NOVELS
Unhinged Trilogy
A Million Tiny Pieces
Inked on Paper
Bad Reputation
Bad Business

NAUGHTY HOLIDAY EDITIONS
2015
2016

Hard to Handle

THE WALKERS OF COYOTE RIDGE, 4

NICOLE EDWARDS

Published by Nicole Edwards Limited
PO Box 1086, Pflugerville, Texas 78691

Hard to Handle
The Walkers of Coyote Ridge, 4
Nicole Edwards

This is a work of fiction. Names, characters, businesses, places, events and incidents either are the products of the author's imagination or used in a fictitious manner. Any resemblance to actual persons, living or dead, business establishments, events, or locals is entirely coincidental.

COVER DETAILS:
Image: © Wander Aguiar | WanderBookClub.com
Model: Jonny James and Desiree Crossman
Design: © Nicole Edwards Limited

INTERIOR DETAILS:
Formatting: Nicole Edwards Limited
Editing: Blue Otter Editing | BlueOtterEditing.com

ISBN:
Ebook 9781939786821 | Paperback 9781939786814

SUBJECTS:
BISAC: FICTION / Romance / Contemporary
BISAC: FICTION / Romance / General

Dedication

To Jonny James

You are one of the nicest, most genuine guys I have ever met. I have had the honor of working with you and hanging out with you. If you don't know it already, you are an inspiration to many. Keep being you!

Dear Reader,

This story contains elements of domestic abuse. If you or someone you love is in an abusive relationship, please seek help.

National Domestic Violence Hotline

1-800-799-SAFE (7233) | 1-800-787-3224 (TTY)

Chapter One

WITH THE SONG BLARING THROUGH THE SPEAKERS, a Friday night with absolutely nothing to do but chill laid out before him, Lynx Caine was feeling no pain. He was minutes away from a cold beer with his name on it and good friends to hang out with. "When the line froze, what did I see?" Lynx belted out loudly. There was nothing better than a little Machine Gun Kelly rocking it out with Kid Rock.

"A bad motherfucker standin' next to me."

With September officially underway and August finally behind him, Lynx was ready to get his drink on, and he damn sure wasn't opposed to getting his knuckles scraped a little if some smart-mouthed fucker wanted to go a round or two. With all the shit going on, it was safe to say, stress was a prominent word in his vocabulary. Between some crazy psychopath terrorizing his cousin's girl, and said girl gearing up to blow the whistle on that asshole, Lynx didn't think it was going to get better anytime soon.

But what the hell did he know?

Bad, bad motherfucker 'til the day I die.

Pulling into Reagan's Bar, Kid Rock screaming about being a bad motherfucker, Lynx felt some of the strain ease from his shoulders. This was his fucking theme song. It rang true and he'd damn sure earned the reputation in this small town.

To make it even better, when that song ended, good ol' Brantley Gilbert started rasping about being hell on wheels. Lynx sang along, hopefully doing the song justice. He'd heard more than once that he had the same raspy tone as the kickass country boy who had rednecks everywhere kickin' it in the sticks. Not that he intended to change his career or anything. A singer he was not.

However, Lynx couldn't deny the redneck part. That was a part of who he was and he was damn proud of it.

He drove his big Ford F-250 around to the side of the building.

"Damn. Gonna be a good night." After all, the parking lot was full.

Not at all surprising. Not in Embers Ridge on a Friday night. Reagan's was the hangout for the low-key crowd. She served only beer and pretzels, a few tunes cranking out of the jukebox, and the entertainment consisted of darts or pool. Truth was, no one there needed more than that. Hell, they usually needed little more than some good conversation.

And he suspected there were quite a few people who had come out tonight to get the scoop.

According to the rumor mill, his cousin had officially hooked up with one sweet little filly *and* the big, tough sheriff of their little backwoods town.

Not one or the other.

Both of them.

Little did everyone know, but it wasn't a rumor. Lynx knew it to be true.

And in the small ranching community of Embers Ridge, that was some serious headline news. Lynx had figured Wolfe would go balls to the wall when he did finally settle down. Although he'd never witnessed it, Lynx had always suspected his cousin went both ways.

"Good for him," he muttered to himself.

As long as Wolfe was happy, Lynx didn't give a fuck whose boots were beside the man's bed.

Of course, the town was abuzz with questions, everyone wanting to know how it had happened and what it meant. No one seemed to believe that their little triad was real. Didn't it figure? If it walked like a duck, quacked like a duck, most people just assumed it was a duck. Here in Embers Ridge, it seemed that if it walked like a duck and quacked like a duck, it was probably a cow in costume. The obvious couldn't possibly be real, but the bullshit they made up was.

Granted, Lynx wasn't sticking his nose all up in his cousin's shit, and he damn sure wasn't about to contribute to the gossip pool. He had more important things to worry about.

Namely, the hot little number who ran his favorite bar.

She'd been avoiding him like the plague as of late. Not that he could really blame her. Ever since he'd established residence outside her house a couple of weeks ago, Reagan Trevino hadn't been happy with him. Shit, his *body* hadn't been happy with him. At six foot three, he wasn't at all comfortable sleeping in the front seat of his truck. But Reagan and his tired-ass body would have to deal because Lynx wasn't going to sit back while the crazy fucker who'd killed a detective not even three weeks ago was on the loose. He didn't give a shit if his Walker cousins were now leading the charge against the fucking chief of police of Houston. Lynx wasn't taking any chances. If that fucker thought for one second he was going to do harm to someone Lynx cared about, the asshole would have to go through him first.

Realizing there was no parking to be had, Lynx pulled his truck into the field adjacent to the building, shut off the engine, and hopped out.

"What's up, Lynx?"

Turning toward the sound of his name, Lynx grinned. "Hey, Jimmy Don. How's the ol' lady?"

"Hella good, man." Jimmy Don's smile went wide as the man continued to move toward his truck. "Baby's comin' any day now."

"Congrats, bro!" Lynx made his way to the front doors, continuing to face Jimmy Don across the parking lot. "Holler when she pops that one out. We'll grab a beer to celebrate."

"Sure thing."

With a quick wave, Lynx turned toward his destination.

Stepping inside, he took a deep breath, then let it out slowly.

The tiny, wood-framed bar smelled the same as always. Like beer and stale pretzels, not to mention sweat and a whole lot of verbal bullshit. Sure, that shit had a smell, too. He could usually sniff it out a mile away and it seemed tonight the aroma was extra potent.

"Hey, brotha'," Wolfe greeted from his spot at the bar.

"What's up, hoss?" Lynx gave his cousin a knuckle bump. "Thanks," he told Reagan when she passed him over a beer.

He let his eyes track her from one side to the other. Of course, the stubborn minx didn't respond. But her cute little nose lifted, and the defiant tilt to her chin made his dick hard. Then again, *everything* about Reagan Trevino made his dick hard. All five foot five sweet inches of her.

"We need to talk, Reagan. Come on, babe. *Please.*"

Lynx's gaze snapped to the opposite end of the bar, where he saw Billy Watson leaning on the wooden top, begging like a little bitch. Lynx glanced at Wolfe, who shot him a quick eye roll. Turning back to the scene, Lynx gave them his full attention.

"You know I'm not leavin' till we do," Billy droned.

Looked as though the fucker had finally realized what he'd lost when he let Reagan go a solid month ago. It appeared he was back to the same old bullshit, trying to get in her good graces and convince her to take him back.

Lynx wanted to punch him in the face. The little pussy didn't deserve Reagan. Hell, he didn't deserve any woman. He had absolutely no respect and that shit was what pissed Lynx off the most.

"Come on, honey. I know you ain't serious. You love me. Don't deny it. It's time for you to come back home. Put the past in the past."

The *past* he was referring to was the pussy Billy had been getting for the past thirty-three days — yep, he'd counted — ever since Reagan up and moved out on the asshole. The guy had no qualms about flaunting the fact that he was making up for lost time with any woman who'd give him the time of day.

A killing rage burned just beneath Lynx's skin, his need to do some serious bodily harm ratcheting up a few hundred notches. When a man loved a woman, or even *claimed* to love a woman, he just didn't do stupid shit like that. Ever.

"I told you, Billy. I'm done," Reagan hissed, apparently trying to keep her voice down. "Now, just leave it be."

"Whatever." Billy huffed. "That's bullshit and you know it. Quit fuckin' around and just come home."

Reagan leaned over the bar, getting right up in Billy's face. "It's not my home," she snapped. "I'm done. It's over. Get used to it."

Lynx waited, counting down silently in his head. He knew Billy, knew the man's temper would get the best of him. Lynx had spent the better part of a decade watching as Billy treated Reagan like shit, then sitting back and dealing when she took the sorry fucker back.

As much as he'd wanted to intervene, Lynx knew it wasn't his place. Then or now.

Good news was it looked as though she might be done this time for good.

Lynx could only hope, because it was high time he moved on with his life, and the only way he intended to do that was to have that woman in his bed, where she belonged. However, he wasn't talking for only one night. His intentions toward her were along the lines of forever and a day.

The hardest part was going to be convincing her.

Fortunately, Lynx was always up for a challenge.

"What the fuck you lookin' at?"

Lynx allowed his gaze to slip to the right of Reagan. That was when he realized Billy was talking to him. Unable to help himself, Lynx smiled. "A hairy asshole." Lynx glanced back at his cousin. "Right? That's what you see, too?"

"Yep," Wolfe agreed. "A hairy asshole with teeth."

Lynx turned back to Billy.

It was Friday night.

Everyone in this town knew that the Caines could generally be persuaded out to the parking lot for a little throw-down action. Lynx was more than willing to clear the way for him and Billy to go outside. He'd been itching to beat the guy's ass for a long damn time.

"Don't do it, Billy," Reagan warned.

"Fuck you," he muttered. "I shoulda known you were fuckin' him. Prob'ly been fuckin' him the whole time we were together."

Same shit, different day. Billy always took that route, no matter what. Truthfully, it was getting old.

"Ain't that right?" Billy asked Lynx directly. "You been lettin' her hoover your dick while she was hooverin' mine?"

No one said Lynx was known for his social skills.

Before the dickhead could draw another breath, Lynx was in Billy's face, his fist in the asshole's shirt as he lifted him off the ground. "What'd I tell you about talkin' about her like that?" Lynx dropped him to his feet. "Let's take this outside. You and me. Once and for all."

"Fuck you," Billy spat.

"You get off talkin' shit about a woman? That make you feel like a big boy?" Lynx glared down at him, the rage building inside him. "Make you feel like your dick's bigger'n it is?"

"You been thinkin' 'bout my dick?" Billy countered with a grin that showed off yellowed teeth and the lip full of dip he was known to have.

What the fuck Reagan ever saw in him, Lynx would never know.

"Y'all hear that?" Billy hollered, turning toward the other patrons filling the small bar. "Lynx Caine's over here talkin' 'bout my dick. Maybe he swings both ways like his cousin."

Lynx fought the urge to roll his eyes. "If I did, I can tell ya, I'd have better taste than that."

Billy flipped him off.

Take a swing at his family, Lynx would be the first to beat your ass.

Treat a woman with disrespect, Lynx would be the first to pound you into the ground.

Raise your hand to a child or an animal, Lynx would be the first to knock your front teeth out.

But talk shit to him … Lynx could take it. He wasn't as reactive as he'd been as a teenager. If Billy Watson wanted to prove his IQ was the same as his boot size by talking smack, Lynx was more than happy to let him.

Waving him off, Lynx strode back to his beer. "There's a reason assholes don't have mouths," he said, making sure his voice was loud enough for Billy to hear.

When Billy took a lunge toward him, Reagan intervened, coming to stand between them.

And a second later, when Billy grabbed her arm and jerked her out of the way, Lynx lost every single ounce of his sanity.

"TOUCH HER AGAIN AND YOU'LL BE SHOVIN'" your toothbrush up your ass to brush your teeth," Lynx snarled at Billy, his emerald-green eyes spitting fire.

Lynx Caine was the ultimate badass.

Well, at least by Embers Ridge standards anyway.

Then again, Reagan Trevino was pretty damn sure that reputation would hold up anywhere he went.

But there was more to Lynx than most people realized. He'd proven that a minute ago when he'd walked away from Reagan's ex-boyfriend when he started trash-talking. Lynx could tolerate a lot of shit. He wasn't the same hotheaded guy he'd been back in the day.

Oh, sure, there probably wasn't a Friday night that passed when the man wasn't involved in some sort of brawl. Guys liked to rile him up just to watch him lose his shit. However, they didn't usually do it twice.

In all fairness, Lynx wasn't usually the one starting shit, but he was damn sure willing to finish it. And everyone in this town knew that a man should never touch a woman out of anger when Lynx was around. It was the fastest way to find yourself in the hospital.

Two seconds after Billy grabbed her arm, his fingers digging painfully into her flesh, Lynx ripped Billy off the floor and practically threw him out the door.

The one thing Reagan asked of her customers was that they take the fighting outside. She worked hard for what she had, and admittedly, she didn't have much. Nothing more than the fifteen-hundred-square-foot bar and the permits required to sell and consume beer on the premises. Her personal effects were limited to mostly her clothes and a couple of shotguns. Reagan didn't need much, but what she did have, she fully intended to keep.

Therefore, the boys who wanted to throw down had to take that shit outside.

The Caines had always respected that request. Always.

"Someone call the sheriff!" Billy hollered as Lynx picked him up off the floor with one big, tattooed hand.

"Call the sheriff and you'll answer to me," Wolfe announced, moving toward his cousin.

Since the sheriff happened to be Reagan's brother, not to mention Wolfe and Amy's lover, she figured people weren't going to defy him. Didn't matter anyhow, Rhys always managed to make his way to the bar about the time the boys decided to knuckle up.

Because this pertained to her, Reagan couldn't help but try to calm the waters before the storm raged out of control. After all, she didn't want to see Lynx go to jail. And if it was up to Billy, that was exactly where he'd spend the night.

"Lynx!" Reagan called after him.

The man stopped and turned around, his eyes hard as they narrowed on her.

"Can I talk to you for a minute?"

He shook his head. "After."

"No. Now." Reagan wasn't intimidated by Lynx the way most people were.

He didn't scare her because she knew he would never hurt her. He wasn't built that way.

In fact, because of that — and many other reasons — Reagan was probably more in love with him than anything else. Not that she would tell *him* that. She might have the hots for the sexy, tattooed country boy, but she definitely wasn't looking to spend her days and nights with a man who went through women more often than he changed underwear. She'd spent *far* too long dealing with Billy and his bullshit, which wasn't limited to his infidelity, either. However, he damn sure hadn't been faithful. Not for a minute.

Not that Reagan thought Lynx was the cheating kind, but he'd proven his track record and *love 'em and leave 'em* was synonymous with Lynx.

Now that she'd been single for a whole whopping month, Reagan found it suited her just fine. Less bullshit, more time to watch Netflix.

Knowing he would follow, Reagan slipped down the narrow hall that led to the restroom. A second later, Lynx appeared in the dimly lit hallway.

Okay, so she probably could've picked a better location to have this conversation.

Lynx's dark eyebrows were angled down and his emerald-green eyes glittered with anger. It wasn't aimed at her, but it was there all the same.

"Don't fight him," she said, keeping her tone casual. "It's not worth it."

"Oh, it's worth it," he countered, reaching down and lifting her arm so he could inspect the spot where Billy had grabbed her.

She jerked out of his hold. It was a survival instinct. The man had put his hands on her once and she had never forgotten it. Her *body* had never forgotten how freaking good it felt for this man to touch her. And her *heart* had never forgotten just what being with him could be like. She seriously doubted she ever would forget it, either.

"Just leave it alone," she snapped.

"Why?" Lynx put one hand on the wall above her head.

He was significantly taller than she was, a hell of a lot bigger, too. But Reagan still wasn't intimidated by him. He could offer a pissed-off glare to any asshole in a five-mile radius, but the moment he turned his eyes on her, there was always something softer in them. Something she'd fought to ignore for longer than she cared to admit.

"'Cause I have no intention of bailin' your ass outta jail."

"Aww, darlin'," he crooned, leaning in so that he was far too close. "You worried about me?"

Reagan rolled her eyes and tried not to inhale through her nose. The man smelled so freaking good. He always did and it drove her absolutely crazy. Like sawdust and Irish Spring soap. No, it wasn't something expensive from a bottle, but it affected her all the same.

Another thing that drove her crazy was his lack of respect for her personal space. As he leaned in closer, Reagan had no choice but to back up against the wall. Her entire body hummed as he stood there, staring down at her as though he wanted to eat her for dessert.

She wanted him to. There was no denying that. But Reagan wasn't an idiot. If she thought she could get away with a short-term fling with Lynx, she might be up to the task. Well, except for the fact that he'd slept with damn near every woman in this town and a shit ton more who weren't from around here. Hell, she wasn't even sure his *divorce* was final.

Yep, and wasn't that the shit. Ol' Lynx Caine had up and married some two-bit hussy from fucking Austin, of all places.

The memory of him coming back to town announcing that he'd gotten hitched to that crazy bitch was like an ice bath to her nerves. It shocked her back to reality and caused her to slip out from under his arm.

"Just let it be, Lynx," Reagan told him, not looking back.

Making her way to the bar, Reagan searched the room until she found Billy. Wolfe was keeping him corralled in the corner.

Reagan locked eyes with her ex-boyfriend, then pointed to the doors. "Get out. You're not welcome in my bar."

"Oh, come *on*, Reag—"

"You heard the lady," Wolfe said, his tone ringing with amusement as he grabbed Billy by the shirt and shoved him toward the exit.

"You'll be sorry you did this, Reagan! Goddammit!"

She shook her head. "No. I'm sorry for a lotta things I've done" — mainly wasting nearly a decade of her life with a piece of crap who treated her like shit — "but not this."

Billy's eyes strayed to something over her shoulder at the same time Reagan felt the warmth of Lynx's body as he pressed up against her.

Even from here she could feel how hard his body was, how freaking warm his skin was.

Her traitorous heart skipped a beat and her belly fluttered.

"I ain't worried," Billy told Lynx. "You'll be tossin' her out like last week's garbage in a week tops," he snarled. "Like me, you'll get tired of fuckin' the skank."

Yeah. Okay.

For about three seconds there, Billy had been home free. He could've turned around, head held high, and walked right out that door…

Unfortunately for him, the asshole never did know when to shut up.

This time when Lynx went after him, Reagan didn't bother to stop him.

In fact, she silently egged him on.

Chapter Two

"DAMMIT, LYNX!" RHYS TREVINO SHOUTED. "I TAKE another right hook from you and I'll make sure you spend the night in jail!"

Lynx shoved Billy one last time before taking a step back, his anger burning white-hot. The damn sheriff always showed up and ruined shit for him.

"Chill," Rhys hissed, taking Lynx by the arm and pulling him farther away from Billy.

Lynx didn't even bother to put up a fight when Rhys went to cuff him. Spending the night in jail was definitely worth the ass-whooping he'd just dished out. It was quite possible Billy Watson would be walking with a limp for the rest of his sorry life.

"You're goddamn right I'm pressin' charges," Billy declared, talking to the deputy as he wiped blood from his lip. "The asshole attacked me."

"Just like always," Lynx stated, loving how he could so easily rile the pussy. "Cryin' like a bitch. You still breastfeedin', boy?"

"Fuck you," Billy spat before a devious smirk tilted his lips up in a snarl. "Not sure why you think you're all high and mighty. I ain't the one in cuffs."

Lynx didn't respond; he simply cocked an eyebrow, waiting for the rest.

Sure enough, he wasn't disappointed.

"And I ain't the one goin' to jail tonight. You are." Spittle flew from Billy's mouth. "And just think, while you're takin' it in the ass, I'll be fuckin' Reagan." Billy's lip curled up before he turned and spit on the ground. When he turned back, he was grinning. "Prob'ly just bend her over the back of the couch, that way I don't have to look at her face."

Lynx lunged and Billy stumbled backward. Before he could get close enough — cuffs be damned — Rhys put a hand on Lynx's chest.

Then Reagan's brother — the sheriff of Lee County — spun around to face Billy. "You wanna repeat that?" Rhys rumbled. "'Cause if you do, I'm gonna hand my badge and my gun over to Dean and I'm gonna be the one beatin' your ass into the ground. That's my fuckin' sister you're talkin' about."

"That's the problem with little boys these days," Wolfe stated. "No respect."

The heated glare Lynx's cousin gave Billy said that it wouldn't matter that Lynx was in the tank tonight. Wolfe was still out there.

"Maybe you wanna reconsider pressin' charges?" Dean questioned Billy as he pulled out his notepad. "'Fore you get your ass in any deeper?"

Billy met Lynx's eyes. Lynx cocked one eyebrow. He'd willingly go to jail, but he wouldn't be staying there indefinitely. They both knew it. And when he got out…

"I've got an idea."

Lynx's attention jerked over to Reagan as she sauntered over.

His mouth practically watered as she moved toward him, her dark brown eyes reflecting both frustration and amusement. Those damn low-slung jeans and the body-hugging T-shirt that just met the top of them made his dick twitch. The way her long dark hair hung over her shoulder had Lynx thinking about wrapping those silky strands around his fist while he fucked them both into oblivion.

Goddamn, she made him so fucking hard.

Damn sure didn't help that he'd spent ten fucking years wanting to get his hands on her.

When she got close enough, Reagan turned to Billy. "Why don't you drop the bullshit and I won't get a restrainin' order."

"I don't give a good goddamn about no restrainin' order," Billy retorted.

"Not even if it ensures you'll never come inside my bar again?" she asked, her dark eyebrows lifting. "'Cause I won't hesitate to kick your ass right out the next time you show up here. And I'm pretty sure half the town'll have my back."

That seemed to get Billy's attention. Although, Lynx had to wonder why Reagan hadn't refused to serve him until now.

"You wouldn't do that," Billy told her, although Lynx could tell he didn't believe his own words.

"Try me." She leaned closer but still kept her distance. "And when I go down to the sheriff's department to file that, I'll bail Lynx outta jail, too."

Billy glared, but for the first time all damn night, the fucker didn't have anything to say.

Thank God for small miracles.

"Fine," Billy huffed. "I ain't pressin' charges."

With one final glare in Lynx's direction, Billy stormed off.

When Rhys went to uncuff him, Reagan stopped him with a hand on her brother's arm. "Can I talk to him first? While he's cuffed?"

Rhys glanced between the two of them, but then backed away, turning to talk to Wolfe and Amy, who'd been standing off to the side watching the show.

"I'm likin' the direction this is goin'," Lynx told her, then lowered his voice and added, "Although I'd much prefer *you* were the one in cuffs."

An image of Reagan cuffed to his bed flashed through his mind, making him wince as his dick took up more space in his jeans.

"I wouldn't get too excited if I were you."

Lynx leaned against the deputy's squad car when Reagan moved into his personal space.

"Can we just call it even now?" she asked, her voice low, her expression blank.

"What?" He had no idea what she was talking about.

"You stop tryin' to mess with me, and I'll pretend that you're not gettin' on my last nerve. Then maybe we can both move on with our lives."

The hell he would. Lynx wasn't about to give up what he'd been waiting a hell of a long time for. However, he wasn't above putting the ball in her court. "That what you want?"

She stared back at him.

"'Cause I damn sure don't," he told her forcefully, leaning forward so he could get closer. "You can keep runnin' from me, girl. I'll just keep chasin'." He lowered his voice so only she could hear. "And the day you finally give in, you'll come to understand exactly why they call me a bad boy."

Her eyes widened, her mouth fell open, and Lynx was tempted to kiss her right there in front of half the town.

Yeah. That was what he thought. Reagan talked a good game, but when it came down to it, Lynx knew she was attracted to him. She was fighting it, sure, but she wanted him nonetheless.

"You sure you're not interested?" he asked casually, as though her answer didn't matter.

But just as quickly as she revealed her desire, Reagan regained her composure and leaned in closer. Close enough Lynx could smell her spicy, sexy scent.

"Do me a favor, Lynx?"

"Hmm?" he grumbled.

"Maybe try keepin' your dick in your pants for a while. And when that divorce is final, if you're still interested, perhaps I'll *think* about givin' you the time of day."

"Done." He could do that. No problem.

Reagan chuckled. "Right. Like it's even a possibility."

With that, she spun on her boot heel and headed back inside.

Boy, did he hate to see her leave, but he damn sure loved to watch her go.

KELLY JACKSON KEPT HIS HEAD LOW, NOT wanting anyone to spot him sitting in his car in the parking lot of the trashy little bar. This town was full of a bunch of idiots. If he was that damn sheriff, he would've rounded every damn one of them up and tossed their asses in jail. One reason he hated little hick towns like this.

He only had one reason for being there.

It wasn't the highlight of his week, that was for damn sure, but he knew he had to figure out a way to get his hands on Amy. However, that wasn't proving to be as easy as he'd thought it would be. Seemed she had a couple of bodyguards with her at all times. That damn sheriff and the guy who owned the furniture store where she worked. Plus, whoever's fucking truck that was parked outside her damn house every fucking night. Kelly had no idea who they were to her, but it seemed they were keeping an eye on her, too.

Hence the reason he was having to come up with another plan. Which meant studying her movements and finding the precise time to strike.

Soon.

Very, very soon.

"WHY DO MEN ALWAYS HAVE TO ACT like assholes?" Reagan muttered to herself as she wiped down the bar top.

They were getting ready to close, and as soon as she got the last of the customers out the door, she was more than ready to head home. Well, technically, it wasn't her home, but she was renting a room from Amy, which was the first opportunity she'd ever had to get out on her own since she moved in with Billy nearly six years ago. Amy's little farmhouse, even if it was lonely at times, had started to grow on her. On nights when Amy was there — which were rare — Reagan loved it. On nights when she was alone … well, she felt alone.

Not that she couldn't get used to it.

She would.

She'd spent plenty of nights by herself even when she'd been living with someone. More often than not, in fact.

"Looks like it's about that time," Amy said when she approached the bar.

Reagan looked up to see that there were only two people other than herself and Amy left in the bar. Wolfe and Lynx were sitting at a table near the door, deep in conversation.

"Yep. 'Bout that time." Reagan peered back at Amy. "Why don't you head on out? I've got it from here."

Amy smiled, then placed her apron beneath the bar.

"Oh, and Amy?"

"Hmm?"

"Take *both* of them with you."

Amy giggled. "Right. Like Lynx is going anywhere."

Reagan frowned. She'd figured as much, but she honestly wished he would go on about his life. Ever since the day the Houston detective had come to Embers Ridge to talk to Rhys, Lynx had been Reagan's shadow.

And sure, part of her was grateful in a way. After all, the detective had been killed that night, and only a couple of hours later, someone had tried to break into Amy's house while Reagan was there. They figured Lynx thwarted the guy's plan by showing up to warn Reagan.

That was only a few weeks ago.

But as she'd proven, Reagan could take care of herself. She'd been doing so for long enough now it was second nature. It wasn't like she had anyone to watch her back. Although her family was tight, they were still a little self-absorbed, which usually left Reagan out of their minds unless she was within their sight. And Billy... God, she didn't even want to get into how self-absorbed that man had been during their time together.

"You ready to lock it down?"

Reagan looked up to see Lynx standing on the other side of the bar.

Sex on a freaking stick. So tall, so sexy it was hard to look at him sometimes. And those damn tattoos that covered him from neck to knuckles were almost too much temptation. Yet she'd managed to ignore her body's disturbing reaction to him all this time.

She could see the dark shadow of a bruise marring his cheekbone. Looked as though Billy had gotten in at least one good hit. Granted, the asshole was far worse off than Lynx.

"You don't have to stick around," she told him, moving to the register to pull out the till.

She carried it to the back office, where she secured it in the fireproof safe, then locked the steel door on the office. Damn fools in this town had tried to break in one too many times. It was bad enough they raided her beer, but she worked hard for her money. She wasn't going to make it easy for them. And when she'd finally gotten tired of replacing the damn door, she'd had a bigger one installed three years ago. So far, no one had been able to break through and she hoped it stayed that way.

When she returned to the bar, Lynx was still there, his long, lean body propped against the wood, his eyes raking over her.

She nodded toward the door as she grabbed her truck keys.

"You don't have to follow me home, you know?" She figured it was a waste of breath, but she told him the same thing she'd told him every night since the first night he'd camped outside her house.

Reagan pulled the door shut and locked it. She could practically feel Lynx behind her.

When she turned to face him, he grinned.

"I don't *have* to do anything," he told her. "I *want* to."

Suddenly fueled by a raging case of frustration, Reagan stomped right up to Lynx. "Why?" she asked, trying to keep her tone civil but failing. "Why can't you just leave me alone?"

He stared down at her and she felt the full impact of his heated gaze. The desire that swirled there was enough to make her knees weak, but she allowed the anger and irritation to win out.

"Tell me, Lynx. Why?"

"Because I want you," he professed. "More than my next fucking breath."

God. Those words said in that raspy tone ... they were more than she could handle, and honestly, Reagan felt as though she'd been waiting an eternity for this man. A freaking lifetime.

For years, she'd come up with one excuse after another as to why she had to stay away from Lynx Caine. Her biggest reason being he couldn't seem to keep his dick in his pants. He was always with a different girl and it pissed her off. And she'd used her crappy relationship with Billy as her armor, as a way to keep Lynx at arm's length. All the while, she thought of Lynx endlessly.

And here he was saying things she'd always wanted him to say. It made her want to jump him, to knock him to the gravel and straddle him, right here beneath the moon.

Rather than give in to that urge, Reagan spun on her boot heel and stomped toward her truck. She could hear Lynx behind her and she balled her hands into fists. The man didn't know when to stop. The worst part was, if he didn't, Reagan feared she was going to do something she would likely regret for the rest of her life.

Like give in.

Chapter Three

LYNX KNEW IT WOULD BE IN HIS best interest to let Reagan go, but he couldn't seem to listen to reason. Not from her and not from himself.

He'd waited ten fucking years to get his hands on her again.

Ten years.

Since the first damn time he'd kissed her. Back when he'd been a heartbroken eighteen-year-old. And she'd been ... sixteen fucking years old.

A fucking decade.

That was one hell of a prison sentence, and now that she'd shed the ball and chain, there was nothing stopping him.

Well, nothing except her.

If he'd thought for one second that the banked fury in her gaze was anything more than repressed desire, he probably would've stepped back, let her climb in her truck, drive off into the night.

But he knew better.

This thing between them was a summer storm gathering strength across the open plains. And there was no running from it. Not anymore.

Stopping her with one hand on her shoulder, he said her name as softly, as calmly as he could. What he wanted to do was spin her around and crush his mouth to hers. He wanted to strip her naked, press her up against the side of that truck, and bury his dick inside that sweet pussy. Then he wanted to remain there for the rest of his fucking life.

But he couldn't do that.

Not until she gave him the green light.

When she turned back to face him, Lynx closed the distance between them and cupped her face in his hands.

Damn, she was so fucking soft. Just like he remembered.

He swallowed hard, watching her. He saw the way her eyes darted to his mouth, the way her tongue swiped over her lower lip, even the way her eyelids lowered as he leaned in closer. She was his greatest temptation. Always had been. Yet he'd managed to never cross that line. It hadn't been easy, but he'd succeeded because a country boy did not mess with another man's girl. That was the bro code. An honorable man didn't break it.

And despite the fact that Reagan and Billy had mixed about as well as oil and water, Lynx had held his ground, staying out of the way.

But now…

"Reagan," he whispered as his lips hovered over hers. "I'm so tired of fightin' this."

That little hitch in her breath was nearly his undoing, but Lynx waited, wanting her to give him some sort of sign. As desperate as he was for her, he knew he couldn't simply take because he wanted to. She had to be on board or he'd lose the war before the first battle started.

"Don't fight this," he whispered, his lips brushing hers.

He could practically taste her and it was killing him to hold back. He wanted to eliminate the few centimeters between them and devour her, to slide his tongue over her lips, past her teeth, into the sweet cavern of her mouth. But he needed more than that. He needed this woman to give him everything, because he wasn't going to settle for anything less. Not where she was concerned.

"I can't," she finally said, her tone firm. Those two words caused her lips to brush against his, and he inhaled sharply, his cock throbbing painfully against his zipper, every muscle in his body tense.

He swallowed again, and with an internal sigh, Lynx forced himself to pull back, to stand to his full height.

"Like I told you earlier," she stated, her voice firm, serious. "Keep your dick in your pants and come find me when your divorce is final. Maybe then…"

She let the sentence hang between them, and Lynx filled in the blanks with a million different thoughts.

Maybe then … he'd have her naked beneath him.

Maybe then … he'd get to taste every inch of her.

Maybe then … he'd slide his cock into the warm, wet recesses of her body and drive them both out of their minds.

Maybe then … he'd wake up with her in his arms.

Maybe then…

"Until then, I'd appreciate if you'd give me some space, Lynx." Her eyes were sincere. "I *need* you to give me some space."

Lynx knew when to concede and now was definitely the time. The woman was giving him hope. Whether or not she intended to honor that, he couldn't say, but he could hold out until then.

After all, what was ten more days? Little did she know, but his divorce would be final in ten days. Sure, it seemed like an eternity to him, but he knew it wasn't.

Lynx stepped back and allowed Reagan to get into her truck, the door making a godawful creaking sound when she closed it. She watched him the entire time and he knew she was battling the same desires he was. If she would simply give in…

Then again, maybe this was what they both needed. It gave him an idea.

"Hey," he called out as he tapped on her window.

He waited as it lowered.

"What?"

"Meet me at the diner for breakfast tomorrow?"

She frowned.

"Come on, girl. You gotta eat."

Reagan huffed. "Not gonna happen, Lynx."

"It was worth a shot," he said with a smirk.

He knew it would take time, but the woman would eventually give in. He understood that he needed to prove himself and he would. Easy fucking peasy.

"'Night, Lynx."

Lynx tipped his hat as she rolled up the window. He watched as she backed out of her spot, then he headed over to his truck.

Half an hour later, Lynx was pulling out of his driveway with Copenhagen riding shotgun.

"Sorry, buddy," he told his dog. "Looks like another night in the truck."

Until someone proved to him that Reagan wasn't in potential danger from that crazy bastard after Amy, Lynx was going to sleep in front of her house. He didn't give a shit how long it took. She might not want to give him the time of day right now, but Lynx wasn't about to let anything happen to her.

So what if he had to deal with a crick in his neck in the morning.

As far as he was concerned, Reagan was fucking worth it.

REAGAN KNEW LYNX WAS OUT THERE.

She'd heard his truck when he pulled up last night.

It should've given her the peace of mind to allow sleep to take her.

Unfortunately, she'd slept for shit, dreaming about the man. And they certainly hadn't been bad dreams, although she was starting to question her sanity.

Why? Why the hell did Lynx have to be so nice?

Even after she had turned him down, he was still parked out in front of her house keeping an eye on things the way he had for the past few weeks. She couldn't even imagine Billy doing something like that. Shit, Billy would've probably kept his distance, not wanting to put himself in harm's way.

"Such an asshole," she muttered to herself, tossing the blanket off.

It was hot. And it had little to do with the mediocre air conditioning and everything to do with that damn dream.

It wasn't different than a lot of her fantasies in previous years. All involving the sexy bad boy who she should've been keeping a serious distance from. For chrissakes, the guy was married.

And okay, fine. He was only married at this point on paper. The legal process was working its magic, and sometime in the near future he would be officially divorced. At that point, Reagan wasn't sure what excuse she was going to use, but she knew she had to come up with something.

Peering over at her nightstand, she was tempted to pull out her vibrator. It would certainly take the edge off as she'd learned over the years. She had started with the self-pleasure a long time ago, so it wasn't like it was anything new. Having been with a man who had been focused only on himself, Reagan had gotten used to it.

She briefly wondered if sex with Lynx would be that way. Would she have to resort to getting herself off after?

For whatever reason, she was shaking her head.

No, she didn't think Lynx was a selfish lover. No way would women be falling all over themselves to be with him if he was. And they were. To the point it was almost embarrassing. So much so that the guy had to be some sort of freak in bed to keep them coming back for more although he was ready to move on after one night. Or so she'd heard.

The sound of a truck engine turning over had her jerking her attention toward the window.

He was leaving.

Reagan glanced at the clock.

It was only six twenty in the morning. What the hell was she doing awake?

When the drone of the engine faded away, Reagan reached for her vibrator.

Why the hell not?

No way was she going to give in to Lynx, so she might as well satisfy her own needs. Even if the man was off-limits, the fantasies of him weren't.

Settling back on the bed, Reagan closed her eyes and drew up the mental image of Lynx. The one she always resorted to during times like this. He was shirtless in her mind, walking into her bedroom after having been outside, his chest glistening with sweat, her eyes drawn to all those tattoos.

God, he was sexy.

Before she knew it, she had the vibrator turned on low, the blunt tip pressed to her clit, working her up slowly.

Reagan imagined Lynx turning to her, his heated stare practically undressing her where she lay. She imagined his eyes trailing down to where her hand was tucked beneath her panties. He was watching her as she let the vibration roll over her clit, driving her higher and higher. Then she imagined it was his tongue on her, his mouth driving her closer to the edge.

"Oh, shit!" she cried out, her orgasm slamming into her unexpectedly.

She rode it out, until she was too sensitive for the vibration. At that point, she tossed the damn toy to the bed and stared up at the ceiling. Although the relief was instant, she knew it would never be enough to keep her thoughts from drifting to that man.

And one of these days, she was going to give in.

Which would leave her where?

As another notch in Lynx Caine's bedpost?

Forcing herself to sit up, Reagan sighed. "Yeah. No fuckin' thank you."

Chapter Four

BY THE TIME SATURDAY AFTERNOON ROLLED AROUND, Lynx was ready for … something. He wasn't even sure what, but he needed something to do.

Glancing over at Copenhagen, who was snoozing on the wood floor, he considered taking the dog out, playing ball for a while. They'd spent a good part of the morning doing that after they'd returned from Reagan's, but Cope was always up for a game of fetch.

Lynx clicked his tongue, but the dog didn't move.

Okay, so maybe not. Poor Cope was probably hoping Lynx would give him a little breather.

But he was antsy and he didn't know why. That wasn't like him. Not these days anyway. When he was younger, sure. He never could sit still, always looking for trouble to get into.

In a couple of hours, he could head over to Reagan's to get a beer. That was what he looked forward to most nights and not necessarily for the beer, either. Nope. His reason for going over there had everything to do with Reagan. It had been his own form of hell for the past few years, it seemed. Knowing he couldn't have her, yet still holding out hope. Yeah. He was pathetic.

Only now he needed to up his game.

Maybe he should send her flowers.

Or not.

That seemed weird. Especially since he didn't think Reagan was much into flowers. Then again, he didn't know all of her idiosyncrasies. Sure, he knew plenty about her, but admittedly, Lynx had made a point to stay out of her business. Mostly.

With a heavy sigh, Lynx flopped back on the couch.

Boredom was a bitch.

"Hey, boy," Calvin greeted when Lynx walked into Reagan's a few hours later. "Where you been?"

Lynx shrugged. "Took a nap."

Wolfe's father grinned. "Old age does that to ya sometimes."

"Thanks," Lynx said when Amy delivered his beer to the table. He turned his attention back to his uncle. "You'd know all about that, wouldn't ya?"

"Hey, I ain't complainin'," Calvin replied. "Just be thankful I don't take naps durin' the workday."

Lynx laughed. He'd caught Calvin snoozing in his chair over at the store a couple of times now, but he didn't say as much. Instead, he lifted his bottle and tapped it against Calvin's.

"Where's Wolfe?" he asked, peering around the room.

"Had to do somethin' with Rhys. Asked if I'd hang out for a bit. At least until you got here."

That meant Wolfe wanted someone to keep an eye on Amy. He had to wonder why Wolfe hadn't called him in the first place. His cousin knew he would've done it.

Calvin leaned back and looked around the room. "Looks like there's not much trouble to be had tonight, huh?"

He sure as hell hoped not. One night a week was enough for him. Didn't help that he was sleeping in his damn truck these days. What he needed was about eight hours in his own bed. And didn't that make him sound old. At twenty-eight, he damn sure shouldn't be planning how to catch some z's in the middle of the afternoon. Shit.

Unable to help himself, Lynx glanced over behind the bar. Reagan was there talking to a couple of guys, both from Dead Heat Ranch. She was laughing at something they said, and he suddenly wished he was the one to put that damn smile on her face.

He waited, knowing she would eventually make eye contact. That's what they did. And every damn time, it was a heady feeling, leaving Lynx reeling.

Wait for it.

Wait … for it.

There it was.

Reagan's eyes lifted, darting over the one guy's shoulder, coming to rest on Lynx's. He didn't smile, simply held her stare for a few seconds as he sipped his beer. Goddamn, the woman made him want things he had no business wanting. Not from her anyway.

"You made your move yet?"

Snapping his attention back over to his uncle, Lynx frowned.

Calvin chuckled. "Oh, come on now, boy. I might be old, but I ain't blind. I know you're sweet on that girl."

Lynx took a long pull on his beer, choosing not to say anything to that. He was sweet on her. Always had been.

"That one's gonna make you work for it," Calvin continued. "But that's not a bad thing. Wolfe's momma…" The older man smiled. "God, she had me chasin' her every-damn-where. Best time of my life."

Lynx glanced back at Reagan again. Yeah, he could see her being the best time of his life, too.

"Take her out," Calvin suggested, his gaze discreetly moving in Reagan's direction. "But I'm bettin' she's not the fancy-restaurant type. I know. Invite her to the lake tomorrow night."

"Tomorrow night?"

"Yeah. Monday's Labor Day. Y'all are plannin' a party out there, right? It's tradition, after all."

It was tradition, but not something he'd even thought about this year.

The door behind him squeaked open, but Lynx didn't bother to turn around. He was too busy trying to figure out how to put together a party in less than twenty-four hours. Sure, Labor Day was on Monday, but their party would start Sunday night and go until people passed out. That's how they rolled out in the country.

A firm hand gripped his shoulder, causing Lynx to glance over his shoulder.

"What's up?" he asked Wolfe.

The man was grinning from ear to ear.

Suddenly, Lynx had a good idea what was so urgent for Wolfe to take care of with Rhys. He smirked at his cousin, enjoying the way the man couldn't maintain eye contact.

"So, Lynx was just tellin' me how y'all are gonna put together a party at the lake for Labor Day."

Wolfe's gaze slammed into Lynx's.

He offered his cousin a one-shoulder shrug. "I can make it happen."

Wolfe nodded. "I think that'd be cool. We need somethin' to break up the tension right now."

Damn right they did.

With a smile on his face, Lynx got to his feet and clanked his beer bottle on the table to get everyone's attention.

"Hey, y'all hear about the party we're throwin' at the Caine lake tomorrow night? Well, if you didn't, it's on like Donkey Kong."

A couple of people groaned at his terminology. It only made him laugh.

"So, get your friends and meet us out there, yeah? And bring somethin', too. Ice, coolers." He grinned. "Beer's good, too."

A chorus of cheers erupted.

And just like that, Lynx had single-handedly set up a party.

Now he just had to get some beer for them.

And the girl.

The first he could worry about tomorrow, the latter he would take care of tonight.

More like right now.

REAGAN KNEW LYNX WAS COMING TO THE bar before he even turned toward her. It was a feeling she had, something she couldn't shake.

Of course, her nerves decided to riot, even though she was willing them to chill the fuck out.

The second he had mentioned the party by the lake to everyone in the bar, memories of so long ago had come roaring to the forefront of her brain. Fortunately for her, she was able to push them back, tamp them down. She didn't have time to be reminiscing about the time she'd spent with Lynx all those years ago.

"Hey," he greeted, stepping up to the bar and resting one arm on the top. He had tucked himself into the corner where he normally spent his time. She'd come to think of it as his space, and anytime someone else took it, she got irritated. No one said her thoughts were ever rational.

"Hey," she said, trying to sound as nonchalant as possible. "'Nother beer?"

"Sure."

Reagan grabbed a Coors Light and passed it over. Lynx Caine was a relatively simple man. She knew he didn't particularly care for Coors Light, but considering she didn't have any of the fancy brews in her bar, he took it without complaint.

Lynx cocked his head in that way that invited her to come closer.

Hesitantly, Reagan moved toward him, leaving the two guys she'd been chatting with to carry on their conversation without her. Not that she'd been particularly interested in their topic of the day they'd spent on the ranch, but she did like to talk to her customers. Plus, being engaged in conversation always kept men from hitting on her. She wasn't so full of herself to think that every guy wanted to hit on her, but she had her fair share. She knew some of it had to do with the fact that she owned the place.

"You comin' out to the lake tomorrow night?"

She shrugged, wiping down the bar top. "Don't know yet."

"You got other plans?"

Reagan lifted her gaze to his, holding it for a second before she exhaled slowly. "You askin' as friends?"

"Of course."

The way he said that didn't make her believe him.

"What? Can't a guy invite a girl out to the lake for some beer around the bonfire?"

"He can," she told him. "As long as the guy knows the girl's not goin' as a date."

"'Course not."

Again, she didn't believe him.

Of course, maybe Lynx was wholly serious. Maybe he *was* just inviting her as a friend.

What if he had a date? Would she be able to handle seeing him with another woman while she was that close? It wasn't above him to do that. Not that Lynx would try to rub it in her face, but she knew him. He didn't chase women. They generally were the ones chasing him. And she'd never seen him lacking in the female companion department.

She had to give the guy a little credit. He had been spending damn near every night at the bar until closing time, then sleeping in his truck in front of her house for the past three weeks. She couldn't imagine he'd had much time to be mixing it up with the ladies as of late. Unless...

"Tammy gonna be there?" she asked, hating that she sounded jealous.

Lynx frowned. "That's over, Reagan. She ain't gonna be around."

"You gonna have a date?" God, could she seriously just stop?

"Just you, girl."

"Not a date," she reminded him.

"Exactly." He tilted his beer to his lips and grinned.

She hated that even *that* move was sexy. It had her eyes trailing down to his neck, watching as his Adam's apple bobbed when he swallowed. Hell, the man's neck was freaking sexy.

Ugh.

"So?"

"Yeah," she said on a huff. "I'll be there." What else would she be doing? Sitting at home watching Netflix?

"Good. Maybe you can save me a dance."

Reagan rolled her eyes. She should've known there would be a catch.

"Don't count on it," she replied, trying to keep her tone dry although she was smiling.

It was hard not to smile at Lynx. There was something about him. He was just so damn likeable.

"See you tomorrow night," he said softly.

Reagan nodded, moving away from him. She needed to put some space between them. Lynx Caine was dangerous to her sanity. Especially now that she was single and didn't have an excuse as to why she should ignore his advances. Once his divorce was final, she knew she would have absolutely no reason.

Her eyes darted over to him once more. Her belly fluttered as it always did when she saw him watching her. She liked that he did, even if she didn't want to admit it to anyone.

"Can I get another beer over here?"

Reagan tore her eyes from Lynx and turned toward her customer.

At least she had something to do to keep her from entertaining the notion of letting this man get under her skin. She knew it would be so easy.

Lynx was right about one thing.

Reagan couldn't handle what he wanted from her. Even if she thought she was tough enough.

She wasn't.

That she could admit.

Chapter Five

"HOW IS IT YOU CAN GET A party together with one announcement in a bar?" Rhys asked Lynx as they stood in front of the bonfire the following night, Dustin Lynch blaring through the speakers.

"It's a gift," Lynx told him.

"Your gift," Rhys chuckled. "My curse."

"Oh, come on now. You ain't here as the sheriff tonight. Let loose a little."

Rhys's gaze cut over to him, his grin wide. "As long as you don't let loose too much."

"Deal." Lynx tapped his beer bottle to Rhys's as he peered around, looking for one woman in particular.

"Who're you lookin' for?"

Lynx shook his head. "Nobody. Just seein' who's here."

"She's not here yet," Rhys said, lifting his beer bottle to his lips and regarding Lynx intensely.

Frowning, Lynx shot a look at the sheriff. "Who?"

"Oh, don't play dumb. Whose house have you been camped out in front of for the past few weeks?"

"I don't know what you're talkin' about," Lynx said, amused by Rhys's accusation.

"I know you got a thing for my sister."

Most people knew he did, so it wasn't like Lynx could deny it.

"Don't you think she needs some space?" Rhys asked.

Lynx met Rhys's gaze, waiting.

"She was with that dipshit for long enough. She needs to try on single for a while."

Dropping his gaze, Lynx took a long pull on his beer.

"You don't think so?"

No way did he want to have this conversation with Reagan's brother.

"I think we'll let her make that decision," he stated.

Thankfully, the sound of more trucks pulling down the dirt road leading to the lake had Lynx turning his attention to the newcomers. He counted five ... six ... seven. Yep, seven in total, all pulling into the field and parking. He waited, wondering who would emerge.

"Well, I'll be damned." Lynx chuckled, grinning to himself.

Rhys turned toward the group at the same time Lynx pivoted to face them.

"That Travis?"

"Yep. And his brothers." It'd been a while since Lynx had seen the whole clan. The last time had been at the family reunion they'd pulled off at Dead Heat Ranch last year. Considering they were only half an hour apart, they didn't spend all that much time together. Then again, everyone was busy doing their own shit these days.

"What're you doin' over here by yourself?"

Lynx turned to see Wolfe approaching Rhys.

"I ain't alone," Rhys retorted. "I'm keepin' your cousin in line."

Lynx snorted at the same time Wolfe said, "Like that's even possible."

"I'll be back," Lynx told them, moving toward his Walker cousins.

"What's up, man?" Zane Walker hollered as he strolled toward him, a pretty brunette on his arm. "You remember my wife?"

"I do," Lynx said, holding out his hand to Vanessa. "Nice to see you again, V."

"Thanks for invitin' us."

"Yeah," Sawyer chimed in. "We've all been itchin' to get outta the house for a bit." He nodded toward the pretty redhead at his side. "You remember my wife, Kennedy."

Lynx nodded. "Nice to see you again."

"Same. Where's Copenhagen?" she inquired.

"She's a veterinarian," Sawyer said with a chuckle. "Always thinkin' about the four-legged ones."

"Took him over to my old man's house. Things can get kinda rowdy out here."

"That's an understatement," Brendon said, stepping up and holding out his hand to Lynx.

Brendon's twin brother, Braydon, moved up beside him.

"Where's your ol' lady?" Lynx asked Brendon.

"She's on the road," Brendon said with a frown. The man happened to be married to one of the hottest country music singers out right now. "She said to tell you hello."

Lynx grinned. "What about Jessie?" he asked, glancing over at Braydon.

"She's back at the house. She's not feelin' all that well."

Brendon leaned in. "Mornin' sickness."

Braydon flipped off his brother. "She ain't pregnant again." He smiled widely. "Yet."

Lynx knew that the Walker brothers had all settled down as of late. Some of them even had popped out a baby or two in recent years.

"Hey, man," Travis greeted. "Kylie, you remember Lynx."

"I do," Travis's wife said with a grin. "The troublemaker, right?"

"Yes, ma'am."

The rest of the clan moved in, and Lynx greeted Ethan and his husband, Beau, along with Kaleb and his wife, Zoey.

"We left the munchkins with the grandparents," Kaleb informed him. "Thought maybe we'd get some adult time."

"Glad y'all could make it on such short notice."

Another truck headed down the drive, and Lynx followed the headlights until he could make out the truck.

"If you'll excuse me," Lynx told the others. "My date just arrived."

All heads seemed to turn toward the newcomer, but Reagan was still in her truck.

"Wolfe's over by the fire," Lynx told them. "And there's beer on ice, so help yourself."

Travis smacked him on the shoulder as he passed, the rest of them falling into step with the eldest Walker.

Lynx strolled over as Reagan was hopping down from her truck.

"Hey," he greeted, moving right up to her as she shut her door.

"Hey," she answered, slowly turning toward him. "What? Were you waitin' for me?"

Lynx chuckled. "Of course not."

"How did I know you were gonna say that?"

He grinned. "Come on, girl. Let's get you a beer."

Reagan's eyes lingered on his face for a few seconds, and Lynx saw the moment she decided not to fight him. Whether or not she was going to give in was still to be seen, but at least he wasn't going up against a brick wall first thing.

He considered that progress.

"Holy shit," Reagan said with a whistle. "You invite the whole town?"

"Yep."

"Looks like most of 'em showed up."

"Good turnout," he agreed.

"That means less people at the barbecue tomorrow, huh?"

He laughed. "Probably."

It didn't take much to put together a party in this town. It was one of the things he loved about Embers Ridge. For as long as he could remember, they'd been having parties out in the empty fields, plenty of them right here on the Caine land.

"Amy here?"

"Yep."

"She doin' all right?" Reagan's eyes were full of concern.

"As good as can be expected, I suppose."

"Still no sign of that crazy man?"

Lynx grabbed a beer from one of the many coolers and passed it over to Reagan. "Not yet."

The crazy man Reagan was referring to happened to be Amy's ex-boyfriend. The bastard who'd tried to kill her a little over a year ago. Thankfully, he hadn't succeeded, but it appeared he was now looking to finish the job. It was the very reason the stress level had ratcheted up a few notches in the past few weeks.

One of the many reasons that a night like this was just what the doctor ordered.

Good friends, beer, bonfire, and laughter.

What more could you ask for?

REAGAN HAD HAD RESERVATIONS ABOUT COMING OUT to the lake tonight.

But a couple of hours in, she was wondering what she'd been worried about. After only one beer, she was feeling lighter than she had in a long time. The conversations weren't hurting, either. Everyone was having a good time, laughing, joking, telling stories about the many parties they'd attended right here on the Caine lake.

"Remember that time Lynx decided to streak around the lake?" Wolfe asked, pointing his beer bottle at his cousin.

"Died out halfway around, if I recall," someone added. "Didn't y'all send someone to get his ass?"

Wolfe and Lynx both roared with laughter.

"No one wanted to pick his nekkid ass up," Wolfe said. "Ended up drivin' the truck around and makin' him ride in the back."

"I had chigger bites on my fuckin' balls," Lynx grumbled, making everyone laugh.

Reagan giggled, she couldn't help it. And when Lynx smiled shyly over at her, her damn heart kicked in her chest.

"Those were some crazy times," another guy said. "Good times."

"Yep," Wolfe agreed.

"I recall a time when Wolfe decided to steal Old Man Gardner's tractor," Lynx said.

Rhys laughed.

"You were just a rookie back then," Wolfe said to Rhys.

"Green as shit. Still, I managed to talk your ass down from that tractor." Rhys glanced at Reagan. "He was nekkid. Said he didn't want to drive drunk so he hijacked the tractor."

Wolfe chuckled. "Avoided a DWI that night."

"Only 'cause I didn't want your bare ass in my truck."

The look Wolfe shot Rhys was hot enough to catch the dry grass on fire. Reagan instantly looked away, embarrassed that she'd caught the look passing between the two men.

The song on the radio changed and a couple of guys turned to their girls, grinning. Reagan watched, somewhat jealous that they had someone to dance with.

Not that she wanted to dance, but there were plenty of times she'd wished for someone to look at her the way Travis Walker was looking at his wife. Truth was, she'd never had that. Certainly not with Billy. He preferred spending his time with his boys, leaving her to herself. And based on the way he treated her when they were in public, Reagan had preferred it as well.

She glanced up to see Lynx staring at her. The next thing she knew, her beer bottle disappeared from her hand and the man was leading her out to the open spot where other couples were dancing.

"What're you doin'?" she asked, trying to pull away from him. "I told you no dancin'."

Especially not to a slow song like this.

"One dance," he said softly, tugging her closer.

"Lynx…"

He didn't force her; instead, his steady gaze settled on her face as he waited. Reagan could feel the eyes of others on them, and she didn't want to look like a total bitch, so she finally gave in. At least, that was the excuse she was going with. Definitely not the fact that she wanted to get close to him.

She blamed the beer. The one measly beer.

Right.

"Thanks for comin' tonight," he whispered softly, staring down at her as he pulled her in close.

Reagan nodded, not sure what to say to that. Hell, she was having difficulty breathing just being this close to Lynx. Forming words was not going to happen.

This man overwhelmed her. He always had, even if she played it off. How well she succeeded was anyone's guess. But if she was even remotely believable, it damn sure wasn't easy.

For one, he smelled so good. And perhaps it was because it wasn't an expensive bottle of cologne that had her mouth practically watering. Billy had always doused himself in that shit and it gave her a headache. Not Lynx.

Add to that, his beautiful eyes, his perfectly crooked nose, and chiseled jaw, which had just the right amount of stubble to be sexy and not make him look like a mountain man. Then there were his tattoos and his hands ... big, wide fingers. God, she could practically imagine his hands on her.

Shaking off the thought, Reagan cleared her throat, wishing the song would hurry up and end. Chancing a look up, she found Lynx was still watching her, a sexy smirk on his mouth.

"What?" she snapped.

"Nothin'. Nothin' at all."

"You know this doesn't change anything," she told him.

"Of course not."

Reagan narrowed her eyes. "Why do you always say that?"

His answer was in the form of a mischievous smirk.

"I'm not one of your playthings, Lynx Caine."

He leaned in, his mouth close to her ear. "Never that."

The way he rasped those two words had a shiver dancing down her spine. There wasn't even a hint of teasing in his tone, which both pissed her off and made her ache. This man confused her in so many ways. She knew him to be a playboy, never with the same woman for any length of time. Yet he seemed to have set his eyes on her and she had no idea why.

Reagan was nothing special. She couldn't offer this man anything, so she had no clue why he would even be interested. Perhaps it was because she hadn't slept with him. If she had, Lynx probably would've been long gone by now, moving on to the next girl in line.

She was lost in her thoughts when the song ended, but her self-preservation instincts were obviously on the mark, because she instantly pulled back, ready to extricate herself from his arms before she started to actually like this guy.

That was the last damn thing she needed right now.

Chapter Six

"WHERE'RE YOU GOIN'?" LYNX ASKED, TEASING REAGAN as she pulled back when the song ended.

"You're bad for my health, Lynx Caine," she grumbled.

"Hmm. That sounds like a compliment."

"It wasn't."

Getting close to this girl wasn't easy, but he hadn't anticipated it would be. However, the fact that she'd let her guard down even a little was promising.

Baby steps.

"I need another beer," Reagan murmured as she started toward one of the many coolers.

Lynx fell into step with her. "Thanks for the dance."

"It was against my better judgment," she countered, not looking at him.

Still, it made him laugh. He could tell she was admonishing herself for dancing with him. But the feel of her against him, the smell of jasmine from her shampoo would stick with him for a while. So, he couldn't complain about her snippy attitude. She *had* given in with very little resistance, which was far more than he'd thought he'd get this soon.

Grabbing a beer and twisting off the top, Lynx passed it over to her. He watched as those walls fell back into place, and the Reagan who turned toward him was the acquaintance he'd had all these years. He couldn't call what they had a friendship because neither of them had tried hard at it. That was all thanks to the douchebag she'd been dating for so long. At least on Lynx's part.

But now…

"How's your dad?" Reagan asked, pulling him from his thoughts.

"Good."

"Really?" She looked sincerely curious.

"He is. Still home, still workin' in that garden of his."

"I need to stop by there sometime," she said, her gaze drifting past him.

"He'd like that."

She nodded, lifting the bottle to her lips.

"How's your mom?" he asked, keeping the conversation at her comfort level.

"Same. Always workin'."

"She still doin' accounting or whatever?"

"She is. Same place, too."

"And your grandfather?" he inquired.

"Still an ornery old fart."

Yeah. Lynx knew Vic Trevino and ornery was putting it nicely. The man was a grizzly. And he didn't much care for the Caines. In fact, it had shocked Lynx when he found out that Wolfe and Rhys were … doing whatever they were doing. Mainly because he knew how the Trevinos felt about the Caines. It wasn't what he'd call a rivalry, but there was a little animosity there. Hell if he knew why.

Lynx maneuvered Reagan around to one of the open tailgates, then held her beer while she hopped up. Once she was situated, he joined her, keeping a good foot between them so that he didn't send her running.

"Things good at Amy's?" he asked, trying to keep the discussion open.

"Yeah." Reagan smiled. "Unless you count the fact that I ran out of hot water this mornin'."

"Long shower?" He tried not to think about Reagan in the shower. He tried really, *really* hard.

"Actually, no. I think it's the water heater. I need to have it checked."

"Did you tell Amy?"

Reagan shook her head and took a sip of her beer. "Nah. She's stayin' with Wolfe and Rhys most of the time, so I don't wanna bother her."

"I'll check it out if you want me to," he offered.

Her head snapped over and he could see the battle brewing in her eyes.

"For free," he added with a grin.

"I'll see how it's doin' later on. If I still have a problem…"

She didn't finish the sentence and Lynx knew she had no intention of asking him for help. Didn't matter. He'd look at it anyway.

"You comin' out for barbecue tomorrow?" he asked when she was quiet for too long.

"Probably not. I need to go see my mother. Check in. She wants to talk about … you know."

He didn't know. Lifting his eyebrows, he silently encouraged her to continue.

"About breakin' up with Billy."

Lynx looked away, the familiar anger shooting through his bloodstream. He hated that bastard, hated that he'd sat back all these years and watched Reagan get shit on by the guy.

"She thinks I should give him another chance," Reagan added, her tone soft.

He jerked his attention her way. "What?"

Her smile was sad. "I know. I don't get it either. But that's her way of thinkin'. After all, she stayed with my dad all those years and God knows neither of them was happy."

Lynx couldn't think of anything to say to that. Nothing that wouldn't make him look like the world's biggest prick. Billy Watson didn't deserve Reagan. She was far too good for that asshole and she deserved a hell of a lot better.

"But it's a lecture I've been expectin'. Once I get that outta the way, we'll be fine."

"You gonna take him back?" He hated that he had to ask that.

"Fuck no," she barked. "For the first time in my life, I feel like … I don't know. I feel like I'm my own person. That I don't have to dread goin' home. I'm done with Billy and his shit."

Lynx had to look away, not wanting her to see the relief he felt. Every damn time she'd broken up with Billy over the past decade, Lynx had hoped she would move on for good. He'd always been disappointed when she took the loser back.

He still wasn't entirely sure she wouldn't get back with him, but he was holding on to hope this time. After all, it really was all he had left when it came to Reagan Trevino.

REAGAN HAD NO IDEA WHY SHE WAS sharing such personal details with Lynx. But he'd asked and she had no one else to talk to these days, so it had come rushing out of her. It felt good, too. Getting it off her chest, sharing some of the shit she had to deal with.

Truth was, she didn't have any close friends. Partly because she'd always been that way, not getting close to anyone who she wasn't related to. And partly because her relationship with Billy had caused her to alienate most people. Not many people liked Billy. He had some good buddies, but he treated most people as though they were beneath him.

Which left Reagan without anyone to bounce things off of.

And no, she couldn't talk to her mother. She had tried plenty of times, but her mother insisted that she had committed to Billy, therefore she had to take the good with the bad. Didn't matter that Reagan continuously reminded her mother that she hadn't married Billy and had no intention of ever doing so. According to her mother, that didn't even matter. She was old-fashioned like that. Which was probably the reason she had stuck by Reagan's father until the day the man died.

"Well, don't you two look all cozy."

Reagan's head snapped around to find Billy walking toward them. She chanced a quick glance at Lynx, realizing the man had hopped down off the truck already.

She followed suit, getting to her feet. "What're you doin' here?" she asked.

"It's a party, right? Everyone's invited?" Billy peered over at Lynx, as though he expected him to confirm that.

"Not everyone," Lynx said, his tone deep, raspy.

"But my girl's here. Figured maybe I'd come check on her."

When Billy moved closer, Reagan took a step back, inadvertently moving closer to Lynx. She didn't mean to, but she did not want to do this here. Not tonight. She was so tired of the fighting. And truthfully, she just wanted to be as far from Billy as she could be.

"What's wrong, honey?" Billy moved another step closer.

"Don't," she hissed when he reached for her.

"Don't what?" Billy grinned. "Don't touch what belongs to me?"

"I don't belong to you," she retorted. It was then that she realized Billy was drunk.

"The hell you don't," he snarled. "I've put up with your shit for ten years. That makes you mine."

When he reached for her again, Lynx growled beside her. It was a dangerous sound, something most people would've been backing away from.

Not Billy. The guy wasn't only drunk, he was also an idiot.

Reagan put her hand on Lynx's arm. "It's fine. We're not gonna do this tonight."

Of course, neither man listened to her. Billy moved closer, practically toe to toe with Lynx. For a second, Reagan wanted to laugh. Seeing the two men square off was a sight. For one, Lynx had a good four or five inches on Billy. His biceps alone were probably bigger than Billy's thighs.

"You been after my girl for years now, Caine. You can't have her though." Billy's lip curled. "For one, she thinks you're a dog. Fuckin' every skank that blows through town."

Lynx didn't move, but Reagan hadn't expected him to. Billy should've learned a long time ago that needling Lynx wouldn't work. The man didn't care what anyone said or thought about him.

However...

Billy reached for her and Reagan managed to jerk her arm back at the last second, avoiding his touch.

"Let's go," Reagan said to Lynx, turning and taking his hand, pulling him away from Billy.

Her brother had perfect timing, too. He stepped up, glancing between the three of them.

"Problem here?"

"Nope," Reagan told him, pulling Lynx's arm. "No problem. We were just goin' somewhere else." She glared at Billy. "And you're leavin'."

"Hell no," he said, spitting on the ground beside his foot. "Just got here. I'm ready to get my drink on."

Ignoring Billy, Reagan turned, still pulling on Lynx until he started to follow. She realized then that they'd drawn a crowd. A couple dozen eyes were on them, and just like always, Reagan felt shame ignite in her chest. She hated that Billy could so easily embarrass her with his actions. Even if she wasn't with him anymore, it still bothered her. She couldn't even blame these people for thinking she was as much of an idiot as Billy.

"I'm sorry about that," Reagan told Lynx when she managed to get closer to her own truck. "I didn't know he'd show up."

Lynx frowned, coming to stand in front of her, crowding her between him and the driver's door. "What're you apologizin' for?"

"He's an asshole," she said, as though that would excuse his actions.

"But he's not your problem anymore."

"Maybe not, but I know what these people think." She shook her head and stared at the ground.

She saw his hand before she felt the warmth of his finger beneath her chin. "These people think you're an incredible woman."

Reagan snorted, meeting Lynx's eyes. "Right. An incredible woman who puts up with a lot of bullshit." With a sigh of defeat, Reagan moved away from his hand and dropped her gaze. "I really should go."

"You good to drive?" he asked.

She wasn't sure the last time anyone had worried about what she did. "I'm good. I nursed those two beers." Reagan smiled up at him. "But thanks for askin'."

Lynx's hand curled beneath her chin again and she held her breath. If he kissed her, she wasn't sure she would be strong enough to resist him.

Not right now.

Thankfully, he didn't kiss her.

His hand dropped and she instantly missed his touch, but she forced a smile and turned to open the truck door.

Lynx pulled the door open and waited for her to climb inside. "I'll see you later?"

She nodded. "Yeah." Smiling at him, she put the key in the ignition. "Probably at the bar on Friday?"

"You're not comin' to the barbecue tomorrow?"

Reagan shook her head. No way could she chance spending that much time with Lynx. It was hard enough to turn away from him now. "I've got … things to do." It was a lie, but hey, self-preservation and all that bullshit.

"If you wanna chat, you know where to find me," he said.

Reagan frowned.

"Outside your house, sleepin' in my truck."

Reagan smiled. "You know you don't have to do that."

"I don't have to," he began, and she finished it for him, "but you want to."

"Exactly."

"Well, I'll … talk to you later on then. I'll see you at the bar?"

His smile was warm, and she could see the heat in his eyes.

"For sure on Friday," he added.

As she drove away, Reagan had to wonder if he took her comment as an invite. Did it sound like an invite?

"Jesus Christ, woman. You're just a magnet for trouble, aren't ya?"

Chapter Seven

THE ONLY THING THAT COULD'VE POSSIBLY MADE the Labor Day barbecue any better would've been if Reagan had been there to join him. Lynx had spent the entire day downing ribs and beer while chatting it up with family and friends. At one point, he'd even sent Reagan a text, inviting her to come join him, but he'd gotten a polite no in response.

The woman was nothing if not stubborn.

However, that didn't mean that Lynx couldn't go to her.

And that was exactly what he and Copenhagen were doing. The small cooler on the passenger seat held two beers, two brisket sandwiches, and some chips. He figured she couldn't possibly say no to dinner at her place. He was even willing to eat it out on the front porch if she didn't want to invite him in.

As he pulled up to the little white farmhouse, Lynx noticed Reagan sitting on the porch. Her eyes swung over to his truck and a frown settled between her eyebrows.

Damn woman.

Plastering a smile on his face, Lynx climbed out of the truck, then walked around to the passenger side and grabbed the cooler, letting Copenhagen out in the process.

The dog trotted directly over to Reagan, who proceeded to pet the animal. Lynx couldn't help but be slightly jealous of his own damn dog.

"Hey," he greeted, lifting the cooler for her to see. "Brought dinner."

A strange look appeared on her face, but Reagan didn't say anything.

"Have you eaten?" he asked, stopping directly in front of her.

Reagan shook her head.

"Good. Then I came just in time."

Taking a seat on the top step beside her, Lynx set the cooler between them, then lifted the lid.

"Nothin' fancy," he told her. "However, it's good, if that's any consolation."

"You're a pain in the ass, you know that?" she said, a teasing smirk on her face.

"That's my goal in life," he admitted. "Glad to know I'm living my dream."

Reagan chuckled as he passed her a beer.

"So, how're things? We missed you at the barbecue today."

"No you didn't," she quipped. "You probably didn't even notice that I wasn't there."

Oh, he'd noticed. Every few minutes, in fact. But he decided not to tell her that, figuring the fastest way to get booted off the porch would be by turning on the charm.

"People asked about you," he said. And that was the truth.

"Did they now?"

"Yep." He passed her one of the brisket sandwiches wrapped in foil.

"They did, actually."

"Like who?"

"Amy, for one."

Reagan frowned, then turned her attention to the food in her hand. "How's she doin'?"

"She was smilin'. Does that count?"

"I can't imagine what she's goin' through," Reagan said softly, taking the bag of chips he handed her.

Lynx moved the cooler out of the way.

"I think she's doin' better now." And he really did think that. After hearing her story, after wanting to strangle the asshole who treated her the way that he had, Lynx had managed to suppress the violent rage. He still didn't understand how a man could hurt a woman like that. And to find out from Travis that Amy wasn't his first victim… Lynx hated even thinking about it.

"She's happy with my brother and Wolfe," Reagan said thoughtfully.

"That she is."

Reagan glanced over at him. "How does that work anyway?"

Lynx lifted an eyebrow, needing her to elaborate.

"That whole ménage thing. You know, two guys and one girl."

Chuckling, Lynx took a swallow of beer. "You got me. Not my thing. But as they say, the heart wants what it wants."

"I guess so."

Lynx took a bite of his sandwich when Reagan took a bite of hers. They sat there in silence for a few minutes, eating their dinner and staring out into the twilight.

"Do you think people plan for that to happen?" Reagan asked.

"What?" He was lost.

"The threesome thing. Do you think people set out knowing that they want to be with two people?"

Lynx shrugged. "Maybe."

"I guess if someone likes men and women, they probably would, huh?"

Chuckling, he took a sip of his beer. "Best of both worlds, maybe."

"But how does Amy end up with two men?"

Lynx turned to look at Reagan. "Is that what you were out here doin'? Pondering the wonders of the universe?"

Reagan chuckled. "I guess it is deep, huh?"

"Maybe you should read those books Amy reads."

That seemed to catch Reagan's attention. "What books?"

"Some romance shit," Lynx told her, opening his chips. "She mentioned some author… Can't remember who. Anyway, I guess people write about that shit."

"Really?"

The way she said that sounded oddly curious.

"You into that sort of thing?" Lynx wasn't sure he wanted to know the answer to that.

"God, no. One man would be more than enough for me."

Especially if that man was him, Lynx thought.

Thankfully, he managed to keep that inside his head.

REAGAN WAS SURPRISED TO SEE LYNX PULL up to her house before dark. However, she wasn't even a little disappointed.

The man confused her in so many ways.

And oddly enough, before he had arrived, she'd been thinking about him. Wondering how today would've gone if she had accepted his invitation to the barbecue. It probably would've been a better day, that was for sure.

"So, what'd you do today?" he asked, his tone casual.

"I was supposed to go see my mother," she admitted.

"Yeah?" Lynx's dark brow lifted. "That didn't happen?"

She shook her head, nibbling on the sandwich. "I actually got in my truck and drove over there," she admitted. "But when I saw Billy's truck in my grandfather's driveway, I turned around and came home."

The dark scowl that descended over Lynx's features didn't really shock her.

"Then the asshole had the audacity to show up here." She sighed. "I spent the better part of twenty minutes waiting for him to leave. I didn't answer the door." Reagan smiled to herself. "But the front door was unlocked and I prayed he didn't simply invite himself in."

Lynx's gaze was focused on her.

"He didn't," she assured him, although she wasn't sure why she was divulging quite so much information. "He finally left."

She didn't bother to tell Lynx that Billy had then pretty much blown up her phone for the two hours that followed. She finally had to turn the ringer off and he had successfully filled up her voice mail during that time. Reagan was pretty sure she just needed to block his number and avoid the hassle altogether.

"Not like I didn't need an excuse not to see my mother," she said after a few seconds of silence. "We aren't gettin' along much right now anyway."

"Why not?"

Reagan shrugged. She knew exactly why, however, she wasn't in the mood to talk about it.

Instead, she took another bite of her sandwich. When she was finished chewing, she turned toward Lynx.

"Thanks, you know, for bringin' this." She smiled. "I was wonderin' what I was gonna have for dinner. Peanut butter and jelly was my original choice, but this is so much better."

His gaze held hers for several seconds, his smile both sexy and sweet at the same time.

Reagan had no idea what she was going to do with this man. She couldn't get him off her mind, and now that she seemed to be spending more and more time with him, she knew which direction this was going to go.

Unfortunately, she just wasn't sure if she was ready for it to go that way.

Not yet.

Chapter Eight

FOR THE FIRST TIME IN A LONG time, Lynx had spent an entire Friday night without getting into a brawl in the parking lot. In fact, the entire week had been relatively uneventful. Nothing more than work and sleeping in his truck out in front of Reagan's house, anyway. Same old shit.

He figured tonight's lack of excitement had a lot to do with the fact that Rhys was in attendance at Reagan's. The good ol' sheriff was hanging out with Wolfe while they chatted it up with their woman. No one seemed to be in a particularly snarky mood, and Billy hadn't graced them with his presence, so Lynx hadn't had to fend any dumb asses off.

Kind of nice if he was being honest.

Then again, Reagan was avoiding him again. She'd made sure to do so every time he'd seen her this past week after he'd shared dinner with her on her front porch. Once at the diner, twice at the gas station. She was polite but distant and he found it cute as hell.

And now that Amy and Reagan were closing things up, Lynx was waiting with Wolfe and Rhys near the door.

"You still sleepin' in your truck?" Wolfe asked.

"Until you catch that asshole, I ain't leavin' her alone out there," he told his cousin, his gaze swinging to Rhys to include him in that statement.

"Holy fuck, man. Why don't you ask for her couch?" Wolfe suggested.

Rhys frowned at the man and Lynx chuckled.

"I doubt she'd be too keen on the idea," he said truthfully.

"It's just a damn couch."

Right. As though Lynx could be under the same roof with that woman and not be tempted to crawl in her bed with her. Hell, he'd wanted her for so damn long he wasn't sure he'd be able to handle having a single wall separating them. It was hard enough with a locked door.

"Y'all can go," Reagan shouted as she turned toward the hallway that led to her safe. "I'll be done in a minute."

Amy joined them and Wolfe met Lynx's gaze. He nodded once, letting his cousin know he was good. He would wait for Reagan as he had every damn night. He had nowhere else to be anyway.

"See ya later then," Wolfe told him, throwing his arm over Amy's shoulder. "Be good."

Lynx smirked. "I'll try."

Rhys shot him a look, which had Lynx laughing out loud. "Don't worry about your sister," he told the man. "She can hold her own."

That didn't seem to settle the sheriff down any. If Amy hadn't taken his hand and tugged him toward the door, Lynx suspected Rhys would've given him some sort of warning. He figured it would be coming sooner or later and he welcomed it.

When Reagan appeared again, her eyes shot to him instantly. "You really don't have to wait for me."

"I don't *have* to," he said, just as he did every time. "I *want* to."

She rolled her eyes and grabbed her keys from beneath the bar. "You're such a pain in the ass."

"But you like me," he countered, following her to the door and opening it for her.

"Not really. I *tolerate* you."

Right.

He stepped out of the way while she locked the door. When she started down the steps to the gravel parking lot, he followed.

"Lynx, seriously. I'm a big girl. I can take care of myself."

She could, he knew.

"Why're you doin' this?" she asked, spinning around to face him. "I'm not gonna go out with you. Not now, not ever."

For whatever reason, she sounded as though she had to force herself to say those words. And that only amused him.

When he didn't say anything, she spun around and headed toward her truck.

He followed again.

"You're like a damn puppy," she grumbled. "I'm not interested, Lynx."

He opened her door for her.

Reagan sighed heavily. "You just don't quit, do you?"

"Not when it comes to you, no," he admitted, meeting and holding her stare.

"Is your divorce final yet?"

He shook his head. "Couple more days." The fucking waiting period was almost over. For all intents and purposes, he was divorced. In fact, he didn't even talk to Tammy anymore. Thank God for that.

As he expected, Reagan started shaking her head instantly, yanking the door shut.

Lynx tapped on the window and waited for it to lower. When it did, Reagan sighed.

"What do you want?" she asked, her frustration evident. "I already told you—"

Before she could lecture him about the divorce, he held up a hand. "Meet me at the diner for breakfast tomorrow."

He didn't pose it as a question because he knew she would easily say no if he did.

She didn't respond.

"Come on, girl. You gotta eat," he said, almost the same words he'd said the last time he'd asked her to breakfast.

Lynx waited, holding her stare. It was clear she wanted to refuse him again, but to his surprise, she finally agreed. "Fine. But it's not a date."

"Of course not." She could call it whatever she wanted or didn't want. It was a date. And it was the first of many to come.

Reagan frowned.

Tapping the truck, he smiled. "Cool. See you in the mornin'. How 'bout nine?"

She nodded, then rolled up the window.

Lynx knew he'd won this one, but he wasn't going to gloat.

That wouldn't happen until he got the woman wrapped around his little finger. After all, it was only fair, considering he was solidly wrapped around hers.

After grabbing his phone from his pocket, Lynx dialed Rhys's number as Reagan's truck kicked up dust on its way out of the parking lot.

"What's up, Lynx?"

"Do me a favor?"

"As long as it doesn't require bailin' you outta jail."

Lynx climbed in his truck. "You have the power to *keep* me out. Why would I need you to *bail* me out?"

Rhys chuckled. "What do you want, Lynx?"

"Keep some patrols runnin' by Amy's tonight, would ya?"

Another gruff laugh. "Tired of sleepin' in your truck?"

"Naw. Just thought I'd give Reagan some space. But only if I know she'll have someone watchin' the house."

What he needed was a solid eight hours of uninterrupted sleep. At least then he might have a chance of bringing his A game tomorrow at breakfast.

"I'll keep a deputy out there tonight," Rhys said.

"Thanks. And I'll talk to RT and Z tomorrow, see if they can get someone closer to her. If that bastard comes back to that house, I don't want her alone in it."

"Agreed. And understood."

"Thanks."

Lynx tossed his phone in the center console and turned the engine over. He'd give Reagan a little time to herself. After all, he wasn't going to push his luck.

But three days from now … all bets were off.

───────────

BY THE TIME THE SUN CAME UP, Reagan had been awake for at least half an hour.

And didn't that seriously rankle? Absolutely no reason she couldn't sleep in this morning and her brain wouldn't cooperate.

It was Lynx's fault.

Rather than roll over and drift back into dreamland, she'd spent all that time, plus what it took to finally nod off last night, thinking about Lynx. The damn man had even invaded her dreams. Again.

The bastard.

She should've been home free seeing as he hadn't parked out in front of her house. That should've eased some of her tension. Instead, she had wondered where he was, what he was doing. Who he was with.

Damn man.

Why did he have to make her feel so much? Think so much? *Want* so much?

Reagan didn't need a whole hell of a lot. She wanted a simple life. One that involved working and spending time with her friends and family. Not necessarily in that order. No, she didn't have a lot of money, but she had enough to pay the bills. Sure, her truck had seen better days, but it still got her from point A to point B just fine. She had a roof over her head and food to eat. She didn't need any more than that.

Most importantly, she didn't want the headache of a relationship, of worrying what a man was doing or where he was all the damn time. Been there, done that. The headache wasn't worth it.

Not that she thought Lynx would be anything like Billy. When she really thought about it, she knew that her relationship with Billy had been more about convenience. They had lived under the same roof, but they hadn't actually been together in a really long time. It hadn't been ideal, but it had given Reagan the independence she needed with him always gone.

She was just now settling into her new life, the real independence that she had now that she'd booted Billy to the curb.

And then Lynx Caine went and infiltrated her thoughts.

And boy, did he. Every freaking thought in her head seemed to be about him. Most of them involved the sexy man naked, fucking her, claiming her in a way she seriously doubted she would walk away from. Lynx was the dominant kind, the type of man who went after what he wanted and didn't stop until he got it.

It certainly didn't help that Reagan hadn't had sex in…

God. Did she even know how long it'd been? Valentine's Day? No, it was before that. Hell, it might've been Christmas. At least nine months, probably more.

Kind of ridiculous considering she'd been in a committed relationship with a man.

Well, not entirely committed. She'd been faithful, but Billy… Yeah, right.

She couldn't remember exactly when she'd been with him last, but Reagan knew she'd put a halt to having sex with him once she'd suspected he was stepping out on her. And then she had stuck around because it had been easier than leaving. Her stubborn streak had kept her rooted in that house, refusing to move back home with her mother and grandfather. Billy had been the lesser of two evils. Again, mostly because he had been gone more often than not.

The bottom line was, she'd been an idiot.

A great big honking idiot.

Then Lynx had to go and stir up her hormones, send her libido on the fritz. Make her wish for things that were beyond her reach.

As she lay there, Reagan thought back to that night by the lake all those years ago, the first time she'd gotten a taste of Lynx, the first time she'd realized she was so far in love with him she would never be able to be happy without him. Ten painfully long years ago.

Up until that night, they'd rarely said anything more than the required pleasantries, but Reagan had always had a crush on Lynx Caine. Always. He was the tough guy no one wanted to mess with, the bad boy all the girls swooned over. Him and his cousin, both. Some of the girls considered the cousins interchangeable, but Reagan had only had eyes for Lynx.

That night, after his mother's funeral, Reagan had gone looking for him. She'd borrowed her brother's truck and driven out to the Circle C. Back then they hadn't had a fancy solar-powered gate to keep anyone off the property, so she had ventured past acres of dry grass, then past Lynx's house.

She'd found him down by the water, sitting on his tailgate, staring out into the darkness. Alone. So freaking alone it had broken her heart to see him like that. Rather than run the other way, Reagan had shored up her nerves, climbed out of the truck, and joined him. For a good ten minutes, neither of them had spoken and Reagan had been okay with that. But when he finally turned his attention on her, Reagan's heartbeat sped up, her body igniting from the mere sound of his voice.

"What do you wanna do after you graduate?" Lynx asked, his raspy tone *making her body warm significantly.*

"I've still got two years," she told him.

"I know." He peered over at her. *"But when you do graduate?"*

Reagan shrugged. "Not really sure."

"You wanna leave Embers Ridge?"

Reagan shook her head. That was about the only thing she knew for certain. She was a small-town girl through and through. There wasn't enough money in the world to get her to move to the big city.

Lynx grinned, but it was sad. "You gonna settle down, have lotsa babies?"

As she stared out at the water, Reagan's belly flipped. Only if they're your babies, *she thought.*

"What about you?" she asked, changing the direction of the conversation. *"You wanna leave Embers Ridge?"*

"Nope," he told her with certainty. *"Plan to open a furniture store with Wolfe later this year."*

"Yeah?"

"Yep. We already got it all mapped out."

For a few minutes, they stared at one another, sparks bouncing back and forth between them. Reagan had always felt them, but she knew it wasn't the same for Lynx. He was the type of boy who didn't have one girlfriend. He had several, and never anything serious.

"Why're you here, Reagan?"

She shrugged again. "I was worried about you."

That seemed to confuse him.

At some point during that conversation, they had moved closer, until Reagan's thigh was pressed up against Lynx's. They sat on that tailgate, under the stars and the full moon while country music filtered out from the cab of Lynx's truck. It had been the best night of her life. And then, when Lynx had kissed her...

Throwing the blankets off her legs, Reagan bolted out of bed. She couldn't lie there and think about him forever. She needed to get a move on. Not that it would take her long to get ready to meet him for breakfast, but she needed something to do to keep her mind occupied. A shower was a good start.

Two hours later, Reagan was pulling into the diner. She noticed Lynx's big blue Chevy was already there, and the flurry of butterflies erupted in her belly. She hated those damn butterflies. They irked the shit out of her. Why couldn't they keep themselves contained around him?

Climbing out, she kept her eyes trained on the gravel, which was the very reason she didn't notice Lynx climb out of his truck and head her way. Before she could reach the door handle, a big hand shot out around her, opening it for her. She was mesmerized by the ink that covered his arm, the back of his hand, his knuckles.

"Mornin'," he crooned softly against her ear.

Goose bumps prickled her skin and Reagan fought off the shiver that threatened to race down her spine.

This was such a bad idea. She should be at home, tucked into bed, dreaming about...

Yeah. Okay. So that didn't help.

Lynx Caine seemed to be invading her thoughts. Asleep, awake, it didn't matter.

"Mornin'," she mumbled, stepping inside as he held the door. "Thanks."

A warm hand gently pressed against her lower back, and she inadvertently sucked in a shocked breath, hoping like hell Lynx hadn't noticed. She peered over at him, trying to keep her face shielded by her hair. It didn't help. He noticed and he was smiling.

Jerk.

When he pulled out her chair, Reagan tried not to even think about it. She'd spent so long in a relationship with a man who put himself first, she wasn't used to someone opening doors or pulling out chairs. It shouldn't surprise her. That's the way Lynx was. He could charm the underpants right off a nun.

"Sleep well?"

She jerked her eyes up to his. "Yes. Actually," she lied effortlessly.

When it came to Lynx Caine, a lie wasn't a bad thing.

It was self-preservation.

Chapter Nine

"WHAT CAN I GET Y'ALL?" DONNA ASKED when she approached the table.

Lynx peered up at the diner's owner and grinned.

Recognition dawned on the older woman's face and a rare smile tilted her thin lips.

"Well, I'll be. Just when I thought nothin' stranger than seein' your cousin with a guy *and* a gal could happen." Donna grinned over at Reagan. "Then the two of you show up together and prove me wrong."

"We're not together," Reagan countered.

Lynx winked at Donna.

"The usual?"

"Yes, ma'am," Lynx confirmed.

"And you, dear?"

Reagan nodded, clearly not pleased with Donna's reaction. Or lack thereof.

"Yeah. The usual. Please."

Donna chuckled and wandered back to the counter.

"You know this is your fault, right?" Reagan hissed softly, her eyes pinned on him.

"What's my fault?" Lynx watched as Reagan brushed her long, silky hair over her shoulder.

"These people are gonna think we're together."

He was banking on that. But he said, "And that's a bad thing?"

She glared at him. "I'm not gonna be your flavor of the week, Lynx Caine. No matter what you think."

Her sassy tone made him smile. The woman sounded as though she couldn't even fathom the two of them together, yet here she was, sitting across from him.

Leaning in, Lynx waited until she met his eyes. "Trust me, darlin'. A week would never be enough for me."

Some women would've swooned if he'd said that to them. Not Reagan. The girl was stubborn as all get out.

"Sweet-talk a nun outta her panties," she muttered, her gaze focused on the silverware wrapped in a paper napkin.

"What was that?"

Reagan shook her head. "Nothin'." She lifted her gaze to his. "So, why'd you wanna meet me for breakfast?"

"'Cause I like your company."

"Pfft. Now I know you're fulla shit."

Although he probably should've been offended, Lynx couldn't keep the grin off his face. Reagan had always been sassy. For as long as he'd known her. It was one of the reasons he was so into her. She wasn't the type of woman to let a man sweet-talk her out of her panties, that was for damn sure. If a man wanted to be with her, he'd have to work for it.

And Lynx knew he'd have to work twice as hard because his reputation when it came to women wasn't one he was necessarily proud of. However, explaining to Reagan that he'd been trying to fill the void because he wanted her more than he wanted air probably wouldn't gain him any points.

"Tell me, Lynx. When's the divorce gonna be final?"

Ah. Fantastic. His least favorite topic.

Leaning back, Lynx toyed with the paper ring that held the silverware inside the napkin. "Monday."

"Really?" She didn't sound convinced.

"Yeah." Lynx held her stare. "It was filed a while back. Just had to wait it out."

Reagan sat stone-still, her eyes locked with his. He could tell she was processing that information, probably trying to find a way to verify it. When she finally broke eye contact, shaking her head slightly, Lynx held back a smirk.

Reagan sighed and Lynx waited. He could see her brain working, knew she was coming up with a sassy retort.

"I'll believe it when I see it," she finally said under her breath.

He didn't say anything. What could he say? It was true. And come Monday, Reagan wouldn't have a reason to push him away. Sure, she would probably come up with something, but at least she didn't have her usual excuses working for her anymore.

"What made you marry that woman, anyway?" She relaxed somewhat. "I've always wanted to know."

"What made you stay with a dumb ass like Billy Watson?" he countered.

Reagan's dark eyes narrowed. "That's none of your business."

"No?"

Donna returned with a cup of coffee for Lynx and a Dr. Pepper for Reagan, but the older woman didn't stick around, quickly moving to the next table and refilling coffee mugs.

"No," Reagan stated firmly. "Plus, I ain't with him anymore, so it doesn't matter."

"Sure it does. Same as it matters to you why I married Tammy."

If Lynx wasn't mistaken, there was something territorial about Reagan's heated stare. She certainly didn't like the idea of him being married. Whether it was to Tammy or anyone, Lynx couldn't tell.

Leaning forward, he decided to clear the air between them. "I'm gonna say this one time and one time only. You do with the information what you want."

"I'm all ears," she responded in that snarky tone that made his dick hard.

Keeping his voice low enough that it didn't carry past their table, he said, "I married Tammy because she said she was pregnant. And yes, before you ask, I did glove up. I've never had sex without a condom."

He noticed a blush creep into Reagan's cheeks. The talk of sex and condoms was clearly not something she was used to.

"But I took her at her word and yes, I fucked up. I married her."

"Did you love her?"

He didn't even hesitate when he said, "No. Did I think I would eventually? No, but I had an obligation. I thought maybe we could make it work for the baby. But it didn't. She lied about bein' pregnant *and* she was screwin' around behind my back. I learned my lesson."

What he didn't say was that he knew he could never love Tammy because there was only one woman he could and would ever love. And she just so happened to be sitting across from him right at that moment.

"I'm sorry about that," Reagan stated, her tone softer this time.

Lynx sat up, surprised by her reaction.

"Regardless of whether you loved her or not, it's not easy when they cheat."

He knew that Reagan had experience in that area. Billy had shit for brains and the dumb ass hadn't even attempted to hide his infidelity. That still didn't explain why Reagan had stuck with him for so damn long.

"Did you love Billy?" he asked, figuring it was only fair. Tit for tat.

"I thought I did. At one point. But no, I don't think so. I cared about him, sure. But even that died a long time ago."

Lynx believed her. Hell, if she'd said she had loved Billy, he would've believed her. He wouldn't have liked it, but he would've believed it.

"What d'ya say we start over?" he suggested after several seconds of painful silence. "How 'bout we forget about Tammy and Billy and just try to leave them in the past, where they belong?"

Reagan's gaze lifted to his face, studying him. It was as though she suspected he had a double meaning for everything he said. Finally she nodded. "Okay. I'd like that."

Good. Because Lynx wasn't sure he could tolerate thinking about Reagan and Billy together. Every time he did, he wanted to put his fist through the fucking wall.

"Here you go, kids," Donna announced as she plopped their plates on the table.

"Thanks."

"Yep." And she was off.

"If we're not talkin' about … you know … then what exactly *are* we gonna talk about?" Reagan asked, forking her pancakes into small bites.

He honestly didn't have the first clue, but hell. They could talk about the damn weather just as long as he got to sit here with her.

For Lynx, that was all that fucking mattered.

SHARING A MEAL WITH LYNX WAS THE most awkward thing Reagan had done in … forever. Maybe *ever*.

Sure, she'd fantasized about what it would be like to spend time with him like this. Although this certainly *wasn't* a date, she'd even thought about that, too. Those damn fantasies had been around since she was sixteen years old. However, she had never thought they'd come to fruition. And certainly not like this.

The tension between them was thick enough to cut with a knife, and she knew that was partially her fault. Even though he'd suggested they leave the past in the past, Reagan knew it wasn't that easy for her.

For one, she'd spent so long watching Lynx parade around town with one woman after another.

Well, okay, so maybe he hadn't paraded, but he'd been seen and she'd heard about it, and her heart didn't seem to know the difference. Every time she thought about Lynx with another woman, it was like she'd ingested acid and it was eating away at the lining of her stomach.

"Where'd you meet Tammy?" she found herself asking before she could think better of it.

Lynx's hard gaze lifted to meet hers. She could see the frustration there.

"It's just conversation," she told him.

"Here," he told her. "In Embers Ridge."

"Really?" How had she not known that?

He nodded, putting his fork down and picking up his coffee mug. "She had a girls' retreat out at DHR. She was at Marla's Bar one night."

DHR was the locals' reference to Dead Heat Ranch, likely the most popular dude ranch in central Texas. People came from far and wide to visit for family reunions, birthday parties, summer vacations, and apparently, girls' retreats.

"Oh."

"Yeah, oh." His tone was a little harder than before. "Now, if you don't mind, I'd like to talk about somethin' else."

"Like?"

"Like you finishin' those pancakes so we can get outta here."

Reagan glanced down at Lynx's plate, realizing he'd already finished his food and she'd hardly even started.

With a shy smile, she picked up her fork.

"What do you wanna do after this?" he asked, watching her as she chewed.

Frowning, Reagan tried to come up with something to say. Something that sounded a lot like, "I don't think we should do anything after this." Unfortunately, that's not what came out of her mouth. In fact, nothing came out of her mouth, but she did manage an indecisive shrug.

"The lake it is," he said quickly.

Reagan instantly shook her head. "No. I can't."

Holy crap. That was the absolute last place she wanted to go with Lynx. Extended lengths of time with him would be hard enough. Somewhere secluded like that… No way could she trust herself then.

As though he had expected her rebuttal, Lynx smiled. "Fine. But I wanna take you over to the shop. Show you somethin'."

Reagan's sex-starved brain instantly thought about him showing her his sexy, naked body, but she shook off the thought. No way was she going that route. Not with Lynx. Certainly not until he held up his end of the bargain. Although two days wasn't a long time, it was still necessary. Once his divorce was final, she would consider an alternate ending, but until then, Reagan had absolutely no desire to get mixed up with the notable bad boy of Embers Ridge.

No matter how much she found herself wanting to.

Half an hour later, after Reagan finished eating and Lynx paid the bill — despite her loud refusal — Reagan was pulling into the parking lot of the warehouse where Lynx and his cousin spent their days building furniture. She had adamantly refused to go, but Lynx had turned on that damn charm and she found herself following him.

It still pissed her off that her brain wasn't doing what her heart wanted it to. She should've been heading home, not willingly spending more time with Lynx, yet here she was.

"Come on, girl," he said, opening her truck door.

With a sigh, Reagan hopped out and did her best not to look Lynx in the eye.

It took a minute or two to get inside because Lynx had to unlock the door and disengage the alarm, then turn on the lights. Once that was done, that damn tension had returned to Reagan's shoulders, only this time, it was threatening to steal her breath from her lungs. It was one thing to go out in public with this man, something else entirely to follow him into an otherwise empty warehouse.

"I wanna show you somethin'," he said, nodding toward the far end of the building.

Reluctantly, Reagan followed, doing her damnedest not to pay attention to the play of Lynx's muscles across his back as he walked. She battled the urge to glance down at his ass or his long legs. She was sure the way the man filled out a pair of jeans was a crime in some countries.

When he stopped suddenly, Reagan plowed right into his back.

"Shit. Sorry."

He turned around, and Reagan had just enough time to jump back. Of course, she couldn't do it gracefully. No, she had to stumble, which then had Lynx reaching out, steadying her with a hand on her arm. Her skin heated where he touched her and her breath locked in her chest.

Why was this a good idea again?

"Do I make you nervous?" he asked in that raspy tone of his that made goose bumps form on her arms.

"What?" She rolled her eyes. "*No.*"

Not that he would believe her since she was suddenly imitating his same raspy tone. Damn it.

When she thought he would pull away, Lynx took a step closer, forcing Reagan to crane her neck to look up at him. Her heart thumped painfully hard against her ribs.

When his hand cupped her face, Reagan had to fight the desire to press against it, to press against *him*. He was so warm and he smelled so good. She just wanted to lean into him, to press her lips to his, see if they were as soft as she remembered from all those years ago. The memory of the other night assaulted her, the way his mouth had brushed against hers...

"Do you know how fuckin' long I've waited to get my hands on you again?"

His words were a dark, guttural rasp that had her clenching her thighs together.

"Ever since that night," he continued, "out by the lake. Damn, girl." His eyes dropped to her mouth, then lifted to her eyes. "I've dreamed about you, Reagan."

She knew she was supposed to pull back, to break the spell he seemed to have on her, but her feet wouldn't listen. Instead, she continued to stare up into his eyes, and she knew for a fact he could see how much she wanted him. It was hard to deny, especially when they were that close.

Reagan was a fraction of a second from throwing caution to the wind, to taking what she'd wanted for so long. When she leaned in, it seemed as though Lynx did, too. Her heart skipped a beat. Hell, it skipped a whole series of beats.

"God, Reagan..."

She was breathing roughly, her hands trembling. She wanted this man to kiss her, to touch her, to erase the last ten years of her life and put her back on even footing. She'd wanted him for so damn long and now he was here, so close—

"But I made a promise," he said, pulling away quickly.

It took a second to see he was smiling.

No, wait.

He was laughing.

At her.

"And I fully intend to keep my promise, girl. No matter how much you want me."

Asshole.

Chapter Ten

LYNX HAD NEVER WANTED TO BREAK A promise more than he wanted to right then.

Although he was laughing, his body was hard as fucking granite, his dick painfully erect, desperate for the woman he'd been waiting what felt like a lifetime for.

However, he hadn't brought her here to seduce her.

He really did want to show her something.

"Come on." He nodded to his left, still grinning despite the fact his cock was throbbing like a motherfucker.

He could see the fire burning in Reagan's dark gaze, both desire and frustration. He liked that about her. The fact that she wore her emotions on her sleeve, that she wasn't afraid to speak her mind. That was hotter than hell.

"Asshole," she muttered.

Yep, definitely hot.

Even when it appeared she was pissed at him.

However, he hoped what he had to show her would take some of the sting out of his backing down, because Lynx was fairly certain he could've kissed her and Reagan would've been hot to trot right along with him. The girl was as flammable as dry grass, anxious for a spark to set her aflame. And he knew without a doubt Reagan Trevino would burn bright and hot. The woman had been neglected for too damn long, and he wanted to be the one to erase her past and show her how a real man treated a lady.

But he couldn't.

Not yet.

Taking her hand, Lynx tugged her along. When she tried to pull away, he linked their fingers together, still chuckling.

Once they were in the farthest corner of the warehouse, he released her hand, then reached for the cloth cover he'd placed there ... a while ago.

"If you've got a bed underneath there, Lynx Caine, I'm—" Her words abruptly ended. "Oh, wow. Those are..." Her eyes lifted to his and he saw the confusion there.

"I made them for you."

"*What?*" She frowned. "When?"

"Oh, I don't know. A while back." No way could he tell her that he made the pair of rocking chairs about eight years ago, a short time after she'd mentioned how much she liked the ones on his father's front porch.

"And you made them for me?"

He could tell she was trying to hide her giddy reaction, so he motioned her toward the chair. "Sit. Test it out."

She swallowed hard but moved closer. Lynx watched as her small hand caressed the polished pine armrest.

"They're beautiful. I can't believe..."

When she sat down, her grin widened. He watched as she pushed back with her booted foot, putting the chair in motion, slowly rocking backward, then forward.

"Thought maybe I could take them out to Amy's," he suggested. "That way you'd have them on the front porch when you wanna sit outside."

Her eyes met his. "You really made these for me?"

He nodded, hating that he suddenly felt shy around her. That was something he never felt. He ruled the roost, prided himself on it. Yet when he was around Reagan, he felt vulnerable in a way he'd never felt before.

"When?" Her gaze narrowed. "When did you really make these, Lynx?"

He shrugged one shoulder. "Hell, I don't remember."

That was a lie. Lynx remembered it like it was yesterday because he'd made the first one right after she'd broken up with that asshole Billy Watson the very first time. She'd been barely eighteen years old, just graduated from high school, and Lynx had been over the fucking moon. Because of her age, he'd been forced to take a step back from her when he'd first kissed her, and the next thing he knew, Reagan had started dating Billy not long before she graduated. The second he'd found out, Lynx had been pissed, confused. He remembered praying, something he hadn't done in a long damn time. Praying that God would strike Billy Watson down where he stood. No one had ever accused Lynx of being reasonable.

So, that first time they broke up, he'd automatically assumed it was over. Never in his life would he have imagined that relationship would've dragged out for so damn long. Eight fucking years he'd waited for this moment.

"You don't remember?" She clearly didn't believe him.

"Nope. Sorry."

Lynx damn near backed up, but somehow, he managed to hold his ground when Reagan got up from the chair. Hell, his feet were yelling for him to run, but he stood there, watching her, bracing himself.

"Do you remember that night?" she asked.

"What night?" Oh, he knew, all right. But he figured it was far safer to play dumb right now.

"The night I sat on your dad's front porch with you. In those rockin' chairs."

He didn't respond.

"I'm pretty sure I went a little overboard talkin' about 'em." She glanced over her shoulder at the two rocking chairs behind her before turning back to him. Her smile was wistful, as though she was remembering that night. "And you just happened to make these? For me?"

"Yep."

"But you never gave 'em to me."

"Nope."

"Why not?"

He shrugged again.

She took another step closer and Lynx found himself staring down at her.

"Tell me when you made them," she urged, her voice softer, far too seductive for his fragile grasp on his self-control.

"A while back," he offered.

"How long's a while?"

He shrugged.

She stepped closer.

This time he did take a step back.

She took another step closer.

"Reagan…"

"Tell me, Lynx."

"Eight years," he admitted, his voice rough.

Something softened in her eyes and he knew without a doubt, for the first time in his life, Lynx was about to go back on a promise.

EIGHT YEARS.

Reagan couldn't believe her ears.

Lynx had made these rocking chairs eight years ago.

Back around the time when she was eighteen years old. Old enough for…

"Why?" she asked.

Another shrug.

"Why'd you stay away?" That was a question she'd wanted him to answer for so long.

"You were too young," he grumbled.

She knew that. She had been young. Not that she'd liked that conclusion when she'd come to it all those years ago. In fact, Reagan had convinced herself that Lynx hadn't really wanted her in the first place. Her irrational brain wouldn't allow her to believe he'd kept his distance because she was underage.

Unable to help herself, Reagan reached out and touched him. She gently caressed the side of his face, the rough rasp of his stubble abrading her palm and sending a shiver down her spine. She had wanted to do this for so long, the memory of that long-ago night slamming into her. The same emotion, the same urgent need fizzed under her skin, thrumming in her blood.

Something about Lynx made her body heat, every cell hypersensitive, eager for him to touch her again. It'd always been like that. But he had rejected her so easily, made her feel as though she wasn't worth his time. Then again, Lynx hadn't actually done anything to make her feel that way, aside from keeping his distance, but she had allowed the irrational thoughts to grow roots, to become the truth. Hence the reason she'd put that much needed space between them, refusing to think on it too much.

"Why didn't you give them to me?" she probed. "And don't tell me you don't know." Reagan narrowed her eyes. "I know you, Lynx Caine. You don't forget anything."

"Because you were with Billy."

The way he said it, the gravelly rasp of his voice had her belly fluttering. Although she'd insisted that he give her space until his divorce was final, Reagan couldn't seem to fight the overwhelming urge to close the distance between them. And what was another day, anyway? She had waited ten freaking years for this.

"Reagan..."

The way he said her name was a warning, she knew.

She ignored it.

Sliding her hand behind his neck, she urged him down toward her, their eyes locked together until her eyes crossed from his nearness. At that point, she let her eyelids lower and leaned in, pressing her lips to his.

Warm, soft.

And Jesus, he smelled so good. Like laundry detergent and soap.

Lynx didn't kiss her back. In fact, he didn't move. She could feel the tension in his entire body.

Pulling back slightly, she forced her eyes open only to find his were closed.

"Why won't you kiss me?"

"Because I promised," he whispered as his eyes opened and he focused on her.

She studied him momentarily, allowing her gaze to bounce from his lips to his eyes, then back again.

"But you want to?" She had to ask; she needed to know.

"More than anything," he rasped.

Holding his gaze for another second, Reagan let that sink in. If he wanted her and she wanted him...

"Fuck that promise," she murmured before grabbing him roughly and jerking him toward her.

This time Lynx didn't resist, and the second his mouth was on hers, Reagan's world lit up like the Fourth of July back in the day when the only thing that mattered was shooting bottle rockets and lighting up the sky, her body buzzing like that one time her brother dared her to stick a fork into the electrical socket in their kitchen.

Quick, powerful. All-consuming.

It was a kiss to rival all, and it only took seconds before she realized she wasn't in control here. In fact, when it came to Lynx, Reagan was completely out of control.

"Fuck," Lynx groaned, his arms coming around her, his hands cupping her ass and lifting her off her feet.

Reagan felt nothing except for the warmth of his mouth on hers, the confidence in his tongue as it plunged past her teeth, dueling with hers. She inhaled him, unable to get enough. There was nothing sweet or seductive about this kiss. It was fueled with years' worth of pent-up desire, the sexual frustration finally finding an outlet.

Wrapping her legs around his waist, she lifted herself with her arms around his neck, trying to get closer, trying to take everything this man was willing to give her.

The rough growl that rumbled in Lynx's chest had her pussy clenching tightly, the emptiness inside her never more apparent than that moment. He held her so easily, as though she weighed nothing. She liked it, for whatever reason. Lynx Caine made her feel feminine in a way she'd never felt before.

When her back met an unmoving force, Reagan grunted, but didn't pull away. He'd pushed her up against one of the steel beams holding up the second floor, which ultimately allowed their bodies to press more tightly together. Reagan ground against him, the seam of her jean shorts rubbing deliciously against her throbbing clit, a zing of pleasure slamming through her. She could feel his erection, thick and hard, grinding against her most sensitive spot.

"Christ, Reagan," he groaned against her mouth. "This is dangerous. You know that, right?"

Oh, she knew. She knew exactly what he was feeling and she was grateful Lynx didn't pull back. There was a fire burning out of control inside her, and every second that he kissed her, it heated until she was consumed by it.

When his fingers slipped beneath the hem of her shorts, Reagan sucked in air and pulled back abruptly. He was touching her, and heaven help her, it felt so damn good. His rough fingers against her skin, searching, seeking.

"Lynx! Oh, fuck... Oh, yes..."

"So fucking wet," he growled against her neck, his mouth doing delicious things to that sensitive skin while his fingers probed beneath her panties, finding her slick entrance.

Rather than pull away, Reagan tried to move closer although she was pinned between his hard body and the steel beam. "Don't stop," she hissed when his fingers stilled. "Please don't stop."

"Not sure I can handle it," he rasped roughly. "Feeling you come on my fingers might do me in, girl."

The way he said that ... *girl*. There was a sexiness in it, almost like a term of endearment. It made her hotter, wetter.

"Once I start, I won't stop," he insisted.

But she needed that. She needed him to make her come. If he didn't, she was going to spontaneously combust.

"Make me come," she pleaded.

When he pushed one finger inside her, she moaned long and loud. It was all she could do to not move, her body desperate for the friction that only he could provide right then.

Oh, who was she kidding? It wasn't the friction she needed, it was *him*.

"Oh, sweet Jesus," Lynx muttered. "I wanna taste you. Wanna feel this sweet pussy on my mouth."

Opening her eyes, Reagan watched his face. His eyes were so dark, his hunger for her apparent. When he leaned forward, pressing his forehead to hers, Reagan tightened her grip on him.

"Make me come," she repeated, her voice barely above a whisper.

She could tell he was debating.

In an effort to reassure him, she grabbed his hair, pulling his head back so she could look in his eyes.

"Just this once."

His body went stone-still, his fingers, while still lodged in her body, no longer moving.

"Not once," he growled. "If I make you come, Reagan, it'll be the first of many. I won't settle for one fucking time."

Her eyes widened, her mouth falling open as she realized the ferocity behind his declaration.

Could she handle this man and everything he would do to her?

If she'd thought it would only be sexual, Reagan could've easily said yes. Her sex drive was intense and she knew she could match this man orgasm for orgasm. However, when it came to her heart...

"Put me down," she insisted. "Right now."

Something passed in his eyes, but Lynx didn't argue. His fingers slipped from her body and the next thing she knew, her boots were on the floor, her chest heaving as she tried to battle back the mixture of frustration and need.

She righted her clothes and met his eyes once more, fully expecting a mischievous smirk, some smartass retort. But that never came and what she saw on Lynx's face this time...

Looked a hell of a lot like regret.

And her stupid heart squeezed in her chest.

Chapter Eleven

LYNX COULD SMELL HER SWEETNESS ON HIS fingers. His tongue itched to plunge deep into her pussy, to drive her as insane as he'd been all this time just *thinking* about it.

But he couldn't.

More importantly, he wouldn't.

Because once would never be enough.

Hell, a fucking lifetime with Reagan wouldn't be enough for him.

And Lynx damn sure wasn't going to settle. Didn't matter how fucking hot she'd been, how fucking much he craved seeing her come apart in his arms. Didn't even matter how many nights he'd jacked off to thoughts of Reagan.

Only once wasn't an option.

"I should go," she finally said.

Unable to find his voice, Lynx simply nodded. He needed a minute anyway. Some time to process what had just happened, to figure out how she'd so easily dissolved his self-control.

Without another word, Reagan headed for the door. Lynx turned to watch her go, their eyes meeting briefly when she reached the door. It looked as though she had something to say, but nothing ever came. The next thing he knew, he was alone in the warehouse. He took one look at the steel beam and had to battle back the urge to punch the damn thing.

Taking a deep breath, then another, he waited until he managed to get his temper under control. He wasn't pissed at Reagan, he was angry with himself for allowing things to go that far. He should've walked away when she'd first kissed him, held out until the time was right.

But his self-control was so thin when it came to her.

Always had been.

His gaze swung to the rocking chairs and he sighed heavily.

Several more minutes passed, and when his body stopped vibrating, Lynx grabbed one of the chairs and carried it out to his truck. After he'd loaded them both and tied them down, he closed up the shop and hopped in his truck.

He had no idea where Reagan had run off to, but he was going to deliver the chairs to Amy's. They belonged with Reagan, and even if she never spoke to him again, at least she could enjoy the chairs. Lynx knew he had to do one of two things. Go balls to the wall and get the girl, or let go of her completely. This in-between state was tearing him apart.

As he drove, he thought back to that night on his father's front porch. He still didn't know why Reagan had showed up, but after his mother died, it seemed Reagan had established a steady presence in his life. After that first night by the lake, Lynx had never touched her again, but that hadn't stopped her from coming around and it hadn't stopped him from wanting her to.

"Where'd your dad get these chairs?" she asked, *tapping her foot and rocking the chair steadily.*

"I made 'em," he admitted, *not looking at her.*

"You... Really?"

He grinned. "Hard to believe?"

"No. It's just ... these are awesome."

She looked out into the distance and Lynx took a moment to stare at her. She was so damn pretty with her long, silky hair pulled back in a ponytail, that white tank top hugging her perfect tits, showing off her smooth, tanned arms.

"I love it out here," she said softly. *"Sitting on the front porch, under the stars. I've watched my mom and dad sit outside like this. They always look so happy."*

Odd that she said that because Lynx detected some sadness in her tone.

"I think it's the only time they really get along. They're always arguin' and yellin'. Then my dad'll leave and stay gone for a coupla days…"

Well, that explained the despondency.

"Yeah," he said. "My mom used to sit out here with me." He smiled at the memory. "We didn't have these chairs at the time. I made these for my dad. Thought maybe it'd get him outside some."

"He still not leavin' the house?"

"Nope. Not since…" Not since the night his mother died a couple of months back. The pain of the loss still radiated inside him, burning hot and painful. His chest squeezed. God, he missed his mom.

Lynx felt more than saw Reagan's eyes on him, but he fought the urge to look at her. He knew if he did, he'd want something she couldn't give him. She was too sweet for what he wanted from her. More importantly, she was too young.

The technical term … jail bait.

Avoiding Reagan hadn't been easy, and once Lynx found out she had a steady boyfriend, he'd nearly lost his mind. Most people thought that losing his mother was the reason he'd gone off the rails and that was true, but only partly. Reagan had played a big part in it as well. For the longest time, she'd offered him hope, made him believe his world wasn't crashing down all around him.

Turning down the dirt drive, Lynx noticed Reagan's truck was parked outside. He pulled his truck behind hers and then cut the engine. Before he got the first chair out of the truck, he heard the front screen door squeak open. Taking a deep breath, he focused on his task, doing his best not to look at her.

She didn't say a word until he was putting the second chair in place on the porch.

"Lynx?"

He turned away from her, eager to get back in his truck and go home. He'd left Copenhagen at the house that morning and he was eager to see his dog. For whatever reason, Copenhagen calmed him, helped him to reason through his thoughts. He needed that right now.

"Thank you for the chairs."

He offered a curt nod, still not looking at her. "You're welcome."

"And … I'm sorry," Reagan said softly.

"Okay." He didn't know what else to say. He didn't blame her for anything that had happened, but he also didn't want to get into it right now. His control was tenuous at best, and the more he was around her, the more fragile it became.

"Will you look at me, please?"

Swallowing hard, he turned to face her, shoving his hands in his pockets.

"What happened back at the warehouse…" Reagan took a deep breath. "I shouldn't've kissed you, and I'm sorry."

He nodded. The lump that those words caused swelled in his throat and threatened to strangle him. The thought of losing her before he even had her was too much for him to bear.

"Okay, that's a lie," she added, her eyes still locked with his. "I'm not sorry. For kissing you. I'm… I've been wantin' to do that for a long time. I'm just sorry I can't give you what you want. You have to realize what I've been through. Dealin' with Billy…"

Oh, he got it, all right. But he wasn't Billy. Not even remotely close.

Another nod was all he could offer. Although she thought the explanation was helping, it wasn't. Not one fucking bit.

"Please say somethin'," she urged.

Lynx shook his head. "Nothin' to say."

And that was the truth.

He feared if he opened his mouth the truth would come out, and he wasn't sure he could handle much more of her rejection.

Certainly not today.

REAGAN WASN'T SURE SHE'D EVER SEEN LYNX like this. The pained expression was hard to miss, but she had no clue what to say to erase it. The man … he threatened her heart in ways he would never understand. She'd been in love with him for so long, but she'd convinced herself he was off-limits. For chrissakes, he'd even told her she couldn't handle what he wanted from her. She knew that to be true.

And it had nothing to do with sex. She'd had more than her fair share of fantasies about the man, plenty of time spent with her vibrator. She could handle that aspect of it easily. Even now, her body was telling her that being with him would be the greatest pleasure she'd ever known. However, her brain and her heart weren't thinking along those same lines.

No, she was thinking on an emotional level, and the hell Billy had put her through… It was still fresh in her mind. And although she knew Lynx wasn't Billy, there was still the risk of heartache in a different form. Something far greater than any pain Billy could've put her through. No, she wasn't interested in having her heart broken again. Letting Billy go was one thing. If she ever got Lynx within her grasp and then had to let *him* go … Reagan wasn't sure she'd be the same person after that, which was what scared her the most.

Before she could say anything more, the sound of an engine pulling down the drive had them both turning.

Wolfe's big black Silverado rolled to a stop behind Lynx's truck.

She released a breath. A sigh of relief, maybe? Or was that disappointment that was slowly filling her up?

"What're you kids up to?" Wolfe asked when he got out of the truck and walked around to open the passenger-side door.

"*Nada*," Lynx offered, his tone far more cheerful than a second ago.

The huge grin on Wolfe's face said that all was right in his world.

Reagan glanced over at Amy. Her smile was equally big as she held Wolfe's hand and walked up to the porch.

"We came by to get Amy's…" Wolfe glanced down at Amy. "You wanna tell 'em?"

Her smile practically engulfed her entire face and her eyes sparkled when she looked up at the man.

Oh, yeah, that girl was in love, no doubt about it.

Reagan didn't move from where she stood, a few feet behind Lynx.

"Wolfe asked me and Rhys to move in with him," Amy said, her eyes darting back and forth between Reagan and Lynx.

"Very cool," Lynx said, but he very well could've said, "Whatever," for as much enthusiasm as he put into it.

"We're still gonna take it slow," Amy added, obviously picking up on Lynx's tension. "I mean—"

"You don't have to explain," Reagan said, plastering a smile on her face. "Like I told you before, as long as the three of you are happy, it doesn't matter."

"Right," Amy noted, once again smiling as she peered up at Wolfe. "I'll be right back."

Wolfe swatted her on the butt, making her yelp before she trotted up the steps toward Reagan. The woman's eyes scanned the two rocking chairs, but she didn't say anything, for which Reagan was grateful.

Figuring Lynx didn't have anything else to say, and certainly nothing that could be said in front of his cousin, Reagan followed Amy into the house.

"I … uh… Are you gonna sell the house?" she asked, blurting the words out quickly. Like ripping a Band-Aid off.

"Actually," Amy said, turning to face her, "I was thinkin' maybe you could stay here. I really don't want to sell it, but I don't want it to sit empty, either."

Reagan nodded, trying to play it cool although the relief she felt was fierce. "Of course."

"If you could cover the utilities, I won't charge rent if you could … uh … maintain it."

Reagan smiled. She liked Amy. A lot. She considered her a friend, even if they hadn't spent a lot of time together.

"Absolutely," she assured Amy. "I can even mow the yard."

"Thank you."

"Don't thank me. I'm the one who should be thankin' you," Reagan assured her.

"And if you want to move into the master bedroom … I was … uh … gonna leave my bed here."

Reagan grinned. She'd slept in Amy's bed a few times when the futon became too much for her tired body to deal with, but she'd felt weird about it.

"I just might do that."

Amy peered around the room. "And feel free to decorate however you like. Consider it ... uh ... your place now."

"Are you sure about this?" Reagan asked, sobering somewhat. "Not that I'm questionin' how you feel about Wolfe and Rhys, it's just..." She knew the hell Amy had been through, had heard the story more than once, and it still resonated with her.

"I'm sure." Her tone was wispy, like a girl in love. "I know I haven't known them long, but..."

"It feels right," Reagan filled in for her. "Don't need to convince me, Amy. I got your back."

Amy smiled and the next thing Reagan knew, Amy was hugging her. "Thank you, Reagan."

"For what?" she asked, confused.

"For being my friend."

Tears welled in her eyes at the sound of Amy's voice. The woman sounded pained, as though she never thought she would have friends. Reagan could relate somewhat. Sure, she had friends in Embers Ridge, but she'd isolated herself from most people because of Billy. She'd been embarrassed about their relationship, about the fact that she didn't love him but stuck around and put up with his shit. And he had treated her like shit, not caring who knew.

"Like I said, I'm the one who should be thankin' you," Reagan replied softly. "And if you ever need anything, you know where to find me."

Amy pulled back and grinned. "At Lynx's house?"

Reagan rolled her eyes. "Definitely not. We're just friends."

It was obvious Amy didn't buy that line, but whatever.

"Okay, then. I guess I'll grab ... a few things."

Reagan had been over every square inch of the house multiple times, mostly when she got bored and had nothing else to do. Amy didn't have much of anything in the house. Some secondhand furniture, clothes, toiletries, a few plastic dishes in the cupboard, a mop and broom, and one cheap vacuum cleaner. There weren't any trinkets decorating the walls, no pictures. Reagan hadn't gone snooping or anything, but she didn't think Amy even had jewelry of any kind. Granted, Amy had more material things than Reagan owned, but it still wasn't much. She could probably load everything in Wolfe's truck right now if she really wanted to.

"I'm leaving the furniture and all that stuff," Amy said as she turned toward the bedroom. "If you decide you don't want it…"

"It's perfect," Reagan called after her. "I promise, I won't throw anything away."

Amy reappeared in the doorway. "Seriously, Reagan, I want you to feel like this is your home, not mine. So … do whatever you want."

Reagan nodded curtly. "I will." She met Amy's gaze. "And thank you. Really."

Amy would never truly understand what she'd done for Reagan. Giving her a place to stay was more than Reagan had ever had before. She had thought about leaving Billy a million times, but the idea of living with her mother and her grandfather had made her cringe. She loved them, but her grandfather wasn't known for his kindness and her mother did not support her breaking up with Billy in the first place. Amy's offer had been the swift kick in the pants that Reagan had needed to finally move on with her life, something she'd ached to do for so long.

Sure, she could've gone to live with her brother when she finally left Billy, but she knew Rhys. He was her big brother and he was overprotective at times. More so since their father had died. Her brother would've given her a hard time, and Reagan was tired of being under someone's thumb all the time.

For the first time in her life, she actually felt … free.

Chapter Twelve

"EVERYTHING COOL?" WOLFE ASKED WHEN LYNX STARTED for his truck.

"Yep," he answered, trying to keep his voice from reflecting the hurt currently swarming him. "Just dropped off those chairs. Headin' home. What're y'all up to? Besides, you know, shackin' up together."

Wolfe's smile was so fucking bright Lynx almost had to look away. He liked seeing his cousin happy. Not that he wasn't usually, but there was definitely something different about Wolfe these days. The guy seemed to be walking around on a fucking cloud, despite the danger they all knew to be lurking nearby.

"Rhys gonna be packin' his shit up, too?" Lynx asked when Wolfe didn't respond.

"We're workin' it out."

"Right. So that's a yes."

"It's a … yeah. He's got a lotta shit goin' on right now. He's tryin' to stay focused, but that's where I want him."

Lynx chuckled. "I get it. Hard to focus when he's spendin' all his time naked, huh?"

"Shut it."

"Well, I gotta run," Lynx told him. "Gotta go get Cope. He's prob'ly goin' crazy right about now."

Wolfe nodded toward the house. "And I need to get inside, see if I can help with somethin'."

"You do that." Lynx stopped. "Oh, and while you're in there, check out the water heater. Reagan said it's actin' up."

"Uh ... yeah. Okay."

"Check ya later, hoss." Lynx offered a half-ass wave, then hopped in his truck without looking back at the house.

Half an hour later, Lynx pulled up in front of his house. Officially it was his uncle's place, but ever since Wolfe's momma passed away two years ago, Calvin Caine had moved into the apartment above the store. Said it was easier that way. Back when Lynx and Tammy had split, Lynx offered to move into his uncle's house to keep an eye on it. Since he was already doing the upkeep on his grandparents' old place, he'd figured it really was easier, not to mention he had needed to get as far from Tammy as possible. The woman was like a damn tick.

Thankfully, it seemed as though she'd moved on. At least since the day she'd stolen his truck, anyway.

It had only taken Lynx wiping out half the money in his personal account for her to finally stop hounding him, but as far as Lynx was concerned, it was worth it. The money didn't mean shit if he had to spend the rest of his days dealing with the woman who'd personally planned to make his life a living hell.

"You live and learn, Cope," he said to his dog when he climbed out of the truck, greeted by the three-year-old German shepherd. "Whatcha been up to, man? Chillin'? Lickin' your balls? What?"

Copenhagen pushed his big head against Lynx's thigh, nudging him.

"All right, I get it. I won't talk about your balls no more."

The two of them traipsed up the stairs to the farmhouse and Lynx found himself eyeing the porch. There were no rocking chairs on this front porch. Not yet, anyway. Maybe not ever if things didn't work out the way he'd planned.

His mind drifted back to Reagan, to how fucking hot she'd been in his arms. And then her words had hit him like an uppercut, nearly knocking him sideways. The woman was out of her ever-loving mind if she thought once was going to cut it. As it was, when the time came that Lynx got her in his bed, he might not ever let her leave.

"You hungry, boy?" he asked Copenhagen. "Come on, then. Let's get you fed, then we'll run over and check on the old man, see what's up."

After that, Lynx would find something else to do to pass the time. It was Saturday, which meant he should've been planning to head over to Reagan's for a couple of beers later in the evening.

"Not tonight," he muttered to himself.

He couldn't remember the last Saturday he hadn't gone over to the bar, but after today... Lynx figured it was time to give Reagan some of that space she'd been asking for.

If for nothing else, so Lynx could maintain a little bit of his sanity.

Otherwise...

No. He wouldn't even go there.

Not this time.

Patience was key to this game. He just had to remember that.

"What's up, old man?" Lynx called to his father when he and Copenhagen walked into the house. Although it was three in the afternoon, it was dark as hell with all the blinds closed.

"Whatcha doin' here, kid?" Cooter called from somewhere in the house.

Copenhagen took off.

"Hey, Cope! Good to see you, boy."

Lynx found his father in the kitchen, a bowl of fresh tomatoes on the counter in front of him.

"That from the garden?" Lynx asked.

"Yep." The man looked so proud.

97

Cooter hadn't left the house, aside from going out into the garden in the backyard or the occasional afternoon spent on the porch, for ten years now. Not to the grocery store, not to get gas, not even to the doctor. At first, it had seemed odd, but eventually it became the norm. Lynx picked up his dad's groceries, he brought fuel for the mower when it was time to cut the grass around the house, and he'd found a doctor willing to make house calls.

Cooter wasn't opposed to company and plenty of people stopped by. Although Cooter had extricated himself from the world outside of his house, the people in this town hadn't given up on him. That was part of living in a small town. Friends became family.

"Figured you'd be out gettin' yourself in trouble," Cooter said, a smile on his weathered face.

"Takin' a break," he told his father.

"For what? Five minutes?"

Smiling, Lynx nodded. "Somethin' like that."

"You want some tea?"

"Naw. Gonna head over to Nana's real quick. Check things out."

"You seen your cousins lately?"

"Who? Travis and them?"

His father lifted one gray eyebrow, as though it was obvious who he was referring to.

"Not since the bonfire," he told him. "Why?"

Cooter shook his head. "Talked to Iris. She mentioned Travis was helping to deal with that little gal's ... situation." His eyes narrowed. "They find that asshole yet?"

Lynx knew his dad was referring to the Houston police chief, the man responsible for Amy's abuse and the death of the police detective. "Not yet."

Not that they'd proven the man was responsible for the car accident that had killed the woman who'd come out to Embers Ridge in an effort to find Amy. However, it seemed awfully coincidental that that woman had ventured this far to confirm that Amy was in fact the Jane Doe who'd been found on the side of the road a year ago only to wind up dead shortly after finding out the truth.

"He'll fuck up," Cooter said, his tone confident. "And they'll get that bastard."

They would. Not soon enough though. The asshole should've been chilling with the worms six feet under at this point.

"Need anything while I'm here? I can run into town, grab some groceries."

"I'm good right now. Next time you're out, maybe you could pick up some M&Ms?"

Lynx grinned. "Sure thing, Dad."

"Thanks."

"Cope, you ready, boy?"

The dog's ears perked and his tongue lolled out of his mouth as he trotted over to Lynx's side.

"Talk to ya later," Lynx hollered as he headed toward the door. "And I'll grab those M&Ms when I'm up that way. Love you, old man."

"Love you too, kid."

Clicking his tongue twice, Lynx directed Copenhagen to the truck.

Time to find something else to do to keep his mind occupied for a little while longer.

KELLY JACKSON SAT IN THE OLD TRUCK he'd borrowed from a friend, watching the small bar. He'd been there for an hour and had yet to see Amy come out. He knew she was in there, knew she worked here in this shit hole every Saturday night.

And it was a shit hole. Not a place he would ever be caught dead in.

However, he wasn't all that surprised that Amy would be there.

Every time he thought about it, Kelly remembered the day he'd decided he could never marry that girl. She was too young, too stupid, too … weak. No wife of his would've ever worked in a fucking bar. That thought triggered memories of his first wife. God, he'd held out so much hope for her. Unfortunately, he'd found out far too late what a fraud she was. The girl hadn't been classy at all. She'd been … a tramp. Whenever he had hit her, she hadn't fought back. After the second or third time, she had simply thrown herself at him, thinking sex would distract him.

It hadn't worked.

They'd only been married nine months when he finally got tired of it. And he'd set it up perfectly. She'd drowned in the bathtub and no one had even suspected that he'd held her head under the water and watched as the life drained from her body.

Of course, his second wife had been wild and crazy, hot for him in ways he hadn't expected. Their sex life had been intense. She'd thought his dominance was sexy, even turned it around so that she was playing the role of his submissive. Granted, Kelly hadn't been into the real D/s relationships. There were too many rules involved in that shit for his liking.

He'd thought things were going to work there for a little while. He had enjoyed their games, the fact that she seemed to like when he hit her. Then the stupid bitch went and got pregnant. She had forced his hand at that point. He wasn't about to raise a child with that woman. Or any woman, in fact. He'd had to work that one from a different angle. A few strategically timed conversations about her being depressed had worked like a charm. So, when she'd taken too many pills, no one had suspected him then, either.

Amy, on the other hand, was proving to be his biggest challenge yet. Out of the three of them, he'd thought she would be the easiest to break. When he had first set his sights on her, she'd been vulnerable, moldable. Even better, she'd had no one, and at nineteen, she'd still been rebellious against her aunt and uncle. Taking them out had been simple and it had allowed him to take possession of Amy.

However, she had proven him wrong by fighting back. The gleam of defiance he always saw in her eyes had turned him on for a while, but she had never cowered, never understood her true place. That had only incited his temper, making his dick harder than he thought possible. Honestly, he had enjoyed their time together in the beginning. But even that had worn off.

Fortunately for him, he'd figured out a way to handle her.

Little did she know, but tonight was going to be the end for her. Once she was out of the way for good, his life would be back on track, her memory a mere blemish in his otherwise perfect world.

EVERY TIME THE DAMN DOOR OPENED, REAGAN'S gaze darted over. And every damn time the door opened, Reagan was disappointed because the person waltzing in wasn't Lynx.

She still remembered the pained look on his face that morning and it made her stomach hurt. She'd put that look there and she hadn't meant to. The last thing in the world she would ever want to do was hurt that man. Although protecting her heart from him was crucial, he was still a friend. A very cherished friend, at that.

"Get another round over here, ladies?" one of the old cowboys called from the back.

Reagan glanced over at Amy, who was busy wiping down a couple of empty tables.

It was late, closing in on eleven, which meant they'd be shutting the bar down in an hour, and for the first time in forever, Reagan was counting down the minutes until that happened. She was pretty sure today had been the longest day in history. It was time to put it to bed. Not that she had anything to do after she left, but tonight she really didn't want to be here. She was tired of listening to everyone laughing and joking, chatting it up about nothing important.

What she wanted to do was curl beneath the blankets in her bed and pretend today had never happened.

It would be easier that way.

Reagan popped the top off three beers and carried them over to the group of men. One of the guys — she'd never seen him in there before — glanced her way, his gaze instantly sliding down to her chest. She fought the urge to roll her eyes.

"Here you go, gentlemen," she said sweetly. "Still good?"

"We're good, honey," the older one confirmed before resuming his conversation.

After making her way back to the bar, Reagan tried to keep herself busy so she wouldn't be tempted to watch the door. Unfortunately, she'd already cleaned everything she could clean. Twice.

"Hey."

Looking up, she saw the man who'd been checking out her tits now standing on the other side of the scarred bar top. He wasn't a bad-looking man. A little older, probably mid-thirties or so. He looked as though he'd been rode hard and put up wet, which likely meant he was a new ranch hand over at either the Double D or Dead Heat Ranch. Not that it mattered. She saw so many come through here and they changed quite frequently.

"What can I getcha?" she asked, knowing he wasn't there for another beer.

"How ya doin'?" he asked.

"Great. You?" She knew her tone didn't sound great, but hey, Reagan was doing the best that she could tonight.

"Name's Tommy. And you are…?"

"Busy, Tommy, but thanks for askin'," she replied coolly.

The guy grinned, clearly not fazed by her obvious brush-off.

"Aww, come on now," he said with a grin. "I was just tryin' to be friendly."

Reagan turned to face him. "And I was tryin' *not* to be rude," she told him flatly.

The man seemed to consider that for a moment. "Somehow, I think we got off on the wrong foot."

"Nope," she assured him. "We didn't. If you need another beer, holler. Otherwise…" Reagan motioned to where she'd left the rag on the bar.

"Got it." He turned and sauntered back to the table.

She'd half expected some sort of snide remark from being spurned, but he didn't say a word. She'd gotten used to that over the years. Most of the folks who came in knew her and were friendly. However, there was the occasional hothead who didn't take kindly to being turned down. And then there was Billy, who had never taken kindly to not getting his way. Whenever she didn't meekly agree with him, she usually endured a rash of shit spewing from his mouth.

She damn sure didn't miss that.

Of course, those thoughts had Reagan replaying the conversation with Tommy in her head. God, she sounded like such a bitch.

Seemed she was on a roll today.

An hour later, Reagan breathed a sigh of relief. Without wasting time, she grabbed the till from the bar and secured it in the safe before locking the rest of the place down. She made her way out to the main room to find Amy and Wolfe standing there, clearly waiting for her.

"I'm good, y'all," she said. "Really. You don't have to wait."

"You're right," Wolfe replied easily. "We don't have to. But we want to."

Same thing Lynx had said the other day.

"Seriously, don't you wanna take your lady home to bed?" she teased, taking off her apron and tossing it beneath the bar.

"Of course," he said with a wicked smirk. "And if you'd get your ass in gear, I could do just that."

"Fine." Reagan knew they wouldn't leave until she did, so she grabbed her truck keys and headed toward the door.

"I'm not sure why y'all can't just—" Reagan pushed the door, but it shifted slightly but didn't open. It should've swung outward. She tried again but was met with the same resistance. "What the fuck?"

She dropped her hands, shook them out, then tried again just in case, you know, she'd forgotten how to open a door in the last few hours.

Nope. Still wouldn't open.

Glancing over at Wolfe, she frowned. "What's wrong with the damn door?"

"Hell if I—"

That was all he got out before the world erupted in a violent explosion. The earth-rattling boom sent the three of them slamming against the front wall of the building. Chairs and tables launched into the air, glass shattering, raining down all around them.

And the noise. Holy shit, it was so loud. *Too* loud.

Reagan landed with a thud on the floor, her head making a solid impact with the hard post that framed the doors. It rang her bell hard, making her see spots momentarily.

Shit.

She tried to push herself up, but she couldn't manage. Her ears were ringing, her eyes unable to focus.

"Wolfe? Amy?" she choked out as smoke filled the building, invading her lungs, making her eyes sting.

Shit, shit, shit.

When Reagan managed to get her eyes open, she noticed…

"Fire!" Wolfe yelled. "Son of a bitch. Get out, Reagan! Now!"

The man sounded frantic, but Reagan was still having a hard time hearing, her ears ringing from the percussion of the blast. What the hell could've exploded?

"Amy? Baby?" Wolfe was shouting now, an ungodly sound that had Reagan forcing herself up, trying to see what was going on.

Fire engulfed the back wall of the bar. The heat from the flames roared toward them as they licked at the rickety ceiling.

"Oh, fuck. Oh, fuck," Reagan hissed, clutching her head as she got to her knees.

Trying to clear her thoughts, Reagan could barely make out Amy unconscious on the floor. Wolfe was cradling her head, but there was a lot of blood.

"Out," Reagan said, talking more to herself. With the roar of the fire, it wasn't like Wolfe would've heard her anyway. "Have to get out."

She glanced at the front door, then at the back wall. Reagan attempted to push the front doors open, but again, they wouldn't move. They were trapped. The only other door was blocked by the flames and the front one wasn't budging.

It took a second to steady herself, and her head was screaming at her the entire time, but Reagan managed to feel her way down the wall toward the bar, keeping low to the floor. She covered her face with the edge of her shirt, trying to breathe through the thick smoke. The room was dark, lit only by the flames, but it was enough to light her path to the bar. Reaching around, she fumbled for her shotgun, locating it instantly.

"Get back!" Reagan yelled, getting to her feet and stumbling toward the door. "Move her back, Wolfe! Dammit!"

The man seemed to process what she was saying, and as soon as he had Amy shifted out of the way, Reagan lifted the gun to her shoulder and aimed at the front door right where the handles were. She sent up a silent prayer that no one was on the other side before she fired off three rounds, hitting her mark effortlessly. It was enough to weaken the wood. With her foot, Reagan kicked in the center, but nothing happened.

"Move!" Wolfe howled, grabbing her arm and jerking her out of the way.

With a well-placed kick by the much bigger man, the doors flew open. Air rushed in and the fire thundered behind them.

"Out! Now!" Wolfe hollered, nudging her with his shoulder.

Her brain was so fuzzy Reagan didn't even realize she'd been standing there, frozen in place.

With Amy in his arms, Wolfe pushed Reagan until the three of them were out of the building, stumbling down the steps to the gravel parking lot.

No sooner had they reached Wolfe's truck than one of the deputy's squads came barreling into the lot, sirens blaring, lights flashing.

"We need an ambulance," Wolfe said, his tone frantic as he spoke into the phone. "We're at Reagan's Bar in Embers Ridge. There's been ... fuck ... an explosion. We've got one injured for sure. Possibly two."

Clearly the guy had the brains to call 9-1-1. Reagan could hardly process what was going on, much less what she should've been doing. Lot of damn good she was doing anyone.

And with that one last thought, everything went fuzzy on the peripheral of her vision. She had to sit down.

So she did.

Chapter Thirteen

"WHERE'RE YOU AT?"

Lynx pushed up off the couch when Rhys's panicked shriek sounded through the phone.

"Home. Why?"

"Reagan's... The bar ... it fucking exploded."

"*What?*" The growl that came out of him was pretty damn close to inhuman as Lynx launched himself off the couch, his sleep-fogged brain working overtime to process the information.

Copenhagen shot up from his spot on the floor, his gaze steady on Lynx.

"Yeah. Fuck. How fast can you get here?" Rhys was breathing hard. "Wolfe insisted I call you. Amy's hurt, Reagan's..."

"Reagan's *what?*" he yelled, snatching one boot as he tucked the phone against his ear. "Goddammit, Rhys!"

"She's... Fuck."

Lynx was tugging on his other boot as he headed toward the door, his blood pounding in his ears. "Come on, Cope. Let's go!" Without bothering to lock the door — he never did — Lynx scaled the wooden porch and took off toward his truck at a dead run, phone still to his ear.

Cope jumped in ahead of him, shooting over to the passenger seat as Lynx hopped in, stabbing his key into the ignition.

When Rhys had been silent too long for his peace of mind, Lynx took a deep breath, tried to calm himself. "Where's Reagan, Rhys? Is she okay?"

"I... I don't know, man. She seems to be, but I don't know. She said they were leavin', but the doors were jammed up. And then the goddamn place exploded. Looks like someone shoved a metal pipe through the front door handles, making it nearly impossible to escape."

Lynx tore out of the dirt drive and onto the main road into town, the back end of his truck fishtailing. His heart was jackhammering in his chest.

"Reagan blasted them with her shotgun, managed to weaken the wood enough... Fuck."

Hell yeah. That was his girl.

"An ambulance is on the way," Rhys continued, his words rushed. "Just get here."

"On my way," he said, his voice louder than he intended for it to be. "Five minutes, max."

The phone disconnected, and Lynx automatically dialed his uncle's number.

"This better be good," the old man grumbled.

"Calvin? How fast can you get over to Reagan's?"

His uncle groaned softly. "What's wrong, boy?"

"Don't know, but there's been an explosion. Wolfe was there..." Lynx exhaled roughly. "Don't know more than that. Can you get over there?"

When the man spoke again, he sounded completely coherent. "Grabbin' my boots and I'm on my way."

"Thanks." Lynx didn't know quite what he was thanking the man for, but he knew for a fact Calvin would be pissed if something happened to Wolfe and no one notified him.

With his due diligence done, Lynx tossed his phone onto the dashboard, then gripped the wheel with both hands and put his foot to the floor. "Hold on, Cope. It's gonna be a wild ride, buddy."

Lynx wasn't sure he'd ever driven that fast. A couple of times he had to reach over and grab Copenhagen to keep him from being thrown into the backseat or the floorboard. By the time they made it to the bar — the fucking bar that was fully engulfed in flames — the place was in utter chaos. Cars and trucks lining the side of the road and the outer part of the parking lot, lights flashing from the emergency vehicles on site, people every-fucking-where.

"Stay," he ordered Copenhagen, leaving the window down after parking on the side of the main road.

Lynx shot out of the truck and ran toward the ambulance, his eyes scanning anyone and everyone.

The instant he caught sight of Reagan, Lynx's breath seized in his lungs. He stopped, skidding on the gravel and changing direction. She was sitting on the tailgate of Wolfe's truck, the ambulance parked beside them.

"Reagan." His voice was nothing more than gravel and dust.

Her wide eyes lifted to his face and he nearly fell to his knees. Somehow he kept himself upright, not stopping until he reached her.

"Lynx." There were tears in her eyes, but it was clear she was holding them back.

His heart didn't start beating again until he had her in his arms, her face pressed to his chest.

"God, girl," he whispered, cradling the back of her head as carefully as he could. He didn't know if she was hurt, or where, and he damn sure didn't want to hurt her.

Unable to help himself, he pulled back, forcing her to look up at him momentarily. He scanned her face, noticing the soot smudged on one cheek. Other than that, he saw no signs of damage. Only when he was satisfied there were no injuries — none that were visible anyway — did he pull her back against him.

While he held her, Lynx glanced around, cataloging all the faces. He knew it wouldn't matter. The bastard who had done this wasn't sitting around waiting for them to catch him. If he had to guess, he was probably halfway to Houston by now.

"Hey, Reagan," Rhys said softly when he approached.

Lynx met her brother's eyes, ignoring the concerned look the man gave him.

When she didn't pull back, Lynx didn't let go.

"They wanna take you to the hospital," Rhys said, talking to his sister. "Said you probably have a concussion. You need to be looked at."

She shook her head, but the movement was shielded by Lynx's body.

"No hospital," she muttered. "I'm fine."

Lynx met Rhys's hardened gaze and held it. "I'll take care of her."

That didn't seem to be what Rhys wanted to hear.

Sure, Lynx got it. His reputation preceded him, and he understood why Reagan's brother would be worried. That didn't mean he gave two shits. He wasn't leaving Reagan, and if she didn't want to go to the hospital, no one could make her.

"Damn hardheaded women," Rhys grumbled.

Lynx glanced over to see Amy shaking her head, her eyes wide, her face as white as the bandage on her head. "I take it she ain't goin', either."

"Nope. They said hers isn't serious. Shallow wound on her scalp from a piece of glass, which bleeds like a bitch."

They did. Lynx knew that for a fact.

"But she was unconscious," Reagan said, pulling back slightly to look at her brother.

"Not from a head wound. They think she passed out from the shock."

Considering all the woman had been through, Lynx could understand that.

Reagan seemed content with the answer because she pressed her face against Lynx's chest once again.

"I'll take Reagan home with me," Lynx assured Rhys.

The man's eyes narrowed.

"I've got two guest rooms, man. Not like I'm gonna throw her in my bed and never let her go." Although he fucking liked that idea. Still, he wouldn't do it. "You can stop by whenever you want and check on her."

Rhys seemed to consider that for a moment before nodding. "I *will* stop by."

Lynx grinned. "I know. I'll even leave the door unlocked."

"You do that," Rhys stated, then slapped Lynx on the shoulder before walking over to the ambulance.

Leaning down, placing his mouth close to Reagan's ear, he whispered, "You good with that? I'll take you home if you want, but I ain't leavin' you alone, so don't ask me to."

Reagan's arms tightened around him and that was all the answer Lynx needed.

For a brief second tonight, he'd thought his entire world had been shattered. Again.

It brought back memories of the night they'd gotten the call about his mother. She'd been on her way home from the hospital where she worked. Her car had skidded off the road and gone headfirst into a tree. They said she'd been going too fast for the corner, probably never saw it coming.

Yep, one woman in his life had been stolen far too soon. He wasn't sure he could handle if Reagan was taken from him, too.

No fucking way was he going to let her out of his sight. Not yet.

Hell, maybe not ever.

HER BAR WAS GONE.

Completely burned to a crisp.

According to Rhys, the fire department said it appeared someone had rigged the above-ground propane gas tank behind the building to blow. However, they wouldn't know for sure until the fire inspector got out there.

Her own gas tank. The one that supplied heat and hot water to the building had been used to blow up her livelihood and damn near kill her and two of her closest friends? Who the hell would do something like that?

Reagan clicked the seat belt into place and took a deep breath, watching the scene before her. It wasn't as chaotic as it had been earlier, but there was still quite a bit going on. She probably should've stuck around, but when Lynx offered to take her back to his place, Reagan hadn't been able to refuse.

"Give her some love, Cope," Lynx urged the dog, his gaze briefly swinging toward her as he pulled out onto the main road.

When the dog's big muzzle nudged her arm, Reagan reached over and gently petted him, leaning her head back against the seat. She was tired. Her body ached from the impact she'd made with the wall. And yes, the paramedic had finally given her a good once-over, telling her she should probably go to the hospital, but at the very least, someone needed to keep an eye on her through the night and not let her sleep for more than an hour or so at a time. Something about a possible concussion.

She was fine.

But her bar was gone.

Reagan sighed.

What she wanted to do was sleep for the next week. Then she wanted to wake up and go back in time to before today. Before she'd had breakfast with Lynx, before she'd known the pleasure he could offer her, and yes, before her entire world had been blown to bits.

"Did you call your mom?" Lynx asked.

"Yeah," she said softly. "She told me to come stay over there."

"You want me to take you there?"

"Nope." She loved her mother, but they didn't get along. Plus, her grandfather was nothing more than a burly old bear who enjoyed berating her every chance he got. She did not need to listen to either of them harp on her right now. "I'll stop by there tomorrow."

"Okay."

He seemed content with that, but Reagan didn't open her eyes to look at him. She couldn't. Not right now. The second she'd seen him racing toward her, Reagan had nearly lost it. And when he wrapped her in his arms, she'd had to fight back the tears that had threatened.

After all she'd said to him that morning, Lynx had still come to check on her in the middle of the damn night. Not only that, but his father had called after Wolfe's dad had informed him of what happened. Reagan had been shocked when Lynx handed her the phone. She had expected it to be her mother, surprised when the deep, raspy voice so much like Lynx's had echoed through the phone.

"Reagan, honey? Are you okay?"

"Yes, sir," she replied softly. "I'm okay."

"Good. Lynx said the bar burned down."

"Yes, sir, it did."

"Well, I don't want you worryin' about that tonight. We'll all be helpin' you to get it up and runnin' in no time at all."

She knew he wasn't included in that "we" because Cooter never left the house, but Reagan appreciated the sentiment anyway. "Thank you."

Cooter grunted. "Put Lynx back on, honey."

Reagan hadn't heard the rest of the conversation. She'd been too busy trying to ignore the paramedic who wanted to shine a light in her eyes to check her pupils.

"You hungry?" Lynx asked, his hand linking with hers and tugging her arm toward him.

"No." She wasn't sure she'd ever be able to eat again. Her heart seemed to have dropped to her stomach and the damn thing throbbed like a bad tooth. She hurt and not only in the physical sense. Her only income had been obliterated in one fell swoop and now she was left with…

Nothing.

It could be worse, the little voice in her head chided.

And yes, Reagan knew that was true. At least no one had been killed. Amy would be fine; Wolfe was fine. Thankfully, no one else had been in the bar at the time.

"He obviously planned this, huh?" she asked Lynx, forcing her eyes open.

"Rhys thinks so," Lynx noted, gently squeezing her fingers.

"To kill Amy?"

"That's my guess."

"At first, when I couldn't get the door open, I thought the guy at the bar had done it," she explained.

"What guy?" Lynx's tone was hard.

"The one who was flirtin' with me. Never saw him before. When I shut him down, he just walked away. I remember thinkin' it was odd. Thought maybe it was a joke that he locked us in the bar."

Then, when the world had exploded, she hadn't given that guy a second thought.

Clearly, she'd been the only one who had thought it was anyone other than Amy's ex.

Reagan had heard her brother talking, knew he suspected the guy was watching Amy. Obviously, the police chief knew Amy worked at Reagan's. Reagan had even briefly wondered if he was still there, watching the destruction. Lynx had sounded completely sure of himself when he told Rhys that the bastard was long gone. Her brother had agreed.

"Do you think he'll be back?" she asked him now.

"I do."

She peered over at him. "Amy said she's gonna take this opportunity to talk to a reporter since they'll be doing news coverage on it."

"I heard."

"Do you think that'll make it worse?" Not that she thought it could really get any worse than this.

"Don't know."

Reagan closed her eyes once again, sighing heavily. She felt defeated.

And the only thing she wanted to do was sleep. For a decade.

Chapter Fourteen

STANDING AT THE DOOR TO THE MASTER bedroom, Lynx watched Reagan sleep. He had no idea how long he'd been standing there, observing the rise and fall of her chest beneath the blankets. He simply couldn't look away. Seeing her in his bed, healthy, strong ... alive. His damn heart jolted every fucking time he thought about what had happened tonight. How easily she could've been ripped from his life.

And every damn time he thought about it, he wanted to put his fist through the wall.

A lot of people accused him of being angry, always looking for a fight. Honestly, that wasn't the case at all. In fact, he considered himself pretty happy-go-lucky most of the time.

Oh, sure, when his mother died, Lynx had been pissed at the world. Who could blame him, though? The most important woman in his life had been taken from him and his father long before she should have been. His heart had been fractured that day. Over the years, as the minutes and the hours passed, the pain lessened, but his heart still had the fissures in it. Always would.

No one knew that Reagan Trevino was the main reason he had held on. Without knowing, Lynx had fallen in love with that girl. Even back then.

Only she'd never been his to have, and spending the past decade watching as she grew up, her life entwined with that son of a bitch had been too much to bear. Ultimately, he'd tried to repair himself with various women. It had never worked.

And now Reagan was right there in his bed.

Only she wasn't his for the taking now, either.

"Lynx?"

"What, darlin'?" he asked, not moving from his spot at the door.

"You okay?"

"Perfect," he answered.

She rolled over, clutching the pillow. "Would you … maybe … hold me for a little while?"

"Sure." He wasn't sure that was the best idea in the world, but it wasn't like he would tell her no, so trying to pretend otherwise was just a waste of time.

He walked around to the far side of the bed and climbed on top of the quilt. He was still fully dressed, except for his boots, and he was grateful for that. Even with the blanket between them, Lynx wasn't sure it would be enough.

Reagan rolled toward him and Lynx froze. She quickly pushed the comforter down to her waist and snuggled up to his side, her hand resting on his chest, her head pressed against his shoulder. He took a deep breath and closed his arm around her. She smelled like his shampoo from when she'd taken a shower earlier. He remembered standing in the kitchen, as far from the bathroom as he could possibly get and still be inside the house, not wanting to hear the shower run, not wanting to think about Reagan naked in his bathroom, the water sliding down her smooth, perfect…

Yeah. Still not helping to think about it.

"About yesterday mornin'," she whispered softly, pulling him back from the brink.

"Don't," he warned, keeping his tone as gentle as he could.

"I'm sorry."

"Reagan."

"I never meant to hurt you," she continued as though he hadn't said a word.

Rather than lie and tell her she hadn't hurt him, Lynx kept his mouth shut and stared up at the ceiling. "Go to sleep."

She sighed, moving closer to him. "It's true, Lynx. I never meant—"

"Not tonight," he said roughly. "We'll talk about it … later."

She sighed again and he waited for her rebuttal.

Thankfully, it never came.

Lynx's entire body had gone rock hard the instant she touched him. He should've stayed in the living room or gone to sleep in the guest room like he'd originally told her he would when he insisted that she take his king bed.

Instead, he was lying here with Reagan beside him, her body so fucking soft against him, her hair teasing his chin where it caught in the stubble on his jaw. And his dick was throbbing, making his damn jeans ridiculously uncomfortable.

Yet this was enough for him. Having Reagan here, knowing she was safe.

It was enough.

A few minutes passed before her breathing evened out. Lynx knew sleep would be a long time coming for him. He'd been asleep when Rhys called, so he was good to go for a while. Plus, he was too fucking scared to close his eyes. He didn't want to drift off, to dream about what had happened, for his stupid subconscious to come up with an alternate ending.

So, for now, he would hold Reagan, pretend that this was his life, that he had the pleasure of holding her every night when they went to sleep, to wake up to her beside him every morning.

After all, it wasn't a far cry from the fantasies he'd had for the past decade.

In fact, it was the *exact* fantasy he'd had for the past decade.

RHYS STOOD IN THE PARKING LOT OF his sister's bar. Well, what used to be her bar. Now it was nothing more than charred remains in the middle of the parking lot. Every single thing was gone, nothing salvageable with the exception of the fire-proof safe that had been in the wall in her office. Sure, it had melted somewhat, but it was still intact.

"We need to bring Billy Watson in for questioning," Dean said from beside him. "And this guy she said hit on her tonight."

Rhys knew that neither of those men were responsible for this. Sure, Billy Watson was an asshole, but he wasn't so much of one that he would try to kill three people. As for the other guy … Rhys didn't know him, but he seriously doubted being turned down by a woman would have him rigging the propane tank to blow.

However, it wasn't like he could tell Dean that the top suspect was the fucking Houston police chief. Kelly Jackson. A goddamn psychopath who was hell-bent on destroying Amy and anyone else who got in his way.

Turning to Dean, Rhys nodded. "Do that. Bring them in first thing in the morning."

While Dean questioned them, Rhys would be checking in with Ryan Trexler and Zachariah Tavoularis. They'd be able to get him some real answers.

And if they were all lucky, they'd soon have Kelly Jackson's head on a fucking platter.

"WHERE'S RHYS?" AMY ASKED AS SOON AS Wolfe stepped into the bedroom.

"He'll be here in a bit," Wolfe told her. "I'll wait up for him, I promise. But you need to sleep."

Wolfe was pretty sure he'd said that at least a dozen times since they got back to the house.

"I can't sleep," she said, her tone soft.

She sounded exhausted and Wolfe imagined she was. It had been a rather eventful night. His entire world had come crashing down when the bar exploded. His only thought had been keeping Amy safe. And he'd thought his world had *ended* when he found Amy crumpled on the floor unconscious. Thank God Reagan had some sense to get that damn shotgun, because Wolfe's brain had gone offline, a blinding rage having taken over, making it impossible to think when the only thing he wanted to do was kill that bastard with his bare fucking hands.

Knowing Amy wasn't going to give in to sleep until Rhys was back, Wolfe shot him a quick text, stripped his clothes off, and crawled into bed with the woman he loved.

"Come here, darlin'," he whispered, pulling her to him.

When she settled against his side, her head on his chest, Wolfe wrapped his arms tightly around her.

"I love you," he whispered in the dark.

"I love you, too. So much. I'm so sorry th—"

"Shh, baby." Pressing his lips to her forehead, he tightened his hold. "Don't apologize for anything. We'll stop him, I promise you that."

"How?"

"Trust me." Wolfe didn't have a plan yet, but he'd already put in a call to his cousin. Travis told him to give him until morning and he'd have something set up. It was time to put a stop to this bullshit once and for all. And if Travis couldn't help, then Wolfe would get Lynx and they'd come up with something.

"Do you think Reagan's all right?" Amy asked.

"I texted Lynx earlier. He said she was sleepin'. I'm sure she's fine."

"But her bar…" Amy's arm tightened across his chest.

"We'll rebuild it," he assured her. "That's what we do."

"I just can't believe he would do that." The pain in her voice was so powerful Wolfe wanted to erase it completely.

"He's crazy," Wolfe told her. That was the understatement of the fucking century.

"I want to talk to that reporter tomorrow," she whispered, her words slurring with her exhaustion.

"We'll talk about it in the mornin'." He kissed her forehead again. "But right now I want you to sleep."

KELLY SAT AT THE SMALL DESK IN his hotel room, his laptop in front of him. He searched the Internet for information on the fire. He knew the damn place had blown because he'd been there to see it.

Well, not *right* there, but he'd been a mile out and there had been no mistaking the solid boom that had shaken the earth and the fireball that had shot into the sky. It had taken every ounce of his honed patience not to turn around so he could watch the place burn. Instead, he'd had to imagine Amy burning to death inside, those stupid fucks she worked for going with her.

So far, he hadn't found anything, but he knew it would come. And this headache would be over once and for all.

TRAVIS WALKER SAT ON THE FRONT PORCH, staring out at the darkness. It was late, but he couldn't sleep. They'd put the kids to bed hours ago and he probably would've been out like a light if Wolfe hadn't called and given him the news about the explosion at the bar. Now, his brain wouldn't shut off. Travis was the take-charge kind and sitting on his ass wasn't working for him.

Only he didn't have many options at the moment.

The screen door squeaked behind him.

"Hey, you all right?" Kylie asked, coming closer.

He reached for his wife, pulling her into his lap. "Better now," he said, pressing his face into her neck, breathing her in. She smelled like baby shampoo, probably from when she'd bathed the kids earlier. He loved that smell.

"Gage is still on the phone," she said softly.

Travis nodded but didn't lift his head. He knew Gage was on the phone, knew he was working his contacts, wanting to control any news reports that went out on the explosion that had burned that little bar to the ground. Their goal was to buy themselves a little time, to announce that there had been casualties, however, ensuring the reporters were told the bodies would take time to identify. That would allow them the opportunity to put a plan in place.

Sure, that crazy fucker might know otherwise, but he wouldn't know that no one had been killed in the blast. Thank the Lord.

120

As soon as the call had come in, as soon as he'd heard Wolfe's voice, Travis had known the shit had finally hit the fan. Not long after that, more calls had come in. One from RT, another from one of the security agents who was working the case, both telling him the details of what had gone down.

The good news was, this guy was on a short timeline. The bad news was that they weren't doing enough to stop him. No way should that bastard have been able to get close enough to set an explosive on a goddamn building in the middle of town. It pissed Travis off that they'd let his cousin down, that some good people had nearly died tonight because they'd mistakenly believed they had some time.

The screen door squeaked again.

"Yes, that's right. And Reese, Travis, and I will be headed that way first thing in the mornin'. I'll need you to manage the resort while we're out. We're gonna meet with Max's sister…" *Pause.* "Yeah, the one in law school… She's on her way down as we speak." *Pause.* "No, I don't know what his plan is, but it's more than we've got, so we're goin' with it."

Travis lifted his head, staring up at his husband. Gage merely nodded when their eyes met.

"Yep, this bastard's goin' down," Gage said gruffly. "Thanks. And let me know how things go."

When Gage hung up the phone, he took a breath and Travis waited.

"Everything's in place." Gage sighed. "Not sure how happy I am that you've got mob ties, but … whatever."

Travis smiled. It was good to have friends. Didn't matter if they were in low places or not. It still helped.

Chapter Fifteen

THE INSTANT HER BRAIN CAME ONLINE, REAGAN knew she was in an unfamiliar bed, an unfamiliar *house*.

She inhaled and the scent of coffee drifted in from somewhere and she was reminded of her grandfather's house. Waking up there each morning before school, the smell of coffee and bacon drifting up from the kitchen. Sometimes Reagan missed those days. Being a kid, not having to *adult* all the damn time. Those were simpler times.

Forcing her eyes open, she squinted against the sun shining into the room and rolled over.

"Oh," she exhaled sharply, her eyes locking on a familiar face. "Mornin', Copenhagen."

The giant dog shifted closer, and she found herself smiling as she reached over and rubbed his head.

"Not used to wakin' up with strange boys in my bed," she murmured.

As soon as the words left her mouth, last night came back to her in a rush, and she sighed heavily.

What the hell was she going to do now?

Well, the first thing she needed to do was call the insurance company. That would have to take place *after* she got out of bed though. Or rather, tomorrow, since it was Sunday. She doubted they were open to take her call. Not that she wouldn't try. The sooner she got that claim filed, the faster she could find a way to rebuild.

Sure, she could probably sit around, whine and cry about all that she'd lost, but she knew that wasn't going to help. And she'd never been that kind of girl. She was the take-the-bull-by-the-horns type. Responsible for herself. As it should be.

Forcing herself to sit up, Reagan felt the aches and pains from last night return with a vengeance. Her head was pounding from where she'd hit it on the wall, and she doubled over, clutching her skull with both hands, fighting the wave of nausea that hit her suddenly.

"What do you think you're doin'?"

The gruff, raspy voice came from behind her, but Reagan didn't move. "Right now? I'm tryin' not to puke my guts up on your pretty wood floor. When that passes, I'm gonna take another shower."

There was a soft grunt that sounded closer. She managed to sit up straight, take several deep breaths, and get the world to stop spinning.

"Here."

She looked up to see Lynx holding a couple of pills and a glass of water.

"Ibuprofen," he added.

"Thanks." Doing her best not to touch him, she took the two pills from his hand and tossed them in her mouth before taking the water glass. Once those were down, she took a deep breath.

"You hungry?"

Her stomach lurched at the mere thought of food. "No. Thanks."

"When you're outta the shower and feelin' better, we'll head into town. Rhys took your truck to the station. We can pick it up there."

She nodded but kept her eyes on his legs as they moved out of her line of sight.

Lynx clicked his tongue twice. "C'mon, Cope. Let's get you some food."

Reagan managed to breathe a little easier when Lynx was out of the room. He seemed to overwhelm her with his presence, not to mention his kindness. Yesterday she'd been a total bitch to him and today he was taking care of her. Honestly, she had no idea why, either.

Twenty minutes later, Reagan was showered and dressed. She had managed to finger comb her wet hair, and she'd used Lynx's toothpaste — her finger sufficed as a toothbrush — to bring herself to a relative state of normal. Her head didn't hurt nearly as bad, nor did her body, which she considered a good thing. She had too damn much to do to deal with that shit right now.

The second she walked out of the bedroom, there was a knock on the front door. She stopped, glanced at it, then over at Lynx, who was standing in the kitchen. He shrugged, as though to say he had no idea who could possibly be there. Since she was closer, Reagan headed that way.

Figuring it was her brother coming to check on her, Reagan pulled it open and came face-to-face with...

"Who are you?" the woman hissed, glaring back at Reagan.

Oh, what a way to start the day. With Lynx's *wife* standing on the front porch.

Reagan gave a small smirk. "The fuckin' maid. Who're you?"

Without waiting for a response, Reagan spun on her heel and headed for the kitchen, rolling her eyes at Lynx as she passed.

"What the hell are you doin' here?" Lynx growled, moving toward the door.

"I heard what happened," Tammy said, her tone sugary-sweet. "I wanted to check on you. Make sure you were all right."

Right.

"You shouldn't be here, Tammy," he snapped.

Reagan turned to face the door, noticing how Tammy tried to peek in the house. One thing Reagan never wanted to be was the other woman. Damn good thing she hadn't acted on her impulses last night. Lying in bed with Lynx, she'd been slammed with a desire so powerful it was a surprise she'd slept at all. However, she'd managed to refrain from jumping him.

And the woman standing at the front door was proof Reagan had no business being here with this man. The guy had a wife, for fuck's sake.

Granted, their divorce would be final in… She had to think on that a minute, counting the days off on her fingers. Today? Or was it tomorrow? It was Sunday, right?

Shit. She had no freaking clue and it didn't even matter.

"Why is the maid here on a Sunday, Lynx?"

Reagan had to slam her hand over her mouth to keep from laughing out loud.

"She's not the maid," Lynx informed her.

Reagan's breath lodged in her chest as she waited to hear him explain who she was. More than likely, he'd launch into a long story about how she was a friend, or even Rhys's sister and he was just helping out.

"Who the fuck is she?" Tammy snarled, sounding more like she did when Reagan opened the door.

"She's my goddamn girlfriend, Tammy. Fuck."

Reagan's eyes flew open and she stared at Lynx's back.

What.

The.

Fuck?

IT TOOK EVERYTHING IN HIM NOT TO turn around and look at Reagan. He wanted to know what her response was to that declaration, but he had to consider his priorities here. And the first on his list was to get Tammy off his fucking property.

ASAP.

"You need to go," he told her roughly, stepping out onto the porch and closing the door behind him.

"You're still married, Lynx Caine."

He cocked one eyebrow lazily. She knew that wasn't true. Sure, there were a few measly hours left until it was all said and done, but so fucking what. Tammy had gotten what she wanted; he'd practically given her every-damn-thing just to get her out of his life. The only thing left was for the waiting period to be over. Then, he'd be free and clear to move on with his life.

And if Reagan had an issue with him calling her his girlfriend, so fucking what. If she wasn't yet, she would be soon, and he didn't give a shit if Tammy wanted to go and shout that to anyone who would listen.

Tammy's face softened somewhat. "So, you're really okay?"

He nodded. "I'm fine. I wasn't at the bar last night."

"Oh. Where were you?"

"Here. Asleep."

"With your girlfriend?"

"No," he told her. Partly because it was the truth and partly because it would get her off his back.

"Lynx..." She took a step closer. "I really am sorry about ... what happened. I was wrong. I shouldn't have ... done what I did."

"What? Fuck some guy in the bed of my fucking truck?" Lynx took a breath. "Or are you sorry for lyin' to me about bein' pregnant?"

Her gaze dropped to the ground.

Lynx took a breath, let it out roughly. "It's done, Tammy. Over. I'm not losin' sleep over it, so you shouldn't, either."

He heard the door open behind him, then glanced over his shoulder to see Reagan leaning against the doorjamb. She was smiling, but the action didn't reach her eyes. This was the very reason she was keeping him at arm's length, and Tammy showing up wasn't going to help matters.

"I have shit to do," he finally told Tammy. "Seriously."

His phone chose that moment to ring. Lynx tugged it from his pocket and glanced at the screen.

"What's up?" he greeted Wolfe, turning his back on Tammy.

"Travis and Gage are on their way here and they want to meet us at the diner in a few. They're bringin' a lawyer with them."

"A lawyer?" Lynx frowned.

"Yeah. And this lawyer…" Wolfe chuckled. "I think she's gonna be the key to bringin' this bastard to his knees."

"That so?" Lynx wasn't sure how a lawyer was going to do that, but hey, he didn't care how it happened. Just as long as it happened.

And the sooner the fucking better.

"Yeah," he told Wolfe. "Reagan and I'll be there in a few."

"Thanks."

The call disconnected and Lynx met Reagan's eyes. She still didn't look amused, but he couldn't very well blame her.

"That's … Reagan?"

Lynx closed his eyes momentarily.

"The girl who owns the bar?"

He didn't respond.

"The one whose name is…"

"You need to go, Tammy," he snapped, his eyes still locked with Reagan's.

She didn't say anything more, but he heard the shift of her feet as she moved. He didn't know if she was coming closer or actually leaving, but he couldn't move, couldn't look away from Reagan.

Seeing her standing there in the doorway of his house…

Every possessive instinct in his entire body roared to life. She was right where he wanted her to be, but he could tell by her expression she didn't care to be there.

To his relief, a car started behind him, then the sound of tires moved down the gravel path.

He waited, still not moving.

"Is she gone?" he asked Reagan.

She nodded.

He took one step, then another. He moved up the stairs to the house, and Reagan remained right there, not moving.

"Your girlfriend?" she asked, her eyes rolling slightly.

Unable to resist, Lynx stepped right into her personal space and put his hands on her hips. She tilted her head back, keeping her eyes on his face.

"Yeah," he whispered.

"I'm not—"

He shut her up by crushing his mouth to hers, thrusting his tongue past her lips when she gasped in surprise. Without hesitation, Reagan kissed him back, and he knew right then, without a doubt, this woman belonged to him. Now and forever.

And if it meant turning the town upside down to prove that to her...

Goddamn, he was up for that challenge, too.

Reluctantly, Lynx pulled back. It wasn't easy, considering he wanted to pick her up and carry her back to his bed, only this time he'd be there with her and she'd be naked beneath him, her thighs cradling his hips while he...

Yeah. Not fucking helping.

"We have to go to the diner," he whispered, his voice rougher than usual.

"For?" He liked that she was as breathless as he was.

Taking a deep breath, he stood tall and stared down at her. "Wolfe called. We have to meet Travis and Gage. Apparently they're bringin' a lawyer."

"A lawyer?"

He shrugged one shoulder. "Yeah. I have no idea, but he wants us there."

She nodded. "I'm ready."

"We gotta take Cope over to the store first."

Another nod.

Lynx didn't want to move from there, but he knew he had to. They had shit to do, and as much as he wanted her, the incident with Tammy was still fresh in Reagan's mind, and he knew she wasn't ready for what he wanted.

And no matter what, Lynx wasn't about to take the next step until she trusted him completely.

For that to happen, he had to prove himself.

Which he would do.

A million times over if that was what it took.

Chapter Sixteen

REAGAN SAT BETWEEN HER BROTHER AND LYNX at a group of tables they'd pulled together to accommodate the large number of people who had arrived at the diner to chat about... Honestly, she wasn't sure what this meeting was about, but she knew one thing. She didn't want to be here.

The introductions had been brief, consisting mostly of first names. Since Reagan knew most everyone at the table, she hadn't been listening, choosing instead to wipe the condensation from her glass with one finger.

"Wait," Rhys said. "Your last name is Adorite?"

Her brother was talking to the beautiful woman they'd been introduced to earlier. Apparently, she was a lawyer, or going to school to be one, but Reagan didn't quite know what she specialized in, nor did she know how her being here was going to help the situation. It seemed they needed more guns, less people since this crazy fuck was on a rampage, trying to kill anyone who was even close to Amy.

The woman nodded.

"As in the Southern Boy *Mafia*?" Rhys questioned. The way he said the words didn't sound as though he was all that impressed.

"Yes," she replied flatly.

"And you're related to Max Adorite how?"

"He's my brother."

"Fuck." Rhys thrust his hand through his hair.

"What?" Lynx asked. "What does that mean?"

It appeared no one, including Reagan, knew what the hell was going on. No one other than Rhys and this woman. Madison Adorite.

"And you asked her to be here?" Rhys confirmed, his tone suspicious as he glanced over at Travis.

"I did," Travis confirmed. "Her brother wanted her here."

Reagan watched the lawyer skeptically. It was obvious she hadn't been told what was going on until this morning. Probably not until she had arrived at the diner, Reagan would venture to guess. She seemed to be eyeing everyone the same way Rhys was eyeing her. With both curiosity and not a small amount of distrust.

"I need to talk to you," Madison told Amy, her eyes softening. "I hate to put you through it again, but I need to get the full story. From the beginning."

Madison Adorite looked confident, despite the fact that she was definitely young. Really young, if Reagan had to guess. Twenty-three, maybe twenty-four. How she was a lawyer at that age was beyond Reagan.

As though she'd read Reagan's thoughts, Madison's tone changed slightly when she added, "I'm here because my brother Victor couldn't be. If this is something Max can help with, my brother will take it on. However, I'll be feeding them information." She peered over at Travis, then back at the group. "It has been requested that my presence here in Embers Ridge be exploited as much as possible. The consensus seems to be that once this man hears the name Adorite, he's going to get curious."

"Why?" Wolfe asked, leaning back and watching them.

"Because she's an Adorite," Rhys mumbled. "As in mafia. No way the chief of police isn't familiar with the name."

That seemed to draw Wolfe's and Lynx's attention.

"That's correct. This man"—her voice lowered—"the chief of police, is going to recognize my name for sure. The man is power hungry. If he thinks he can possibly bring down the Adorites, or the Southern Boy Mafia as you so kindly refer to us, then he'll likely step out of the shadows. It works twofold. If he can work a case, he'll have a legitimate reason to be here, and since he wants to be here for other reasons…"

Reagan still didn't understand what the point of it all was. Why didn't someone just call the guy up and challenge him or something?

"And why would he do that?" Wolfe inquired.

"Because it'll make his career," Rhys stated, as though that was completely obvious.

"But what sort of criminal activity can he possibly get you on here in Embers Ridge?" Wolfe asked.

"He can't," Madison said, her tone a little haughty. "But he doesn't know that. And the overall objective is to get him here."

"And how do you propose we get the word out?" Lynx asked.

"If this place is anything like Coyote Ridge, it won't take much," Gage noted.

Lynx laughed, apparently amused. "True. I did manage to put together a party in a matter of minutes."

"More than once," Rhys grumbled.

"Well, then I'd think it wouldn't take much," Travis said.

Lynx leaned back, his arm coming around Reagan, resting on the back of her chair as he stared at Madison. "Well, I hope you're ready, 'cause you just inserted yourself in the middle of town, honey." He used his free hand to wave around the diner. "This is it, sweetheart. And as of the second you stepped in the building, all eyes went to you. Shit. There's prob'ly gossip takin' place as we speak. Don't let the lack of warm bodies in this place fool ya."

"Good thing is, most of the town's at church right now," Wolfe stated, glancing between Travis, Gage, and Madison. "But that won't last long, so I suggest you get your grins on and we kick this up a notch."

Yep, Reagan knew that, come noon, the diner would be flooded. And by two, everyone would know who Madison Adorite was and they'd likely have a million different reasons as to why she was in town. With Reagan's bar exploding, everyone was going to want to know what happened, and the fastest way to do that was for the busybodies to congregate in town.

Which reminded her, she'd need to call the insurance company first thing in the morning since she'd been right. When she'd tried to call earlier, she'd gotten a voice mail system.

The door opened and the bells overhead jingled. Almost instantly, Lynx sat up, a grin on his handsome face.

"Well, congratulations, ma'am!" he hollered, his tone exuberant. "Hey, Donna! How 'bout we get some more coffee over here. We've got a real live lawyer-to-be in our presence. Madison Adorite is in the house."

Rhys and Wolfe both chuckled, as did Travis and Gage.

However, Madison didn't appear to be fazed by the announcement.

Then again, if her family was really mafia, as Rhys had said, she probably wasn't fazed by much of anything.

BY THE TIME THEY WERE FINISHED CHATTING it up at the diner, Lynx was more confused than when he'd arrived. He had no clue what Travis's intentions were with this whole Adorite-in-town thing. Were they looking to draw this asshole out? By dangling the mafia in his face? How the hell was that supposed to help?

There seemed to be some serious holes in this plan, but Lynx wasn't sure how to voice his concerns. It was as though everyone else was trying to wrap their brains around it, too.

While Rhys and Wolfe remained with Travis, Gage, and Madison, Lynx excused himself. He had sensed Reagan's discomfort when they first arrived, and he knew she was ready to bolt. Personally, he wasn't all that interested in sitting around and shooting the shit right now. He had things to do, starting with getting in touch with some people who owed him some favors.

"Would you mind takin' me to get my truck?" Reagan asked when they stepped outside.

"Sure." He'd known this was coming, knew he couldn't keep her at his side indefinitely. However, he couldn't deny that he'd enjoyed spending the morning with her, sitting by her side, putting his arm around her.

"Thanks."

Lynx walked Reagan to the passenger-side door, opened it, then waited for her to get inside. As he was heading around to the driver's side, his cousin appeared.

"Hey, man," Wolfe called out.

Lynx tilted his chin in question. "S'up?"

"We're gonna head back to the house so Amy can talk to Madison, tell her the story. Was wonderin' if maybe you could stop by there. She's takin' this really hard. It's killin' her that Reagan was hurt last night." Wolfe glanced over at Reagan. "Think maybe you could talk her into comin', too?"

"Absolutely. I'll be wherever you need me, and I'll tell Reagan. I'm sure she'll wanna be there."

"Thanks, man." Wolfe clapped him on the shoulder. "This shit's gonna be over with soon. Then we can all get back to normal."

Lynx wasn't even sure what normal was anymore. Not for him anyway. However, he was looking forward to this shit going down once and for all.

"See ya in a few." After a quick knuckle bump, Wolfe turned and headed back inside the diner while Lynx sauntered to the driver's-side door of his truck.

Once inside, Lynx turned to Reagan.

"Wolfe asked us to come out to his place. Thought Amy would appreciate it. She's gonna talk to that lawyer chick."

"Of course," Reagan said quickly. "Amy's my friend."

"And he said Amy's takin' it hard." He nodded toward her. "The fact that you got hurt last night."

"This ain't her fault," Reagan declared.

No, it wasn't. They both knew that. But guilt could be an evil bitch, not always making sense.

"Let's get your truck," Lynx told her, starting the engine.

Neither of them spoke on the short ride over to the sheriff's department. However, there was a lot to be said once they pulled into the small lot.

"Holy shit," Reagan hissed. "My ... truck."

Yeah. Holy shit was right. Rhys had said he'd taken Reagan's truck over to the station, but he hadn't bothered to mention that he'd had to have the damn thing towed.

Lynx glanced over at Reagan. She looked on the verge of tears, but once again, the woman held them back. She was tough, always had been. It was one of the things he loved about her. One of the many things.

"Hey," he said, pulling her attention over to him. "You can take my truck until we can get yours…" He let that drift off because the charred front end of her truck didn't look as though it was going to be repairable.

"No," she insisted. "I can't do that, Lynx. What'll you drive?"

"My old man's truck," he told her quickly. "Ain't like he's usin' it." Lynx grinned, trying to ease some of the tension. "Trust me, it's no hardship. I happen to be quite fond of that truck."

She took a deep breath, met his eyes, then nodded slightly. "For a few days, maybe. I'd really appreciate it."

He wanted to tell her he'd do any-damn-thing for her.

"Let's head to Wolfe's then," Lynx said, backing out of the parking lot. "And I'll have Wolfe run me over to get it."

Reagan didn't say anything and Lynx wasn't expecting her to, so when she unbuckled her seat belt and shifted over to the middle seat, he found himself holding his breath.

And when she reached over and took his hand, linking their fingers together, he forgot how to breathe altogether. It got even worse when she leaned her head over and rested it on his shoulder.

"Thank you," she whispered. "For bein' my friend."

Friend.

Right.

He didn't bother to tell her that being her friend was only the beginning.

Chapter Seventeen

"JESUS CHRIST," WOLFE GROANED ROUGHLY.

Reagan knew just how he felt.

Every damn time they heard Amy's story, it was as horrific as the first time.

"Son of a bitch," Gage growled, pushing open the screen door and stepping outside.

Reagan didn't move from her spot beside Amy; she didn't let go of the woman's hand. She hated that Amy had to continue to go through this over and over. It was bullshit and they all knew it. What they should've been doing was getting that bastard to show his face. Get him to come out on the Caine property, where they could rightfully take care of him once and for all.

Except that wasn't the right thing to do, even if it was what everyone was thinking.

This bastard was crazy.

"And the night the detective came out?" Madison inquired, still all business. "She was in a fatal crash?"

"That's correct," Rhys told her, his gaze set somewhere outside through the large pane window. Reagan figured he was trying to erase the mental images now swarming his head, the hell Amy had been through at the hands of a madman.

"And someone tried to break into Amy's house," Lynx noted. "Reagan was there. Alone."

Yeah, she tried not to think about that one. Every time she did, she wondered what would've happened if that asshole had come into the house. She would've shot first and asked questions later, she knew that much. That was what her daddy had taught her to do. If they came into the house uninvited, they knew the consequences.

However, that didn't mean she wouldn't have to deal with the repercussions of her actions. Protecting herself was one thing; the thought of actually shooting someone was entirely different. And not something she wanted to dwell on.

"And then the bar?" Madison continued to watch Rhys. "Do you have any leads on that one?"

Rhys raised an eyebrow and pinned her with an angry glare.

"You know assumptions won't hold up in court," she stated in that business-like tone she'd held on to since she'd arrived.

"No, they won't." Rhys dropped his eyes to the floor. "And no, we don't have any solid evidence that leads back to him. We have ruled out other suspects though."

"Other suspects?" Reagan asked, curious as to who they thought would do something so vile.

Rhys nodded. "Dean brought in Billy and the guy from the bar. His name's Tommy."

Reagan shook her head in disbelief. Sure, she might've considered the guy from the bar had locked them inside, but not once had she thought he had blown up the bar. And Billy... He was an asshole but not a murderer.

"Oh, come on," she said, letting her disbelief ring through. "I turned him down. I'm not exactly worth killing over."

Reagan watched her brother, noticed the way his eyes darted over to Lynx. She peered up to see him staring at her. The look on his face said she was way off base on that one.

Waving him off, Reagan leaned forward, releasing Amy's hand for the first time. "So what now? You know the story. This guy should be spendin' the rest of his life in prison with a cell mate named Bubba."

"It seems clear to me that this guy is workin' alone. He's not gonna hire someone to do his dirty work," Madison stated. "Which means we're gonna have to get him to show his hand."

"And how do you propose we do that?"

Madison cocked one eyebrow at Rhys, then smiled. "Without you here."

"What?" Rhys frowned.

"You're the sheriff," she stated. "And although the plan is to get this guy arrested and charged with multiple counts of murder and attempted murder, I can't promise you it'll be aboveboard all the way."

Lynx grinned. "I like this woman already."

The screen door opened and Gage stepped inside. Travis instantly moved toward him and Reagan watched as the two men shared a moment. It was clear by their simple body language that they loved each other. In fact, it was so powerful Reagan had to look away.

"I just got off the phone with RT," Gage announced. "Sniper 1 Security will be sendin' someone down to Houston to keep an eye on this guy. At least we'll know where he is for the time being." Gage peered at Amy. "It won't make this any better yet. But it'll at least give us time to put a plan together."

Amy nodded.

Reagan had to wonder why they hadn't done that in the first place.

"And again, it's important that the Adorite name get around," Travis clarified. "They believe that this will draw him out, make him curious."

Everyone seemed to be tossing that one around mentally, trying to figure out how it would work. Reagan had never heard of the Adorites, or the Southern Boy Mafia. She wasn't sure how it was supposed to lure the police chief out of his jurisdiction. But what did she know.

"What if it simply stalls him out?" Lynx questioned. "If he thinks somethin's goin' on, he'll lie low for a while. How does that help us?"

"It doesn't," Gage responded. "However, we need time to put a plan in place. Without him here."

Lynx didn't seem impressed with the response, but he didn't say anything in return.

"What about the agents already planted here?" Wolfe inquired.

"They'll remain here. All eyes are on Amy." Gage nodded toward her. "They aren't gonna let this bastard get close again."

Reagan felt a little relief knowing that they would be keeping tabs on this guy. As much as she wanted this to be over with, she wanted to get her life back to normal. And that required not having to look over her shoulder every second of the day. No, she wasn't this guy's target, but it appeared he didn't care who was collateral damage, and that meant they were all in the line of fire.

At least now, maybe they could relax a little.

Her eyes cut over to Lynx, who was staring back at her.

Then again, *relax* might no longer be a word in her vocabulary.

LYNX WAITED UNTIL REAGAN WENT OUTSIDE BEFORE he cornered Wolfe, Rhys, Travis, and Gage.

He glanced at each face. "I thought Amy was gonna go public."

Travis shook his head. "Not yet. It'll draw too much attention and only drag things out."

"Drag them out how?" he asked.

"Once this hits the news, people will be all over him. And Amy. We need to lie low for a bit, see what his next step is."

Lynx looked to Rhys and Wolfe, wanting to know if they were all right with this.

They both nodded in agreement.

"I want eyes on Reagan's house then," he demanded. "At all times."

"Understood," Rhys stated.

"When she's there and when she's not," Lynx continued. "While everyone's lookin' out for Amy, I don't want Reagan caught in the crossfire."

Lynx didn't give a shit that he'd gone territorial on the woman. He was going to protect her. Earlier, when she'd mentioned that she wasn't worth killing for, the woman had been crazy. Lynx would take down anyone and everyone if it meant keeping her safe.

"Understood," Travis said, glancing between Lynx and Rhys.

Lynx nodded, then turned to watch as Reagan stepped back through the door. Her eyes met his.

"If you need anything, you know how to get ahold of me," Lynx told Rhys before moving over to Reagan. "You okay?"

She nodded, her eyes studying his face momentarily. "You really don't mind if I borrow your truck for a little while?"

"Not at all." He pulled the key from his pocket and handed it over to her.

"Do you want me to take you to your dad's?" she offered.

"I'll have Wolfe drop me off. Thanks though."

She nodded, but her eyes didn't hold his gaze for long. "I need to get home and take care of some stuff. I'll talk to you later?"

He smiled. "You can bet on it."

This time Reagan smiled and it seemed less forced than before. "Thank you again."

"Any time." And he meant that.

"Hey, old man!" Lynx called out to his father when he stepped inside the house an hour later.

"Kid," Cooter grumbled, sounding as though Lynx had woken him from his nap.

"I need to borrow your truck," he announced when he joined his dad in the living room.

Sure enough, Cooter was leaning back in his recliner, the television muted.

"You know where the keys are," he replied.

"I remember back when I was sixteen and I asked to borrow that truck," Lynx teased. The '65 Chevy was his dad's prized possession. He wasn't keen on letting anyone drive it. "Or what about the time I snuck it outta the garage?" Lynx had made it almost to the road before his father had stopped him on their riding lawnmower of all things.

"Yeah, don't remind me or I might change my mind." The recliner shifted upright.

"I'm gonna need it for a few days."

Cooter nodded, then reached over to pet Copenhagen when the dog ambled up to him. "Somethin' wrong with yours?"

"Nope. I let Reagan borrow it."

This time his father looked his way, his eyes questioning. "She doin' all right?"

"Fine. Her truck was damaged durin' the fire at the bar, apparently. I'm havin' it sent down to Roy's. See if they can get it up and runnin'." Lynx left off the fact that the truck was pretty much toast. He was still hoping for the best. For Reagan's sake.

Cooter turned. "Somethin' goin' on with you and Reagan?"

Lynx automatically shook his head.

"You sure 'bout that?"

"I'm sure." It wasn't a lie. There wasn't anything going on with him and Reagan. Not yet anyway.

"That divorce final?"

"Almost." Come tomorrow, he would be free and clear.

"Tammy stopped by here this mornin'," Cooter informed him.

Lynx sighed. He should've known. She'd probably stopped by after Lynx had sent her on her way.

"She said you had a girlfriend."

Great. He knew one day his big mouth would come back to bite him in the ass.

"I don't have a girlfriend, Dad."

"No?"

Lynx shook his head. "We're just friends. And Dad, please don't talk to Tammy."

Cooter grinned. "She's a nice girl. Got her priorities all mixed up, sure. But a nice kid."

Priorities being her need to lie about being pregnant to get him to marry her in the first place. Or to fuck other men while they were married.

It wasn't that Lynx even gave a shit about it. He didn't care if she screwed every ranch hand who worked in Embers Ridge. He never should've married her in the first place, and no one regretted his actions more than he did. Had she really been pregnant, Lynx could've and would've been a good dad regardless.

"You be careful with Reagan," Cooter stated, his eyes locked with Lynx's.

"I will."

"That girl's been through enough shit already."

"Trust me, I know that."

"And she's always had a thing for you, Lynx. If this ain't real, don't lead her on."

Lynx paused for a minute, staring at his father. He wanted so badly to tell him that it was real, that, in fact, it was everything. However, Lynx had been down this road before. He'd defended himself when he had up and married Tammy, and look where that had gotten him.

"I know you care about her," Cooter continued.

Lynx didn't respond. He couldn't.

"It's obvious to anyone with eyes. Especially these past few weeks."

He offered his dad a one-shoulder shrug.

"Be careful with her," his father repeated.

"I will," he said softly.

It was Cooter's turn to nod, and thankfully, that meant the subject was closed.

For now.

Chapter Eighteen

KNOWING SHE COULDN'T PUT IT OFF INDEFINITELY, Reagan made a pit stop on her way home. Dropping by to check in with her mother was not something she had looked forward to, even if deep down she wished it could be different between them. She couldn't remember a time when there wasn't tension between her and her mother. Even as a teenager — *especially* as a teenager — she'd butted heads with her more often than not.

Then, when Reagan had started dating Billy, her mother hadn't been impressed. However, she'd learned to deal with it as time went by, until one day, her mother started backing Billy more than her. Reagan wasn't sure how that had happened, or why. And she damn sure wasn't going to think about it now.

"Whose truck is that?" her grandfather bellowed through the open window when Reagan stepped onto the front porch.

Reagan sighed, opening the screen door and moving into the dimly lit living room. Her grandfather was sitting in his usual spot, a cigarette dangling from his fingers.

"A friend's," she told him.

"What friend?"

Telling him the truth would likely only make things worse, but Reagan didn't want to get caught up in a lie. So, she took a deep breath and prepared for the worst.

Before she could get the words out, her mother came storming out of the kitchen, her eyes wide.

"Reagan Marie," she said in a huff. "Why didn't you come by last night?"

She didn't have time to answer before her mother threw her arms around her and hugged her tightly.

"I was so worried."

"I'm fine, Mom," Reagan assured her.

"But your bar blew up. With you in it." Her mother sounded hysterical.

"I know. But no one was hurt." Not really anyway.

"Where'd you go last night?" her grandfather asked.

Once again, Reagan found herself tight-lipped.

"Whose truck is that?" her mother asked, peering over Reagan's shoulder through the screen door.

"Lynx Caine's," she blurted, preparing for the worst.

"Why are you drivin' his truck?"

"Mine was damaged in the fire."

"Christ Almighty," her mother said dramatically.

"I hope you're not mixin' it up with that Caine boy," Vic insisted. "He's bad news."

"Where's Billy?" her mother asked, talking over her grandfather. "What does he think about this?"

"About what?" Reagan frowned, trying to read between the lines.

"About you drivin' that boy's truck."

"Mom, Billy and I broke up."

She waved Reagan off. "That won't last forever and you know it."

Arguing wasn't going to get her anywhere, so Reagan opted to take the high road. "I just wanted to stop by, check in. I'm good, I promise."

"You ain't good if you're drivin' that truck," Vic said, his eyes focused on her. "That boy's bad news," he repeated.

"He's not bad news," she insisted. "He's a friend and he's loanin' me his truck until I can get mine fixed."

"Shoulda known you'd go messin' up a good thing," her mother grumbled.

The words, no matter how often her mother said them, still shocked Reagan every time. She knew Billy played a big part in it. He fed her mother lies until Reagan looked like the bad guy every time.

And this was the very reason Reagan stayed away. She hated arguing with her mother, but it seemed inevitable these days.

"It's no wonder Billy had to stray," her mother continued. "If you're spendin' time with other men…"

"Mother!" Reagan took a deep breath. "Billy was steppin' out on me. Not the other way around. He was the one out screwin' other women while I was sittin' at home wonderin' where he was."

"You don't know that," she insisted.

"I *do* know that! He *told* me."

"He was just upset."

The way she said that had Reagan stiffening. Her voice lowered when she pinned her mother with a glare. "Did you talk to Billy?"

"He came by the other night. Wanted to apologize for all that was goin' on. Said he was gonna work extra-hard to get you back. Said it was all a misunderstandin'."

"Like hell," Reagan hissed.

Her mother waved her hand toward Lynx's truck. "I can't help but think that maybe you're the one who's been givin' him mixed signals, Reagan."

Pointless.

The whole fucking thing was pointless.

And with everything going on, Reagan knew she wasn't going to hold it together for much longer. So, in an effort to save some of her sanity, she spun on her boot heel and marched right back out the door.

"Reagan Marie Trevino! Don't you walk out that door!"

Too late.

"You need to go talk to Billy!" she yelled.

"Fucking hell," Reagan murmured as she yanked open the truck door and practically launched herself inside.

Next time she considered coming by to check in, she really needed to have someone give her a brain scan. Because if she ever thought it was a good idea, clearly she wasn't functioning on all cylinders.

LYNX HAD FULLY INTENDED TO HEAD HOME but found himself back at Wolfe's after he picked up his father's truck. Everyone had hung around until a few minutes ago, even Travis, Gage, and the lawyer woman. Rhys had finally had to suggest they give Amy a break, but when Lynx went to leave, Wolfe had stopped him.

"I still don't see how this is goin' to shake out," Wolfe said, taking a long pull on his beer as he leaned against the front porch railing.

"Me, either," Lynx agreed. He propped his feet up on the wood and leaned back in the chair they'd dragged from the kitchen table.

"The fuckin' mob, bro," Wolfe said with a whistle.

"Didn't even know they existed," Lynx told his cousin.

Apparently, living in a small town meant being in the dark about some shit.

The screen door creaked open and Rhys stepped outside.

"You think this plan's gonna work?"

Rhys shrugged, obviously not needing to be brought into the loop.

"Depends on whether or not this guy's interested in bringin' them down."

"But if I didn't know about them and I *live* here, how do they think word's gonna get out? I mean, yeah" — Lynx pointed his beer bottle at Rhys — "people are gonna talk. But it's not like the grapevine's got a hotline to Houston."

That earned him another shrug from Rhys. "I just want him stopped. I don't fuckin' care how they do it."

Now, that surprised Lynx.

Although he was the sheriff, Rhys Trevino was a good guy. And the town really was lucky to have him. He was fair and just, which worked in everyone's favor. But Lynx knew this had to be wearing on him. The woman he loved was in danger. No way could any sane man sit back and wait for something to happen.

"Personally, I'm not worried about what information makes it through the grapevine," Wolfe said. "I want this bastard stopped. Goin' after him ourselves would be the right way."

Rhys's eyes cut to Wolfe.

Wolfe held up his hands in surrender. "Not sayin' I'm gonna do anything."

Lynx shook his head and took another sip of his beer. "I just don't get it. I know Travis wants to help out, but this seems a little extreme."

"Ever think that maybe there's another plan?" Rhys suggested.

Lynx and Wolfe both locked their eyes on the sheriff.

"Such as…?" Wolfe asked.

"I don't know," Rhys said, his frustration evident. "I just get the feelin' that Max Adorite is gonna play a role in this."

"Which means…?" Lynx probed.

Rhys huffed. "Fuck if I know. I just get the feelin' that this is some sort of distraction."

Lynx glanced at his cousin. He didn't know the first thing about the mafia, but he'd seen enough movies to get the gist of it. Perhaps Max Adorite was going to take out the police chief.

And wouldn't that make everything fucking easier?

"I can tell ya," Lynx said, tilting his head toward Rhys, "if the mafia boss wants to take out the crazy bastard, more power to him."

That, obviously, wasn't what Rhys wanted to hear.

Chapter Nineteen

LYNX HADN'T BEEN ABLE TO SLEEP FOR shit last night. It was the very reason he was at the shop early the next morning. He and Copenhagen had even arrived before Wolfe for the first time … well, *ever*.

His first order of business had been to start coffee, which he'd done, then proceeded to drink the entire pot while he pulled the parts out for another pair of rocking chairs. They happened to be the most popular piece of furniture they sold in the store. Seemed no matter how many he made, they never lasted long, and Calvin was always asking him to bring more.

So, after the first pot was gone, he got the second one going and got to work, all the while thinking about Reagan. He hadn't seen or heard from her since yesterday afternoon at Wolfe's house. Not that he blamed her. After having to hear Amy's story again, listening to the pain she'd endured, Lynx had needed some time to himself as well.

Now, he merely wanted to know how they were going to stop a man who seemed to wield all the power. Lynx still didn't understand why Amy couldn't go public so they could get this over with. She'd even said she wanted to, but now they were going back on that. It seemed simple to him. If she went public, there would be a lot of heat on that bastard, which would ultimately keep him from sneaking around trying to fucking kill people.

However, it appeared Lynx was the only one thinking along those lines. According to Madison, the idea was to lure him out and stop him once and for all.

Of course, that made sense to Lynx, too. If Amy went public and the guy stopped making his attempts, it would be Amy's word against his, and Kelly Jackson would likely walk around a free man indefinitely. After all, he was the chief of police. People respected him. Granted, they didn't know he was a monster who should be locked up indefinitely.

And right now, Madison said her brother wanted enough evidence to stick the asshole with multiple charges of attempted murder as well as the murder charges for the man's two dead wives *and* the police detective.

Lynx just didn't want the man to succeed in taking someone else out, and based on his actions, the asshole was bound to get lucky at some point. Then again, if the mafia was after him…

"Holy shit!" Wolfe yelled when he stepped into the shop. "Did hell freeze over and I didn't get the memo?"

Lynx flipped his cousin off, which earned him a grin from both Amy and Wolfe. Copenhagen took off at a trot over to the new arrivals, eager for some attention.

Watching the pair, Lynx grinned when Wolfe pulled Amy against him, their lips coming together.

"Hey," Lynx called out. "None of that kissy-face shit in here."

Wolfe and Amy chuckled as she kissed him quickly before turning to go up the stairs.

"I think there's a rule somewhere that says once you move in with someone, that shit stops," Lynx continued.

"Not in my world, it don't," Wolfe noted. "And you wanna tell me why your happy ass is here before the sun's up?"

"Bored," he said, standing up and leaning against the steel beam. The second he touched the damn thing, the memory of him holding Reagan right here, his fingers buried in her silky heat, assaulted him. That seemed like a million years ago and it had been less than forty-eight hours.

"You get ahold of anyone yesterday?" Wolfe asked as he moved closer.

Shaking off the erotic thoughts of Reagan, Lynx let Wolfe's question sink in. Wolfe had to be referring to the crew he was wrangling together to get started on the rebuild of Reagan's bar. The favors he had called in.

He nodded. "I did. Harlow's gonna loan us his equipment. Got Ben and Ed headin' over this mornin' to clear the lot."

Wolfe frowned.

"Don't worry," Lynx told his cousin. "I talked to Rhys. He gave me the go-ahead. Just said we couldn't touch the propane tank, or what's left of it, anyway, until he signed off on the investigation." Something about ongoing bullshit that Lynx knew wouldn't matter anyway. They weren't going to find anything, but apparently Rhys had to do his due diligence to make everyone happy. "You get ahold of Ron?"

Wolfe nodded. "He's sendin' over a couple of dumpsters this mornin'. Said he'd be able to pick 'em up later today."

"Perfect." Lynx had spent the better part of yesterday evening on his phone, recruiting people to help clear the remains of Reagan's bar so they could start the rebuild.

"She know yet?"

Lynx shrugged. He hadn't told Reagan that they were starting the demolition on the remains of the old building so they could get the new one underway. He'd heard her mention calling the insurance company this morning, and she'd seemed extremely stressed, so he hadn't wanted to add to that.

"How're things goin' with … you know?"

Cocking one eyebrow, Lynx waited for his cousin to elaborate.

"With you and Reagan?"

Shaking his head, he turned to get back to work. He didn't want to talk about him and Reagan right now. For one, he had no fucking clue where they stood. It seemed she'd turned this thing between them into a friendship. And with all the shit going on, he wasn't sure how to move things in the right direction. The only thing he could do was help her out and wait for her to come around.

Wolfe chuckled and Lynx spun around to look at him.

"Man, you got it bad."

His middle finger automatically went up, but Lynx couldn't hide his smile.

"You up for breakfast in a bit?" Wolfe asked, thankfully changing the subject.

"Hell yeah."

"Cool. Give me some time to get shit ready for the day and we'll head over."

An hour later, Lynx was walking into the diner. He'd taken Copenhagen over to the store to chill with Calvin for a bit. When he arrived, Wolfe and Amy were already there, sitting at their table in the back. He glanced around, taking in all the faces, offering up a couple of waves.

"Hey, Lynx."

Turning, he saw Darrell Jameson waving him over.

Lynx lifted his eyebrows in question.

"What can we do to help out at Reagan's? Got a construction crew itchin' to pitch in. You got some plans sketched out yet?"

"Workin' on it," Lynx told him. In fact, he'd drawn up the plans for the new place last night while he'd been sitting on his ass wishing like hell Reagan had stayed over again.

"When you get 'em, let me take a look. I can work on some of the permits, then I'll grab more guys if I need 'em."

Lynx nodded, then held out his hand. "Thanks."

"Happy to help."

Turning back toward the table, Lynx couldn't help but smile. This was what living in a small town was all about.

REAGAN HADN'T BEEN ABLE TO SLEEP AT all last night. Seemed every time she closed her eyes, the memory of the explosion came rushing back. The fire, the heat, the fear … it all resounded in her head and her eyes had refused to close again. At one point, she had gotten up and rearranged the dishes in the kitchen in an order that made more sense to her. From there, she had situated the furniture in the living room on the opposite wall, opening up the space and making it feel a little less like Amy's place.

By then she'd been exhausted, but sleep still wouldn't come.

Part of her had wished she'd agreed to stay at Lynx's when he'd offered, but she knew that was not a good idea.

For one, she was having a difficult time not thinking about him nonstop. Right now, Reagan needed to focus on getting her shit together, to figure out what was up, because her life had been turned upside down in the past few days. Definitely not spending all her time thinking about Lynx, wishing his hands were on here, wanting nothing more than to lose herself in him for a little while.

Which was the reason she was heading over to the bar. Or the parking lot, as it may be. She'd called the insurance company first thing only to be told it would take some time for them to investigate, to get the police report and whatnot. Luckily, she'd taken plenty of pictures, so she shot those over to them via email, hoping they would suffice. However, what she thought would be a simple, quick process sounded anything but. And now she'd added *figure out how to pay the bills* to her list of things to do.

She had some money put aside, but it wasn't like she made a lot. The place had been in their family for decades, but when it'd come time for her father to take over, he had refused, letting it rot. She could still remember the heated argument she had with her father when she told him she wanted to open a bar there. He had insisted she couldn't do it, and that had made Reagan work harder to make it a success.

It cost plenty to keep the bar open and Reagan refused to charge ridiculous prices for beer. When she'd originally opened, she had made a promise to herself that she'd keep it a local hangout. Most of the tourists ventured over to Marla's Bar, where they could get liquor, dinner, and a little dancing. At Reagan's, the highlight of the evening was when drunk fools wagered on their pool game.

But it was hers and she loved it. Now she just missed it.

Pulling into the parking lot, Reagan's jaw dropped when she saw a couple of backhoes and tractors in the process of moving the debris into a dumpster.

She slammed Lynx's truck into park and hopped out, waving her arms to get their attention.

When the tractor stopped, she marched over, her eyes coming to rest on Ed Davis, one of the regulars at her bar. "What're you doin'?"

The man frowned. "Cleanin' this up."

"Why?"

He glanced over at the other man, then back to her. "Lynx Caine asked us to help out."

Lynx.

Of course.

Reagan had to spin away from the man as tears flooded her eyes, her heart squeezing tightly in her chest.

Lynx was taking care of her. The same way he took care of everyone in this town. Anytime something happened — whether it was a new baby, a birthday, graduation, even a funeral — it seemed Lynx was somewhere in there, making things happen for people.

It didn't surprise her, although at the same time, she didn't know what to think.

Without saying another word, she fled to the truck and climbed in, not wanting them to see her cry, because there was no way she could hold back the tears now. Lynx had done this. He'd gotten some people over here to help out already.

What was she going to do with that man? Why did he have to be so sweet?

Of course, then her thoughts drifted to Billy. She hadn't even heard from the asshole, and she knew he was still in town. No way did he not know about the explosion considering he'd been brought in for questioning. Nope, the man she'd spent ten years with hadn't bothered to call and see if she was okay.

"Because he's an asshole," she muttered to herself.

The polar opposite of Lynx. Damn. She was in so much trouble here.

Taking a deep breath, Reagan gripped the steering wheel and fought the tears back. She couldn't cry. It wasn't going to do her any good. Didn't matter that they were from the relief she felt. Truth was, she didn't deserve Lynx's kindness right now. She felt guilty enough about the way she'd treated him. More so about how she wanted nothing more than to hide in the shelter of his arms and let him take care of this mess. He would do it, she had no doubt. That was the way he was. The man looked out for his friends.

But she didn't want to be his friend, no matter what she told him.

She wanted so much more. However, her heart wasn't strong enough for what Lynx would do to it. He was the only man in the world who had the power to break it, and she would rather spend a lifetime alone than to feel that kind of pain again. It'd happened once before. Back when she realized Lynx wasn't within her grasp, that he was more interested in drifting from one woman to another than to give them a chance.

That was the very reason she'd started dating Billy Watson. One day after school, Reagan had spotted Lynx with Angie Chesney in town, watched him kiss her near the gas pumps over at the Pump 'n Go, and her heart had been shattered. His desire to hop from one woman to another was also why she'd continued to take Billy back despite the fact that their relationship had been doomed from the start. Ten years she'd fought her desire for Lynx Caine.

She realized the two men on the tractors were watching her, so she waved, then started the truck. She figured she might be able to catch Lynx at the diner, and if not, he would probably be at the shop.

It was time they had a little heart-to-heart.

After all, the man was now officially divorced, which meant she had no more excuses.

Just as she'd thought, Reagan found Lynx at the shop a short time later. The door was open and she heard the whine of a saw spilling out into the parking lot. When she stepped inside the cool interior, her eyes took a moment to adjust. By the time they did, the saw had shut off and Wolfe was looking her way.

"Hey," she greeted. "Is...?" Her attention was pulled to movement at the far end of the warehouse.

Her gaze landed on Lynx, who was armed with sandpaper and a worried expression on his face.

"Mind if I talk to him?" she asked Wolfe, waving her hand in Lynx's direction.

"Not at all," he grinned, glancing at his cousin. "I needed to talk to Amy anyway."

She knew that was a lie, but she wasn't about to say anything. A few minutes alone with Lynx was all she needed.

Okay, *that* was a lie.

She needed more than a few minutes. Not to mention, somewhere that offered more privacy than this. But right now, this would have to do.

"Thanks."

By the time she reached Lynx, he was leaning against a table, arms crossed over his wide chest as though he was expecting an ass chewing.

"Imagine my surprise," she began, "when I stopped over at the bar and found a couple of guys clearin' things out."

His dark eyebrow lifted slightly, but he didn't speak.

Reagan moved closer, the butterflies in her stomach taking flight.

She closed the distance between them until they were toe-to-toe. Then she put her hands on his waist as she stared up into those gorgeous green eyes. Touching him was a gamble, but her hands didn't seem to hear the warning her heart was giving them.

"I'm not sure..." Her heart squeezed in her chest and she started over. "I'm not sure what I'm gonna do with you."

Her voice was so soft she wasn't sure he'd heard the words. The way his eyes traveled over her face had her body warming. It didn't help that she was touching him, but she couldn't seem to help herself.

"You don't have to help me out, Lynx." She shook her head, knowing that came out wrong. "I appreciate it, sure. But…"

Lynx moved and the words caught in her throat when he cupped her face, then leaned down and kissed her. His lips were soft, warm, and so gentle her heart flipped over.

She wasn't sure if the move was meant to shut her up or not, but it worked. Although he kept it soft and sweet, Reagan couldn't seem to maintain his leisurely pace. Within seconds of his lips touching hers, her body throbbed, her pulse sped up, and she once again found herself trying to climb his body.

The rough groan that rumbled in his chest only made her body heat more, her need for him intensifying. She'd been fighting this for so long and she wanted to give in, to allow him to take her mind off all the crap that was going on right now. Granted, she'd learned not to say as much, because the man was quick to take the offer off the table whenever she mentioned that this thing between them could only be temporary. She wasn't sure what he was after, but she knew he wanted her complete surrender.

Not that she was capable of giving that to him.

But that didn't mean she couldn't pretend so they could both get what they wanted.

The only thing she had to do was make sure her heart understood this wasn't a forever kind of deal and thinking that it was would only cause more pain in the end.

Yeah. That was going to be the hard part.

Chapter Twenty

"REAGAN," LYNX WHISPERED AGAINST HER LIPS, HATING himself for pulling back when he wanted nothing more than to strip her naked and bury himself inside her right here.

The woman was going to push him past the brink any second now. He had actually managed to keep his distance, even come up with a plan to ride this out for a while until she was ready. That plan hadn't taken into consideration what would happen if she approached *him*.

Between the softness of her lips and the warmth of her hands still clutching his abdomen through his T-shirt, Lynx was damn near ready to combust.

The second she'd walked into the shop, he'd been expecting her to let loose on him.

Only, this wasn't how he'd envisioned it going down. Knowing how independent the woman was, he'd been waiting for the shit to hit the fan. After all, the text he'd received from Ed a few minutes ago had been a warning. She'd stopped by the bar to find the charred remains being hauled into the dumpster, and evidently she hadn't been happy about it.

Not that you could tell it by the way she was acting now.

"Can you take a break for a while?" she asked, pulling back and staring up into his face.

"For…?"

She shrugged. "Thought we'd go … somewhere."

"Where?"

Reagan shrugged and a small smile pulled at her lips. "Maybe out to the lake."

Lynx knew this was a bad idea, but again, bad ideas were his calling. He tended to gravitate toward them every chance he got. Didn't matter if the repercussions were jail or, in this case, something a hell of a lot more promising, he couldn't seem to resist.

"Yeah. Give me a couple minutes to clean shit up and we'll head out."

Reagan seemed to be eyeing him hard, and he briefly wondered what was going on in that pretty little head of hers. Whatever it was, he got the feeling it had a lot to do with the two of them naked, translating to: the bad decision he was referring to earlier.

Every man had his breaking point, and apparently, Reagan Trevino was his.

Thirty minutes later, Lynx was steering his truck down the dirt path to the lake, Reagan riding shotgun. He had taken his time cleaning things up, fully expecting Reagan to back out on him. Hell, he might've been hoping she would. This thing between them had been building for years. It was a pressure cooker ready to blow the lid off, and Lynx wasn't sure Reagan was ready for what came next. In fact, Lynx wasn't sure *he* was ready. He wanted it, absolutely, but trying to wrangle a wild stallion was easier than convincing Reagan to take a chance on them.

"Thanks for having those guys clear the lot," she said, her tone soft, her attention out the window.

"They volunteered," he told her. "Actually, a lot of people did."

Reagan's gaze shifted his way. "So, they just called you up and said ... what?"

Lynx grinned as he turned the truck around and backed it toward the lake, stopping beneath the shade of one of the big oak trees. "Okay, fine. I called them, but *then* they volunteered."

"Why?"

"Why what?"

"Why are you doin' this?"

He cut his eyes over to her quickly, processing her disbelieving tone. He wasn't sure what he'd ever done to her to make her keep him at arm's length, to have her thinking the worst of him, but clearly she did.

Reagan appeared to be waiting for an answer.

Unfortunately, he didn't have one, so he led with, "Do you really think I'm a dick, or what?"

Without waiting for a response, he got out of the truck, trying to rein in his temper. Why did it always seem that the woman wanted to jump up and down on his fucking nerves? It was as though she wanted to piss him off and he didn't get it.

"Lynx!" Reagan hollered, the passenger door slamming shut. She rounded the truck, coming to stand a few feet away.

"That's not what I meant and you know it."

No, actually, he didn't.

Reagan put her hands on her hips. "With all the shit I've done, I—"

"We've got a new rule," Lynx interrupted, glaring down at her. "From now on, we don't talk about the shit in the past. Not Billy. Not Tammy. Not any of it."

"But I need to apologize," she declared.

"No, you don't. You need to stop dwellin' on that shit and let's move forward."

"Is that how it is for you?" Reagan's tone was hard. "You forget everything in the past and just look at the future?"

"In a way, sure."

Reagan chuckled, but he could tell it was strained. "Explains all the women."

Lynx yanked his ball cap off his head, thrust his hand through his hair, and groaned, spinning on his boot heel and walking away. "You don't fuckin' get it do you, Reagan?" he called back.

"Get what?"

Pivoting to face her, he locked his eyes with hers, the three feet between them not nearly enough to keep him from wanting to put his hands all over her.

"It's always been you, Reagan. Always."

"*What's* been me?" she snapped.

"Do you remember when you started datin' Billy?"

She frowned. "What the fuck does he have to do with anything?"

"He's got every goddamn thing to do with it," Lynx yelled. "Since before you were eighteen, you've been with that fuckup."

Reagan shook her head. "I don't have a clue where this is goin'."

Lynx took a step toward her. "I have spent... God*damn*! For ten fuckin' years, Reagan ... I have wanted you. And then when you turned eighteen ... I've spent the past eight years *waitin'* for you."

Her eyes widened. "You've got a funny way of waitin'. Fuckin' every woman who crosses your path."

"They were never *you*," he growled, coming to stand directly in front of her. "No matter how fuckin' hard I tried to get you outta my head, it never fuckin' worked. And yes, damn it, I fuckin' tried. Do you understand what I'm sayin'?"

She didn't speak.

Lynx took a breath, tried to get a handle on his temper. When he felt as though his head wouldn't explode, he caught her gaze with his.

"So, yeah," he continued, taking a deep breath, "hold it against me for as long as you want. I fuckin' deserve it. But it doesn't change a thing. I can't go back and do things differently, darlin'. Trust me. If I could, I would."

"What would you change?" Her tone was softer now, her eyes imploring his.

Lynx touched her face, tilting her head back with his thumb. "For starters, I would've told you that first time you broke up with that dickhead."

"Told me what?"

Although the words hung on the tip of his tongue, Lynx couldn't say them. If he did, he'd never get them back, and he knew Reagan wouldn't believe him if he told her. Loving her was something he'd done all this time without anyone knowing. And the first time he told her, it damn sure wouldn't be when they were fighting.

So he said, "That I want you. That I've dreamt about gettin' my hands on you, about pullin' you beneath me." He moved closer, lowered his voice. "Slidin' deep inside you."

Lynx could feel her rapid breaths against his mouth.

"Fuckin' you until neither of us knows our own names. That's what I wanted, Reagan."

"Past tense?" she whispered.

"Not by a long shot."

She blinked, her eyes still locked with his. "Then what're you waitin' for?"

And that was the moment she pushed him right over the edge, his breaking point now nothing more than a memory.

IT WAS A DARE.

Of all the people in the world, Lynx Caine was not the man to dare, because as soon as the words were out of her mouth, Reagan saw the shift in his eyes, knew he was about to unleash on her.

The soft rumble in his chest was drowned out by the pounding of her heart when Lynx crushed his mouth to hers, jerking her to him. And when he lifted her off her feet, Reagan wrapped around him and held on tight, legs around his waist, arms around his neck. And still she wasn't close enough.

She heard the loud click of the tailgate releasing, then found her butt planted on the edge, Lynx standing between her legs, his arm banded around her as his mouth did crazy wicked things to hers. God, he could kiss. Lynx knew just how to coax her mouth open, just how to work her into a frenzy with the devilish flick of his tongue.

"This what you want?" he growled. "You want me to take you right here?"

Reagan figured why the hell not. After all, this was where it had started all those years ago. Why wouldn't it be where they picked things back up?

When he pulled back and met her eyes, Reagan didn't even debate on her answer. Instead, she slid her hands beneath his T-shirt and pushed it up, eager to get him out of it. Lynx grabbed a handful and yanked it over his head, tossing it into the truck behind her.

Then she was staring at all those tattoos on his chest, the beautiful designs that decorated so much of him. She'd always loved those tattoos. Even back when they were nothing more than random designs. Over the years, they'd filled in, merged together until it required effort to make out the smaller ones from his teenage years.

The man was the sexiest thing she'd ever seen in her life.

Running her hands over the smooth ridges of his stomach, she continued upward, leaning forward and pressing her mouth to his skin. When he growled roughly, her pussy clenched. She didn't stop touching or kissing him until he had her shirt up. She only paused so he could remove it because she wanted to feel his skin against hers and she was tired of waiting. It didn't matter that they were outside, that it was probably close to ninety degrees in the shade, that she was sitting in the bed of his truck, or even that someone could wander up at any moment.

None of it mattered because she finally had Lynx all to herself.

Her bra was the next article of clothing to go while she tugged at the button on his jeans.

"Oh, God," she moaned, pulling her mouth from his when his rough hands cupped her bare breasts.

Her eyes shot to his hands, but the tattoos there didn't register. No, she was watching the way he cupped her breasts, pinching her nipples with his thumbs and forefingers, his callused hands abrading her skin in the most sensual way. The various sensations swirled together, escalating into something she'd never felt, an erotic bliss that had her wondering if she would implode.

"Fuck," he hissed, lifting one sensitive peak to his mouth.

Reagan watched as he pulled the hardened point between his lips, his teeth scraping gently before he sucked her fully into his mouth. She clutched the back of his head, holding him to her while he alternated to her other nipple, driving her out of her mind with his lips and tongue. She'd imagined this, but never had she thought it would be this good.

Hell, *nothing* had ever been this good before.

"Lynx..."

One of his hands dropped and she felt him working the button on her shorts free. When the waistband loosened, his hand dipped inside, sliding against her skin but not quite getting to the spot she needed him most.

He groaned, pulling back from her, and Reagan whimpered when the heat of his mouth disappeared.

Relief swamped her when she realized he wasn't stopping.

No, Lynx seemed to be focused solely on getting her naked, and she damn sure wasn't fighting him. He tugged her boots from her feet, then yanked her shorts and panties down until her bare butt was on the warm metal.

"Lean back," he commanded.

Placing her hands behind her, Reagan nearly fell back when Lynx lifted her feet and placed them on the edge of the tailgate before his head dropped down between her splayed thighs. When his fingers separated her pussy lips, she gulped in air, her head falling back as a strangled moan escaped her throat. And when his tongue slid against her clit, she cried out.

Reagan didn't have time to react, to feel even an ounce of modesty, because his mouth obliterated her thoughts, one glorious sensation overrode the next until she was panting and moaning.

It was an awkward position, but it didn't seem to faze Lynx, because he slid his hands under her ass and cradled her as his tongue did wicked things, thrusting inside her, then teasing her clit repeatedly. She was desperate for release, hanging on by a fragile thread when he lifted his head. Unable to help herself, Reagan sat upright, reaching for him as he crushed his mouth to hers. She tasted herself on his lips, once again clutching his head, holding him so he couldn't get away.

She vaguely heard the crinkle of a wrapper, felt Lynx moving, knew he was sheathing himself. She wanted to watch, wanted to see his cock for the first time, wanted to take him in her mouth, but he seemed to have other intentions and she wanted him so much she hurt.

"Reagan... Need to be inside you."

"Yes," she moaned in earnest, her lips sliding against his as they breathed each other's air.

He shifted her back as he crawled up onto the tailgate. He wrestled with his jeans, shoving them lower before settling between her thighs, his big body looming over her. Then she felt the blunt head of his cock against her entrance. When he pushed in, her breath caught in her throat, her body trying to accommodate him. *All* of him. He was much bigger than she'd imagined him to be.

"Girl... Jesus fuck ... this ain't gonna last long."

No, it wouldn't. She was on the verge of climaxing already, her body strung tight as he pushed in slowly.

But she didn't want slow.

"Fuck me," she demanded, holding on to him.

His hips thrust forward and he was lodged all the way inside her. Reagan drew in air as fast as she could, his cock filling her, stretching her. It was too much but not enough. The pain warred with pleasure, and she forced herself to relax around him, to let the pleasure win out.

"Please ... Lynx..." She was on the verge of tears. She wanted him so much she ached with it.

"Hold on to me, girl," he crooned, pulling his mouth from hers.

He propped himself up on one hand, his other hand dropped to her ass, and he held her tightly against him. Then he was retreating, slamming into her hard. Her skin tingled as the pleasure consumed her. And when Lynx began fucking her hard, drilling into her, Reagan knew without a doubt that she would never forget this moment for as long as she lived.

Chapter Twenty-One

FUCKING REAGAN ON THE TAILGATE OF HIS truck had never been his intention. Not for their first time together, that was for damn sure. However, getting to a softer surface would require time and he didn't have it. He needed her with an intensity that robbed him of his good sense.

Lynx had always known that his world would be forever changed once he sank deep inside this woman. He hadn't known how much though.

He prided himself on being an attentive lover, but when it came to Reagan, he couldn't seem to control himself. He wanted to fuck her until neither of them could breathe. Then he wanted to start all over again. His entire body was hard, his muscles straining as he plunged deep, retreated, then slammed into her again. He didn't give a fuck about finesse, only about sating the urge that had been burning inside him for so long.

"Lynx … so close … oh, God."

Reagan's fingernails dug into his shoulders, and Lynx fucked her harder, faster, driving them both closer to the edge. He only prayed he wasn't hurting her, because he was out of control when it came to this woman.

He could feel her pussy milking him, squeezing his cock, her body welcoming him with every grueling thrust of his hips.

"Reagan…" It was a warning growl that he couldn't hold back. He was going to come.

"Yes … Lynx … God, yes. Just … like … that."

Every one of her words was punctuated by a punishing plunge of his cock inside the silky, wet depth of her pussy, and her sweet cries only made him want more, until he knew he couldn't hold on any longer.

Reaching between them, he pressed his thumb against her clit, circling the hardened bundle of nerves until she screamed out his name over and over, her pussy pulsing around his dick, robbing him of air and sanity when his body was rocketed past the breaking point, headfirst into a climax unlike anything he'd ever known.

They were both panting hard, sweat covering their bodies as they clung to one another.

When he finally caught his breath, Lynx pulled out of her, slowly, but he couldn't seem to let go. He *never* wanted to let go.

"Did I hurt you?" he asked, his voice low as he spoke close to her ear.

"God no. That was ... fantastic."

"We're goin' to my house," he stated gruffly, pulling back and meeting her gaze before hopping off the truck to his feet. He removed the condom and tied it off, continuing to look at her. "I'm not done with you yet. And I need a hell of a lot more space to lay you out."

A wicked smile tilted her mouth, and Reagan Trevino had never looked more beautiful than she did right then. Naked and smiling back at him as though he was her favorite dessert and she'd been deprived of it for ages.

It took a little while, but they both managed to get their clothes on, then climbed back into the truck. Neither of them said anything for the few minutes it took to get to his house. And then, after he'd haphazardly parked near the porch, he got out. Thankfully, he still had some manners. After helping her out, he led her into the house, through the living room, and right to the bathroom. He tossed the spent rubber into the trash can, then turned on the shower.

"Naked," he ordered, turning his full attention on her once again.

It was as though he hadn't fucked her not fifteen minutes before. It was as though he'd never had his hands on her before. His body was hard, his cock once again throbbing, eager for anything and everything this woman was willing to give him. He wasn't sure a hundred lifetimes with Reagan would ever be enough.

"This time I'm gonna go slow." He reached for her shirt and helped her to dispose of it once more, then he unclasped her bra, gently easing it over her shoulders, his eyes feasting on her perfect tits.

Letting his hands roam slowly up her sides, Lynx looked into her eyes, holding her gaze. He couldn't tell what she was thinking, but he knew she could read his face like a book. This woman was in total control where he was concerned, even if he was the one calling the shots.

"Your turn," she whispered, pushing his T-shirt higher.

Wasting no time, Lynx jerked it over his head, loving the way her eyes instantly roamed his torso along with her soft hands. He'd waited so long for her to touch him like this. Too long.

Once they both stripped their remaining clothes off, Lynx took Reagan's hand and led her into the shower. He kept the water lukewarm because they were both still sweating from the heat outside. It didn't seem to bother Reagan when the water sluiced over her hair, her skin. He watched as her nipples pebbled. He couldn't resist cupping her breasts, gently kneading them until she moaned softly.

He sucked in a sharp breath when her fingers circled his dick, teasing him with firm, slow strokes.

Reaching for the soap, Lynx was determined to get them washed up and back to his bedroom. It wasn't until Reagan took the bar of soap and lathered her hands that he paused. When her hands resumed their position on his dick, Lynx closed his eyes, letting the sensations roll through him.

"Fuck yes," he groaned. "Never stop doing that."

Forcing his eyes open, he watched as Reagan took a small step back, her gaze dropping to his cock as she continued to slide her palms up and down his length, the water slowly rinsing the soap away.

"Aww, hell." He reached for the tiled wall when she eased down to her knees in front of him. He hadn't been expecting this, but holy fuck, he'd dreamed about this moment plenty of times. In fact, he'd jacked off to fantasies of her sucking him into her sweet little mouth…

"Reagan." He snapped out her name as her mouth closed over the head of his cock, her tongue circling, teasing.

Lynx couldn't resist sliding one hand into her hair, holding her as she sucked him deeper. When her eyes lifted to his, he could see the heat, the need. She wanted him as much as he wanted her and his cock pulsed with the knowledge.

"That's it, girl," he urged. "Suck me. Deeper. Yes… All the way…" Lynx groaned when she took as much of him as she could.

He watched his dick slide over her lips before disappearing inside her mouth once more. He wanted to see his cock disappearing into her pussy, her ass. And he wouldn't be content until he'd claimed this woman in every way imaginable.

However, he had no intention of coming just yet. His orgasm from earlier had taken some of the edge off. Which left him with plenty of time to explore *her* for as long as she would let him.

But in order for him to do that, he had to get her sexy little mouth to release him.

He'd never thought he'd be thinking along *those* lines.

ADMITTEDLY, REAGAN HAD LIMITED EXPERIENCE WHEN IT came to sex. She'd been with one man only, so she didn't have much to compare to, but holy hell, Lynx Caine was a *big* man. One of her hands barely spanned the full breadth of his cock — the tip of her middle finger and thumb barely touching — and as she took the wide crest past her lips, she briefly wondered how he hadn't caused her significant pain when he'd fucked her before.

Apparently, her body was made to adjust to him. And she was grateful for that. Not to mention, she was eager to feel him inside her again.

"Come here, girl," Lynx groaned, reaching for her arm and helping her back to her feet.

"I'm not done," she told him coyly.

"Neither am I. Trust me." He swiped his thumb over her lower lip. "I look forward to havin' my dick in this sweet mouth again, but right now, I need to taste you."

Before she could come up with something to say to that, Lynx shut off the water and grabbed a towel. Rather than dry himself, he slid it over her body.

Slowly.

So slowly.

The soft cotton teased her nipples, as did his tongue when he dropped to his knees and proceeded to dry her feet, her shins, her thighs. And the man was paying close attention to detail, spending more time than was necessary, and driving her crazy in the process. When he dried her ass, he took her breast into his mouth, the suction making her moan as she dug her fingernails into his shoulders.

"Lynx..."

With a soft rumble, he released her breast, then got to his feet. "I fuckin' love when you say my name." His voice was little more than a rough growl and it made her clit throb. "I think that's my new mission in life. To see how loud I can make you say it."

Once again, Lynx took her mouth with his. She could feel him moving, knew he was quickly drying himself, never once breaking the kiss. And when he was finished, he led her back to his bedroom, sitting her on the edge of the mattress, then leaning her back, her legs dangling off the side.

He remained standing as he came over her, his tongue thrusting insistently against hers. But then the kiss ended and his mouth trailed fire down her neck, her chest. Every one of her senses was attuned to him. His sexy scent, the warmth of his skin, his hard body beneath her palms, the intriguing way he growled when something seemed to please him. Yep, she was one hundred percent in tune with this man.

"This time, I'm gonna make you come with my mouth," he said, lifting her knees and pushing them closer to her chest.

His eyes blazed as they drifted down her body. She was on full display for him, her knees wide, his gaze caressing her bare pussy. Reagan wanted to beg him to hurry, but she bit her lip to keep the words in. Although she was eager, she didn't want to hurry. She wanted this to last forever because she'd never felt anything this amazing. His hands, his mouth, even the way he looked at her had new, incredible sensations coursing through her.

When his head lowered between her thighs, she felt the heat of his breath against her skin, the rough rasp of his thumbs as he separated her lips. But the gentle slide of his tongue along her clit was the best part. He certainly wasn't racing to the finish line. No, not Lynx. He was taking his time, feasting on her, fucking her with his tongue, then flicking her clit until she was gripping the quilt with both fists, trying to hold on.

"So wet," he mumbled against her skin.

Reagan's body hummed when he pushed one finger inside her, slowly fucking her while his tongue worked her clit. When two fingers dipped inside, she was panting, her body no longer her own. It belonged solely to Lynx. She was like a puppet on a string, and he was making her feel things she never knew she could feel.

"Lynx…" Her back bowed when his fingers brushed that spot deep inside that she'd only heard about.

"That's it, girl," he urged before his tongue worked her clit again, more insistently.

"Oh, God…" She felt the heat bloom inside her, the electricity sparking in her core. When it started radiating outward, she cried out his name.

"Come for me, Reagan," he commanded, never slowing his sensual assault.

And then her orgasm crested, obliterating her mind, sending her body soaring onto another plane of existence, one where she was suspended in the moment by a pleasure so unreal it bordered on pain. It left her in awe, but it also scared her to death. This man had more control over her than she'd expected.

"That's the prettiest thing I've ever seen," he whispered as he crawled over her. "That sweet pussy coming for me like that."

His dirty words caused aftershocks, her body tingling.

When Lynx's mouth found hers, Reagan adapted to the slower pace, her body still coming down from the incredible high. Thankfully he had more energy than she did, which was the only reason she ended up on top of him, straddling his narrow hips, her breasts crushed to his chest.

His hands roamed down her back, her ass, over her thighs before traveling up again. It calmed her, soothed her. But at the same time, it renewed her need, rekindled the fire banked in her core.

"Put me inside you," he whispered. "I want you to ride me, Reagan. I wanna feel your pussy squeeze my dick. Wanna watch as you come again."

How she managed to move, she wasn't sure, but Reagan reached between them, her hand circling his cock. Only then did she realize he'd suited up. Where the condom came from, she had no idea. Nor did she care, because a second later, he was filling her to overflowing.

Wanting to watch his face when he came this time, Reagan pushed herself up, her hands pressed to his chest as she rocked her hips, her body adjusting quickly to the intrusion. His cock glided against delicate nerve endings, and her nipples pebbled as more pleasure detonated inside her. Her skin felt too tight for her body, chills breaking out along her arms as the sensations rocked her.

"Beautiful," he whispered, their eyes locked together.

Reagan didn't look away. She couldn't. She was trapped in his beautiful green eyes, lost to him, to *this*.

She began to rock faster, then lifting and lowering, fucking him, sending them both to that ethereal place she'd been before.

"Aw, fuck…" Lynx's hands gripped her hips, pulling her down on him, his cock filling her. "So fucking perfect."

It *was* perfect.

Beyond perfect.

And that, more than anything, was the most terrifying part.

Reagan knew it would be so easy to fall completely in love with this man.

In fact, it was quite possible she was already there.

Chapter Twenty-Two

LYNX KNEW WITHOUT A DOUBT THAT NOW that he'd had a taste of Reagan, he was completely hooked. And watching as she rode him, he wanted to stay just like this for the rest of his days. She looked like a fucking goddess atop him, the long, wet strands of her hair hanging over her shoulders, brushing his chest with the motion of her body. Her soft pink nipples hardened into points, her golden skin gleaming.

"Come here, girl," he whispered, pulling her mouth down to his.

When she rested atop him, Lynx gripped her hips, holding her still as he thrust deep inside. Their tongues met, sliding against one another as he took the reins and fucked her from underneath.

"Lynx…" Reagan pulled her mouth from his.

He didn't slow, punching his hips upward, driving into her while he watched as she threw her head back and cried out, her pussy squeezing him as her orgasm raced through her. He didn't stop thrusting, merely slowed as she rode out her climax. And when she was finished, he rolled them both so that he was on top.

"One more, girl. I want you to come for me one more time."

"I…"

Before she could argue, Lynx slammed home, retreated, then slammed in again. With every powerful thrust, she moaned, her nails digging into his arms as she held on to him.

"So hot … so wet… Come for me, Reagan. Come all over my cock, girl. Let me—"

"Lynx!"

Damn, he fucking loved when she said his name. And he'd been serious. His new mission was to have her screaming his name as loudly as possible.

Reagan's pussy clutched him tightly, this time strong enough to drag his release from him. It stole his breath as he slammed into her one last time, his dick pulsing deep inside her body. Lynx watched her face, loving how uninhibited she was, how fucking beautiful she was.

Although he was tired, his body wrung out, he'd be damned if he wasn't ready to go again. Like a fucking teenage boy who'd gotten his first taste of pussy, Lynx wanted to keep going, but he knew she was exhausted.

He eased from her body, then headed for the bathroom to dispose of the condom. When he returned, Reagan was in the same place, her eyes tracking him as he moved toward her, a sexy smirk on her lips.

So fucking beautiful his heart squeezed.

Although they probably should've gotten up, gotten dressed, and headed back to the shop, Lynx couldn't resist crawling back in bed with her. The tension in his body eased completely when she curled up against him, her head on his chest the way she'd done the other night when she had stayed.

"A nap sounds perfect right now," she whispered.

He grunted softly. Being here with her was the perfect part. Awake, asleep, it didn't really matter.

Lynx brushed her hair away from her face and gently stroked her back while she breathed against him. She probably felt the steady thump of his heart against her cheek, but she didn't say anything.

And right before he drifted off, Lynx couldn't help but think that this was exactly where Reagan belonged. Right where *he* belonged.

Together.

The sun was still shining when Lynx stirred. He glanced over at the clock, doing his best not to move so that he didn't wake Reagan.

Three hours.

They'd slept for three hours but he felt as though he'd slept for three days.

The ringing of his cell phone sounded from somewhere, and Lynx lifted his head, glancing around, trying to figure out where the damn thing was.

Bathroom.

Where he'd ditched his clothes earlier.

It stopped ringing but started up a few seconds later.

Shit.

Lynx eased Reagan off him before swinging his legs over the side of the bed. He was naked, his cock already perking up at the sight of the naked woman in his bed, but he ignored it. Shutting the bathroom door, he took a piss, then washed his hands and splashed water on his face. He then took a good long look at himself in the mirror. He looked like the same guy, but he damn sure didn't feel like the same guy.

Not after Reagan.

He scrubbed his hands down his face once more, then grabbed his jeans and fished his phone from his pocket before pulling them on.

The phone rang in his hand, so he hit the button. "What's up, hoss?" he greeted Wolfe, keeping his voice low.

"Thought I'd check up on you."

"You called multiple times so you could check up on me?" Lynx chuckled.

"Oh, you know how it is. I look for opportunities wherever I can find 'em. Reagan with you?"

"Yeah." He knew Wolfe already knew the answer to that or he wouldn't be calling to give him a hard time. "So, what did you need?"

Wolfe chuckled. "Not a damn thing. Just wanted to give you shit. Later."

Shaking his head, Lynx grinned.

His cousin was a pain in his ass, that was for damn sure.

But for right now, he could forgive him.

REAGAN WOKE IN LYNX'S BED FOR THE second time, but this time was vastly different than the first. For one, Copenhagen wasn't the one greeting her. And two, it wasn't the morning after her bar blew up.

Nope. This time she awoke to a warm, solid man lying by her side.

"Evenin'," Lynx greeted in that dark, raspy baritone that made her skin tingle and her insides glow.

"What time is it?"

"Six thirty."

Reagan closed her eyes again and sighed. She shifted closer to Lynx, and she felt the unfamiliar twinge of her muscles. It brought back memories of what they'd done earlier. What she wanted them to do again.

"Anything happen while I was asleep?" she asked, her voice rough from sleep.

"Wolfe called to give me shit," he said, amusement in his voice.

"Yeah?" Turning, Reagan peered up at him.

"Yeah."

"So, it's safe to say he knows I'm here?"

"He does."

"Which means my brother probably knows I'm here."

Lynx frowned, which made Reagan laugh.

"Are you scared of Rhys?"

A snort came from the sexy man beside her.

Reagan chuckled, her body warming. "Oh, wait. Lynx Caine isn't afraid of anyone."

He shifted, the movement forcing her onto her back. "Oh, I'm scared of someone."

"Yeah? Who?"

"You."

His mouth lowered to hers in a sweet, gentle kiss. "Is that right?"

"Absolutely."

"Why's that?"

His eyes met hers and Reagan could tell he was contemplating saying something, but she had no idea what. However, nothing came out, but a seductive smirk tilted his lips.

Damn, the man had perfect lips.

In fact, he had perfect everything. Lips, eyes, hair, body. And his tongue. She wouldn't even get started about that wicked tongue that had done delicious things to her.

Reagan's hand slid down his stomach, over the ridges of his abs, then lower.

"What're you doin', girl?" he asked, grinning at her from above.

"Who me?" she teased as her hand closed around his cock.

He had a perfect cock, too. Long, thick, and oh so hard right now.

Lynx's eyes closed momentarily and he groaned low in his throat. It was a sexy sound, one Reagan could listen to every day of her life and never tire of.

When he rolled onto his back, Reagan continued to stroke him, watching the movement as she did. Peering up at Lynx's face, she watched him as he watched the action, too.

"Love that," he whispered. "So fucking much."

"Yeah?"

Reagan didn't stop stroking him, certainly not when he covered her hand with his and assisted her movement, tightening her grip around his steely length. She pressed her lips to his chest, right over the tattoo that inked over his heart. It was a flower. A lily, in fact, which made sense. His mother's name was Lily. The script below read: *Forever with me. Always in my heart.*

As she continued to visually feast on his beauty, Reagan noted the various other tattoos. There were so many, some of them hard to make out, but her eyes locked on one that was inked down his side.

Her gaze darted up to Lynx's face and she saw that he was watching her. She couldn't seem to look away, her heart in her throat, even as she continued to stroke him slowly, leisurely.

"When?" she whispered, her heart in her throat, tears burning behind her eyes.

He gave one of his famous one-shoulder shrugs. "Years ago."

Reagan's attention shifted back to the tattoo. The one of her name in beautiful script. And right then, her heart burst open in her chest, warmth unlike anything she'd ever known infusing her.

This man…

This beautiful, imperfectly perfect man had her name tattooed on his body.

She knew, right at that moment, that Lynx Caine was it for her. No matter what she tried to tell herself, this man was who she wanted. Who she'd wanted since she was a naïve teenager.

Accepting that was the easy part.

The hard part was figuring out what that meant.

For her.

For him.

For *them*.

Chapter Twenty-Three

LYNX WAS HOLDING HIS BREATH.

Not only because Reagan's soft, warm hand was gliding up and down his rigid erection, either.

No, he was holding his breath because the woman had just located the tattoo of her name on his body. He'd gotten it years ago. And it hadn't been an accident.

In fact, none of his tattoos had been an accident. He hadn't gotten any of them during a drunken bender. He'd been sober and lucid for every single one, drawing most of them out himself beforehand. Many of them inked directly from his sketches. All of them having meaning to him in some way.

His breath locked deeper inside him when Reagan leaned forward and kissed his chest, her little tongue gliding over his skin. It was an erotic sight, one he'd fantasized about plenty of times over the years.

When her head continued to move south, his stomach muscles tightened. As she traced the muscles that arrowed down between his legs, he finally sucked air into his lungs. But the moment those sweet lips wrapped around the head of his cock, Lynx's entire body jerked from the heat of her mouth.

Yet he watched, loving the way she laved him with her tongue, the gentle squeeze of her hand around the base of his shaft. She moved her hand in tandem with her mouth, stroking, sucking, driving him absolutely crazy. His cock should've been in desperate need of rest after their marathon sex from earlier, but no. It seemed that that part of him was as eager to have this woman's attention as the rest of him was.

Reagan moaned and electricity sparked through every one of Lynx's nerve endings, the vibration causing his dick to twitch.

For several minutes, he watched her, loving the way she teased, not quite sending him over the edge, although he was definitely grasping it by his fingernails. He was close. So fucking close.

Then she did something wicked with her tongue, her fingers lightly grazing his balls.

"Ah, girl," he groaned. "You're gonna make me come."

She moaned, and more vibrations shot through his shaft, his balls tightening against his body.

"I'm gonna come in your mouth, Reagan," he warned.

Another moan.

He inched closer to his inevitable climax.

"Fuck…" he hissed, his legs tensing when she applied the perfect amount of suction to make his eyes cross. "Reagan…" Reaching for her, Lynx twined his fingers in her hair, pumping his hips gently, not wanting to take control but desperately chasing his release now.

When her hand tightened, her tongue swiping over the head before she sucked him as deep as she could, his control snapped.

He roared as his release barreled down on him, stealing his breath as he came, spurting into her mouth. Lynx didn't close his eyes, wanting to watch as she swallowed him down. It was so hot he couldn't seem to stop the damn thing from twitching.

While he attempted to recover, Reagan crawled up his body, her tits grazing his stomach, his chest, until her mouth was hovering above his. Didn't matter that he could hardly breathe, Lynx grabbed her, crushing his lips to hers, darting his tongue into her mouth roughly.

She chuckled and pulled back before he could deepen the kiss.

"I think we should probably get out of this bed for a bit."

His stomach rumbled as though that was the best suggestion he'd ever heard.

Reagan laughed. "And maybe we should eat somethin' while we're at it."

"I know what I wanna eat," he told her, grinning.

"Down, boy."

Sage advice, sure. But Lynx was finding it nearly impossible to do with Reagan around.

Not that he couldn't get used to walking around with a perpetual hard-on.

He could. Especially if she was going to do those wicked things with her tongue again.

But for now, he could rein it in, give her a breather.

For a little while anyway.

Half an hour later, Lynx dished up fried bologna sandwiches and chips. He'd been shocked when Reagan suggested them, considering that was one of his favorite meals. He wasn't a complicated man by any means. He wasn't a gourmet chef, either, but he knew his way around a kitchen. Hell, he was twenty-eight years old. If he didn't know how to cook at this point, he'd be pretty well doomed.

They were eating at the small table in his kitchen when his phone rang.

After glancing at the screen, he peered over at Reagan, then answered.

"What's up?"

"We got the entire lot cleared," Ed told him. "The dumpsters were hauled away, so we're ready for whatever comes next. Wanna meet up tomorrow mornin'?"

Lynx kept his eyes on Reagan. "Yeah. How 'bout you come over to the shop around nine. I'll have Reagan there with me. She can tell us what comes next."

"Sounds like a plan. See ya then."

Reagan was eyeing him suspiciously when Lynx set his phone on the table.

"Why will I be at the shop tomorrow?" she asked, gripping her iced tea glass.

Lynx held up one finger, signaling her to hold on. He got up from his chair, then headed out to his truck. He grabbed the spiral sketchbook he'd been using, then went back in.

"Now, don't think I'm tryin' to take over," he began. "I was just messin' around and came up with this. Obviously, you can do whatever you—"

Reagan held up a hand, smiling. "Just show it to me, Lynx."

He flipped open the notebook and pushed it toward her.

Once again, his breath was lodged somewhere in his chest as he watched Reagan study the rough sketch. Her eyes popped up to meet his, then dropped back to the notebook.

"You *drew* this?"

He nodded.

"Wow. This is…"

When she looked up at him again, Lynx noticed tears in her eyes, and he instantly wanted to kick himself. Tears weren't his thing. He didn't handle them well at all. And to see Reagan cry … that was his worst fucking fear.

"This is…" She exhaled roughly. "Amazing."

"*Really?*" That wasn't what he'd expected her to say.

"Yeah." A smile formed, then grew bigger. "This is *my* bar," she said in a soft whisper.

"Of course it is," he assured her.

"No." Her eyes met his. "What I mean is this is *me*. This is *my* style. It's… Holy shit, Lynx. This is incredible."

Probably for the first time since he'd drawn the damn thing, Lynx felt the pressure on his chest release. He'd figured it could go one of two ways. She'd like it or she'd hate it.

This, of course, was what he'd hoped for.

But not at all what he'd expected.

REAGAN FELT AS THOUGH SHE WAS IN some sort of alternate universe.

And once again, Lynx Caine had rocked her already unstable world with his kindness.

Turned out, the bad boy of Embers Ridge had the biggest heart of anyone she knew.

And to think, she had wasted all this time running from him.

As she stared at the sketch — the really *good* sketch — of what his vision was for her new bar, Reagan couldn't help but think this man really knew her.

"The old bar," she explained, "it wasn't really mine, you know?"

She looked up to see him watching her.

"I mean, it was mine according to the piece of paper I have showing it is. However, it never really felt like mine. But this…" Reagan glanced down at the notebook again. "This is incredible."

"It's a rough draft," he said, his voice soft.

"No, it's perfect, Lynx. It's everything I've ever wanted." Reagan frowned. "But I don't know when the insurance company'll be able to pay out."

"We're not worried about that right now," he said.

Her gaze snapped to his. "Of course we are. I can't build this when I don't have the money to do so."

"Like I said, Reagan, we're not worried about that right now. There're a lot of people willing to help, plenty of donations coming in."

Reagan shook her head. "No. Absolutely not. I will not take handouts."

Lynx sighed heavily. "Jesus Christ, girl. It ain't a handout. Do you realize how many people come into your bar on a weekly basis? Hell, half this town stops in at least once a week. Some damn near every day."

"I get that," she countered. "But that doesn't mean they have to help me rebuild." Reagan shook her head again and got to her feet, but not before Lynx was on his.

When he pulled her toward him, she started to push him away, but resisting him was impossible.

"What happened to you that night … it happened to the whole town, Reagan." He lifted her chin with his finger. "Don't offend them by refusing their help."

"You don't get it," she argued. "I don't have the money to do any of it. Shit, I'm lucky I even have a place to live right now."

His eyes narrowed. "You've got everything you need. Just ask."

This time she did push him away. "No. No way." Reagan turned and walked to the opposite side of the room. "I am not askin' you for help, Lynx. Certainly not when it pertains to money. No fuckin' way."

Reagan prided herself on being able to take care of herself. Sure, she had lived with Billy all those years, but she had paid the bills herself. Half the time, Billy's paycheck was spent before he ever made it back home from a job, and he certainly hadn't spent it on her. She'd learned to live with that. And yes, they had argued every damn day about money, but in the end, Reagan had accepted the fact that she had to take care of herself.

"I need to go home," she insisted.

She needed some distance, some time to herself.

Reagan needed to think long and hard about all of this. About what she wanted, what she didn't want. She'd just gotten out of a long-term relationship. She wasn't sure she was ready for another. Even if it was with Lynx, a man she loved despite herself.

However, love was one thing. Money was something else entirely. And she damn sure wasn't going to be indebted to Lynx.

No way. No how.

That was the fastest way to ruin a good thing.

When she met Lynx's gaze, she realized he was holding out his truck keys. However, when she reached for them, he didn't hand them over.

Instead, Lynx cupped her chin, forcing her to meet his gaze.

"You are the most stubborn woman I've ever met." He was smiling as he said this. "But I already knew that about you. So, do what you need to do, Reagan. But just know, I'm gonna do what I need to do."

"What does that mean?" she countered hotly.

He dropped his hand from her chin, then pulled her against him. Reagan flattened her palms against his hard chest.

"It means I'm gonna take care of you, whether you like it or not." His green eyes narrowed. "And like I told you. I'm not lookin' for a one-time thing from you. So, you can be scared and you can be ornery, but that doesn't mean I'm gonna back down."

He pulled her tighter against him and her heart melted in her chest. This man knew all the right things to say.

"You knew what you were in for when you came to the shop this mornin'," he stated firmly. "Yet you showed up there anyway."

"I came to talk to you," she said, although it was a lie.

"Right." His smirk was both sexy and irritating. "I told you before that you couldn't handle what I want from you," he continued. "But you still came to me."

"I came for sex," she said, another lie. Good Lord, she probably shouldn't go outside if there were any clouds.

Lynx chuckled. "Oh, girl. You're gonna get that and more. Every fuckin' day for the rest of my life."

Reagan's eyes widened at his words. She wasn't even sure he knew what he'd just said, but it sounded a hell of a lot like commitment.

"Yeah," he said softly, leaning down and pressing his lips gently against hers. "And I mean that exactly as it sounds."

She felt him press the keys into her hand, but Reagan had a difficult time moving from where she stood, still leaning against him. She searched his eyes, trying to figure out what the hell was really going on here.

But in her heart, she already knew.

The question was whether or not she was strong enough to handle him.

For some reason, she seriously doubted she was.

Chapter Twenty-Four

THE FOLLOWING MORNING, LYNX WOKE AT HIS normal time.

Normal being whenever his eyes opened.

Just so happened that he was always awake in time to meet Wolfe at the diner. That was a tradition engrained in him, something he wasn't willing to let go of.

So, after dropping Copenhagen at the store, he headed over to meet his cousin.

"Where's Amy?" he asked when he joined Wolfe at the table.

"She stayed with Rhys this mornin'," he said, a smirk on his face.

"She takin' the day off?" Not that Lynx cared what Amy did, but it hadn't been the norm thus far. Then again, his entire life was far from normal, despite his daily breakfast.

"Nah. Said she wanted to spend some time with him and she'd be in after breakfast."

"Rhys finally moved in?"

Wolfe grinned. "Mostly, yeah. But baby steps."

Lynx waved his hand behind him. "Seems everyone's takin' it well."

He hadn't heard anything negative regarding Wolfe's relationship with Amy and Rhys. Then again, he'd been wrapped up in his own shit these days.

"Most," Wolfe said, his eyes dropping to the table.

"Who the fuck has a problem with it?" Lynx growled, his automatic instinct to protect his family kicking in, his body coiling tight, gearing up for a fight.

Wolfe rolled his eyes. "Not everyone gets it, Lynx. No big deal."

Leaning back, Lynx rested one hand on the table and fiddled with his spoon. "That what Rhys's worried about? People not likin' that the sheriff's in a relationship?"

Wolfe chuckled, but there wasn't much humor in it. "A relationship with a man and a woman, Lynx. That's not natural."

Lynx frowned. "For who? And who gives a fuck? It's natural for you or you wouldn't be in it, am I right?"

Wolfe simply stared at him.

"I'm so fuckin' tired of everyone bein' up in everyone else's business," Lynx grumbled. "If it doesn't affect them, they should keep their fuckin' noses out of it."

Wolfe grinned. "Always the protective one, aren't ya?"

It was the way he was. Lynx couldn't change that about himself and he wouldn't anyway. He liked who he was. And he honestly did not give a single fuck who liked it or not.

"Here you boys go," Donna said, delivering their food. "Oh, and in case you haven't heard, Jimmy Don's wife went into labor this mornin'."

"Hot damn," Lynx said with a grin. "Gonna have to go grab us some cigars."

Donna smiled, then shook her head and walked away.

"What's goin' on with Reagan's? Couple people stopped by yesterday after you left. They wanna help out."

"She didn't hit me when I showed her the sketch," he admitted, reaching for his fork and leaning closer to his plate.

"Well, that's a damn good sign."

Yeah, it was. With Reagan, her reaction was anyone's guess. She was stubborn and hardheaded, and truth be told, he loved that about her. She was spunky and sassy and so fucking hot, just thinking about her made his mouth water.

"I was thinkin' that maybe I could design and build the new bar for the place," Wolfe noted.

"Yeah?"

"If she'd be cool with that."

"Prob'ly have to ask her, but shit, I'd say go for it. The girl can use all the help she can get right now."

Even if she didn't necessarily want it.

Taking a bite of eggs, Lynx chewed as he pointed his fork at Wolfe. "She'll be over at the shop in a bit. Ed's stoppin' by to see what's what. And DJ … you know, Darrell Jameson." He chewed some more.

"The general contractor?"

Lynx nodded. "Yep. He's gonna take a look at the plans, help out in that regard. Work on permits."

"And Reagan's cool with this?"

Lynx shrugged. "Until she tells me to stop, I ain't gonna. She needs that bar open. It's her livelihood, but you know Reagan. She ain't gonna ask for help."

Thinking back to their argument last night, Lynx smiled to himself. The woman was nothing if not independent, and she made sure everyone knew it. One day, she'd learn that some people weren't looking for something in return. They simply do for others because they could.

"Nope. She won't." Wolfe grinned. "Good thing she's got you."

Lynx couldn't help but smirk at that.

She did have him.

Even if she wasn't quite ready for all that he wanted from her. She'd get there.

He had faith.

REAGAN HAD TOSSED AND TURNED ALL NIGHT long. She wasn't sure if it was due to the long nap she'd taken with Lynx yesterday or simply because she hated that she'd been in her bed alone. When she finally did doze off, she'd thought she'd heard a sound outside the bedroom window, and she'd ended up pacing the floor for half an hour, shotgun in hand.

Now, as she drove to the shop to meet Lynx, her exhaustion was replaced with an anxious flutter in her belly.

Truth was, she missed seeing Lynx.

Not that she wanted to get addicted to him or anything, but she still wished she could spend more time with him. Sure, it was her own damn fault. That stubborn streak was hard to beat back, and sometimes it didn't do her any favors. Okay, *more often than not* it didn't do her any favors. Hell, her own family gave her a hard time about it.

According to her mother, stubborn was her middle name. She always said that it was probably the reason Reagan would be with Billy forever.

"I showed *you*, Mom," she muttered to herself.

Stubborn and stupid were two very different things, she knew. And she'd proven her stupidity by staying with Billy for so long.

"Ugh." She hated thinking about that asshole.

However, stubborn was a trait she had been born with, something she had a hard time overcoming.

And now, Reagan figured Lynx would eventually get tired of it, and she couldn't very well blame him. Problem was, she had no idea how to change that part of herself. Or if she even wanted to. Yes, she could be the equivalent of a brick wall in an argument, but she was who she was. And if people didn't like it, they could shove it. That was her thoughts on it anyway.

Then again, when she thought about Lynx, she didn't want to be the brick wall that stalled out this thing between them. It was intense. Insanely so. But he was right. She was the one to provoke it every time she tried to put some distance between them.

Not that she intended to spend too much time thinking about long term with Lynx Caine. The guy was a sweet-talker through and through. As much as her heart yearned to be important to someone, she wasn't sure Lynx was the steady, long-term kind, no matter how many sweet words he whispered. Sure, she wanted to believe. Reagan just wasn't sure she could.

When she pulled into the shop shortly after nine, she was surprised to see several additional trucks in the parking lot, besides Calvin's and Lynx's dad's, which Lynx was currently driving. After squeezing the big F-250 into a vacant spot, Reagan climbed out and headed toward the door.

"Damn straight," someone bellowed, their laughter drifting out of the building. "That's what we do 'round these parts. We help when we're needed."

Reagan stepped inside and all the voices cut off almost instantly, leaving a deafening silence lingering.

"There's my girl," Lynx noted, a strange prideful tone to his voice.

He smiled as he moved toward her.

Of course, she blushed. How could she not? The man was already staking his claim on her in public. For whatever reason, she didn't want to contradict him, so she returned the smile and hoped he didn't see how red her cheeks probably were.

Certainly not a good look for her.

When Lynx leaned down and kissed her quickly, another flutter of unrestrained butterflies took hold of her stomach. She found herself staring up at him, slightly in shock. His response: a sexy, crooked smirk.

Of course.

"What's goin' on?" she asked, her voice sounding ridiculously like a croak.

"Well, it looks to me like your bar's gonna be goin' up in the very near future."

Reagan cocked an eyebrow and glanced around at all the faces. She was familiar with most of them. What got her was the fact that they were all smiling like this was something that made *them* happy.

"I ... umm ... really don't know what to say."

Last night she'd spent hours thinking about what Lynx had said. About how they wanted to help her because the bar meant something to them, too. She had tried to come up with a reasonable argument, but had failed each and every time she thought she was getting somewhere.

"It's our pleasure," Ed spoke up.

"We gotta get that bar up and runnin', you know. It's like not havin' television at the house. It just ain't right," Doug Maxwell added with a wide grin.

"And the day the doors open," Lynx added, his arm still comfortably around her shoulders, "the first round's on me."

"No," Reagan said quickly. "The first round's on *me*."

"All right, then," Lynx conceded. "The *second* round's on me."

The grins seemed to widen at the mention of free beer.

"Anyone heard from Jimmy Don? How's the baby doin'?" Ed asked, his eyes swinging to all faces, then over to Lynx.

"They had a little girl," Lynx said. "She's healthy as a horse, he said. Momma's doin' fine, too."

"That's great news." Ed turned, glancing between Reagan and Lynx. "Let us know when we're good to go. We're ready to pour concrete whenever the permits are taken care of and the plumbing's inspected."

Lynx nodded. "Will do."

"I'll check back in with you in a bit," Calvin stated, calling Copenhagen to his side. "Mind if I take the boy with me?"

Lynx shook his head.

As the guys filtered out, they waved. Reagan offered a smile although her head was spinning at everything that was going on around her. She still couldn't believe that these people were coming together to help her rebuild.

Okay, so maybe she could believe it. Embers Ridge was that sort of town. It was the very reason she'd never had any desire to leave. However, she knew she had put a rift between herself and most people due to her relationship with Billy all this time. Most of them, quite frankly, weren't big fans of Billy. Not that she could blame them. But then again, she had been the one to stick with him for so long, so they probably figured she had a few screws loose as well.

Which she probably did.

Once they all cleared out, Reagan realized she and Lynx were the only two left.

"Where's Wolfe?"

Lynx grinned. "He headed home for a bit after we had breakfast. Somethin' about a phone call from Rhys regarding somethin' Amy was doin'." He shrugged. "No clue."

"So what now?" she asked and as soon as the words were out of her mouth, she knew exactly what Lynx was thinking.

It was the same thing *she* was thinking.

When he stepped closer, Reagan lifted the straw Stetson from his head.

"What're you doin'?" he asked, his voice a low growl.

Reagan slipped the hat on her own head.

"You know what it means when a girl wears a man's hat?"

Reagan nodded. She did know.

"You think I won't?" he asked, his eyes boring into hers.

"I'm hopin' you will," she whispered back, her body warming from his nearness.

She also knew that she would not be able to tell the man no. And she damn sure didn't want to.

Chapter Twenty-Five

"COME HERE, GIRL," LYNX SAID, TAKING REAGAN'S hand and leading her toward the stairs. He continued to watch her, wondering if she was going to back out at the last second. He could tell she was thinking about it.

Shit, the woman was already blowing his damn mind. Taking his hat ... putting it on her head. It was a signal that she wanted him. That she wanted him to do some wicked dirty things to her.

And fuck, he wanted that so badly he could taste it.

Only, he was going to wait until she made the next move.

She surprised him — as she was good at doing — when she took the lead, moving in front of him as they ascended the stairs. He followed as his cock went stiff in his jeans. He'd told her yesterday that he intended to get his hands on her every single day. He hadn't been blowing smoke, either. That was his plan. Any day she'd allow him, Lynx intended to be all over her. And maybe, in fifty years or so, he'd be able to cut back to every couple of days.

Then again, he doubted it.

Especially if the woman continued to wear those damn short shorts with boots. It was Reagan's signature style, and it had been her thing long before it'd become a fashion statement for the rest of the country.

"Right here," he told her, opening the door to the break room.

Once inside, he closed and locked it. He didn't know if Wolfe was coming back, but he damn sure didn't want any interruptions.

Before she got too far into the room, he tugged her back toward him, then pressed her up against the door. His mouth found hers in seconds, their bodies colliding. He loved the way Reagan's arms went around his neck, the way one of her legs wrapped around his. It was as though she couldn't seem to get close enough. He knew how she felt.

"Fuck, I missed you," he whispered against her lips before diving in for more of her taste.

Lynx pulled back when Reagan's hands slipped beneath his T-shirt. Their eyes met and held as she slowly pushed it up. He finally gave in, gripping the cotton behind his head and tugging it off and tossing it onto the counter. To make things easier, he grabbed his hat from her head and tossed it alongside his shirt.

"I missed you, too," she said sweetly, her lips pressing against his chest, moving slowly across his pecs.

"My bed was damn lonely last night."

Her cheeks turned a pretty shade of pink. "I know the feelin'."

"Maybe that means you should spend more time there." Like every fucking night.

Damn, but she made him feel things he'd never felt before. Just the way she touched him was something new every time. Admittedly, he'd been with plenty of women, but he'd never met a single one who did things to him the way Reagan did. She was meant for him and he'd always known it.

"I like that idea," she whispered, her lips grazing his jaw.

While she trailed wet kisses lower, moving down his neck, then across his chest, Lynx worked loose the button on her shorts, slipping it from its mooring, then working the zipper down. Her tongue moved to his nipple, her teeth sending shards of electricity firing down to his cock.

Slipping his hand down the front of her shorts, he eased his fingers beneath the edge of her panties, working his way lower until he felt the warm, wet heat he was seeking. Lynx dipped one finger between her smooth lips, her slickness nearly making him moan.

"So fucking wet for me," he groaned.

Reagan peered up at him, a hunger unlike anything he'd ever seen reflecting in her dark eyes.

"You're so damn pretty," he mumbled, leaning down to meld his lips to hers.

While his tongue glided against hers, he slid one finger into the hot depths of her pussy, fucking her gently. His cock was hard as iron, desperate to have her sweet pussy sheathing him once more, but this wasn't only about him. And focusing on her was his main priority. Hopefully in the near future, he'd be able to do that. But he wasn't sure now was that time.

Fueled by his overwhelming need for this woman, Lynx broke the kiss. "Need to be inside you. Right fucking now." The words were rough, gravelly, and ringing with the truth, but he couldn't help himself. Lynx needed this woman. He fucking ached for her.

Reagan never ceased to amaze him. And she took him by surprise once again. First when she toed off her boots, then pushed her shorts down while he focused on releasing his cock from the denim torture chamber. He did manage to wrangle a condom from his wallet and roll it on before he hefted her up against the door and guided himself into the sweet haven of her body.

"Don't wanna hurt you," he growled.

"Just fuck me," she countered, her words as raspy as his.

Reagan clutched his head, then crushed her mouth to his at the same time he thrust deep inside her. They both groaned, the pleasure intense, damn near overwhelming.

Holding her to him, Lynx stumbled over to the counter and set her butt upon it before driving into her again. Holding her was no hardship, but he couldn't seem to control himself right now, which meant this was a hell of a lot easier.

Not to mention, the counter put her at the perfect height. One of these days he was going to turn her around so he could fuck her from behind, gripping that perfect little ass in his hands while he did.

Kissing wasn't an option because he was slamming into her, holding her head with one hand, keeping her cheek pressed to his while he thrust into her over and over.

"Yessss," she hissed, her fingernails digging into his biceps as she held on to him. "Feels good, Lynx. So good."

"Lift your knees," he ordered.

Reagan shifted, her knees coming up against his ribs, changing the angle just slightly... Her pussy clamped down on him.

"Fuck, girl. You're gonna make me come."

Ignoring his impending orgasm wasn't easy, but Lynx focused on sending her over the edge. It was the absolute least he could do considering he was acting like a fucking caveman. He slammed his hips forward, pulled back, slammed home again. Their bodies slapped together and the erotic sound only made it that much harder to hold on.

"Lynx ... oh ... shit... Oh, yes!"

Reagan's pussy squeezed his dick, the muscles rippling over his cock as she came. Her nails dug deeper into his arms, and the extra bite of pain sent him spiraling, his release hitting him like a Mack truck, stealing his breath.

He pulled her hips closer, keeping his cock lodged deep inside her as they both fought for breath.

If he could stay right here forever, buried inside her, holding her against him...

Oh, yeah. He definitely would.

Best fucking place *ever*.

IT WAS SAFE TO SAY, REAGAN WAS putty in this man's hands.

She hadn't even batted an eyelash when he'd led her upstairs. Hadn't hesitated even a second when he guided her into the breakroom. Nor had she paused when he'd kissed the daylights out of her.

Truth be told, she couldn't get enough of him. Even now, as he drove them over to the lot where the new bar was going to go up, Reagan was already plotting her next move. Maybe this time she could take him back to her place and...

"Where'd you go, girl?" he asked.

Reagan realized they'd reached their destination and Lynx had shut off the engine. She glanced over at him to see he was grinning, a knowing smirk tilting his mouth.

"If I had to guess, based on that sexy gleam in your eye," Lynx rasped, "I'd say you're thinkin' about gettin' me naked and inside you again."

She couldn't help it, Reagan groaned. The man's mouth was wickedly dirty and she liked it.

However, she wasn't above playing a little hard to get. She grinned. "Maybe."

His eyes flashed with heat. "Then we should get this outta the way right quick. 'Cause I've got a long list of things I intend to do to that sweet body of yours."

Her stomach fluttered, her pussy clenching.

"Come on," he insisted, opening his door, then helping her across the seat of his dad's cherry-red '65 Chevy.

She knew Lynx loved that truck. In fact, half the town admired it, and they had for as long as Cooter had owned it. However, she also knew that she needed to give his truck back to him. Unfortunately, the phone call earlier had been to inform her that her truck wasn't salvageable. On a positive note, her insurance said that due to the fact it was damaged during the bar explosion, it would be considered in the settlement. What that meant, she wasn't exactly sure, but she was hoping she'd know more in a day or two.

Lynx helped her to her feet, then led her over to what appeared to be a staked-off section situated just a little farther back than the original bar had been.

"Afternoon," Darrell Jameson greeted. "Wanted to talk about placement real quick."

Reagan nodded, smiling.

"We were thinkin' that we could situate the place back here to give more space for the parkin' lot in front. It takes away some of the space behind, but it'll still have room for the dumpster."

She felt Lynx's eyes on her.

Reagan nodded. "I like that idea."

"Good deal. Now I'm takin' Lynx's design over to get it drawn up by an architect friend of mine."

Geez. That sounded expensive.

Darrell must've read her mind because he smiled sheepishly. "He's doin' it for free. He owes me a favor."

Once again, Reagan felt tears forming behind her eyes. She was still trying to wrap her head around all these people wanting to help her out.

"Thank you," she said, forcing the words past her dry throat. "I really appreciate it."

"Anything, kiddo," he stated. "That's what friends are for." Darrell glanced over at Lynx. "That really is all I needed. I'll be in touch and if all goes well, the rest of the plumbin' will go in by the end of the week."

Lynx shook the man's hand and they stood there as Darrell sauntered over to his truck.

When the parking lot was once again empty, Lynx turned to face her. "You still good with this?"

Reagan met his eyes. "I am. It's a little overwhelming... I just don't know how to react, how to thank everyone."

"No thanks needed. Like I said, your bar was home to a lotta people."

Taking a deep breath, she willed the emotions down. She wasn't about to fall apart in front of this man. She'd save that for later, when she was alone.

"What now? You hungry?"

Reagan nodded. "I could eat."

"Good." He took her hand and steered her toward the truck. "You need your energy."

"For?"

The crooked smirk he shot her was all the answer she got.

Then again, it was all the answer she needed.

Chapter Twenty-Six

"WE REALLY SHOULD GET OUTTA THIS BED and get back to work," Wolfe mumbled, although he didn't move an inch.

Being sandwiched between Rhys and Amy was a place he was hesitant to ever leave. Mornings were especially hard when he woke up to them beside him, all warm and sexy... And these moments worked, too. The second Rhys had called him, telling him all the dirty things their girl was doing to him, Wolfe had lit out of the diner like the hounds of hell were on his ass. Screw work, these two were far more important at the moment.

Hence the reason they were naked in bed.

"Ready to run off already?" Rhys joked, his hand sliding down between Wolfe's legs.

Wolfe grunted. The warm hand curling around his dick had his blood pumping faster.

"Keep that up and I'll be ready for a replay of what we just did," he said, turning his head and looking at the sexy naked man lying beside him.

Wolfe groaned when Rhys's fist tightened around his cock. "Fuck..." He inhaled sharply. "Love when you touch me."

And he did. He fucking loved every second of it.

Despite the fact that their relationship was relatively new, with each passing day, Wolfe knew right where he belonged. Here with them. Forever and always.

With all the shit going down, it would've been easy to get his priorities mixed up, but Rhys and Amy were keeping him grounded. And the same could be said in reverse. Life could so easily swallow you up, make you forget the little things such as moments like this. And Wolfe refused to allow that to happen to them.

Amy shifted beside him, her hand sliding down his stomach, lower, until she was cupping his balls while Rhys continued to stroke Wolfe's now fully erect cock. He'd just come not ten minutes ago, but he was already raring to go again.

"What were you saying about work?" Amy asked, her tone sweet and teasing.

Wolfe grunted, his arm tightening around the beautiful woman beside him. "No fuckin' clue," he moaned.

Closing his eyes, he allowed the sensations to slam into him. His thigh muscles tightened, his abs contracting as his breaths sped up. Rhys's lips pressed against his chest, and Wolfe tightened his grip on the man, holding him closer, never wanting to let him go.

When those warm lips started traveling lower, Wolfe hissed, turning his head toward him. "Get on up here and ride me," he urged Rhys. "Let me feel that tight ass squeeze my dick."

He felt the shiver that racked Rhys's body.

Amy's hand fell away, but she didn't disappear. Nope, the woman was grabbing a condom, and Wolfe was reduced to little more than a puddle of sensation as the two of them continued to tease him. Amy rolled the condom down his rock-hard cock before returning to her spot beside him. Rhys got to his knees, then straddled Wolfe's thighs while Amy took over the hand job, sliding lubricant over Wolfe's cock.

"Fuck…" He could hardly breathe.

Although it took some effort, Wolfe assisted Rhys by holding his dick rigid as the man sank down on him.

Wolfe's back bowed as pleasure so intense slammed into him.

And then the man was riding his cock, impaling himself while Wolfe and Amy watched. Thankfully, Rhys did all the work.

"Stroke his dick," Wolfe ordered Amy. "Jack him off while he rides me, darlin'."

Her small hand shifted to Rhys's thick cock, stroking in a rhythm that matched Rhys's movements.

"Fuck, yes…" Rhys groaned, his eyes closing.

Unable to help himself, Wolfe gripped Rhys's thighs, punching his hips upward to meet Rhys on the down stroke.

"Close…" Wolfe warned. "So fucking close."

And a few seconds later, he proved that point, coming in a rush as the pleasure stole his breath and more than half his brain cells.

WATCHING RHYS AND WOLFE TOGETHER HAD BECOME one of Amy's absolute favorite things. Seeing the intense pleasure on their faces … it left her feeling a rush of love so deep it was sometimes painful, and always scary. But in a good way. The sort of way that made her breath hitch and her insides quiver. She had never known that something could feel as good as being in love with both of these men.

When Wolfe roared his release, Amy's eyes were fixated on the spot where they were joined. It was probably the reason she didn't realize Rhys had moved, coming over her.

She smiled up at him as his warm weight covered her. Cradling his hips with her thighs, she sighed deeply when he easily pushed inside her, his cock filling her so perfectly.

"Heaven," Rhys whispered, his mouth hovering over hers. "You feel so fuckin' good."

"Ditto," she said on a breathless moan.

"Need you," Rhys mumbled against her lips. "Right now."

She knew exactly what that meant and Amy was completely on board. Although they'd thoroughly taken care of her earlier, it seemed her body was always ready for more. Always.

And over the course of the past few weeks, ever since they'd declared their love, it was as though they couldn't get enough of each other. Both Wolfe and Rhys had become a welcome distraction in her life. Even though fear still flooded her as she waited for that monster to return, it was hard to dwell on it when she was finally living a life she'd never thought she'd have.

"Love you," Rhys whispered again, lifting his head and meeting her gaze.

Amy smiled. "Love you, too," she said softly.

His hips jerked forward, driving him deeper. She sucked in a breath and tightened her hold on him.

"More," she pleaded. She loved the tender sides to these men, but when they lost their control … that was what she longed for. More and more every day.

Rhys gave her exactly what she asked for, slamming into her, retreating. Harder, faster. It was the ultimate high, her nerve endings lighting up until she was trying to catch her breath.

"Rhys!" Her body tensed as her orgasm plowed through her, stealing the air from her lungs.

"So fuckin' beautiful," Wolfe growled from beside them.

Seconds later, Rhys came, his hips stilling, his body settling over her. And though his warm weight pressed her deeper into the mattress, Amy held on tight and refused to let go.

AFTER A QUICK SHOWER, RHYS GOT DRESSED for work. Although Amy and Wolfe had played hooky this morning, Rhys didn't have that luxury. Granted, he also didn't have to be to work until later, so it worked out for them.

As he was holstering his gun, his cell phone rang. He pulled it from the case and glanced at the screen before shooting a quick look to Wolfe, who was standing in the bedroom doorway watching him.

"Trevino," he greeted.

"Hey. It's RT."

"What's up?"

"I just got word that Kelly Jackson has slipped past the agent we have watchin' him."

"And that means what?"

"One minute he was havin' breakfast at a small diner and the next he was gone. His car's gone, too."

"Again," Rhys said, trying to hang on to his patience, "what does that mean?"

"I have a sneakin' suspicion he's on his way there."

"Why's that?"

"I've got another agent watchin' his house and he's not there. He seems to be a creature of habit. Work and home, those are the only two places he goes regularly."

Rhys waited, knowing there had to be a point.

"This mornin', he went into the office earlier than usual, but he didn't stay long. Woman we've got on the inside said he was quiet, cancelled two meetings for the afternoon." RT sighed. "Add to that there was a report this mornin' that revealed the full details of the explosion…"

"Fuck."

"We knew we couldn't keep the truth completely outta the news forever. Some nosy reporter figured out there were no dead bodies."

Shit. And now Rhys was at a loss. It wasn't like he could call his deputies and tell them to keep an eye out for this bastard. Hell, he couldn't even drop the guy's name.

"I'm movin' people as we speak," RT stated. "Z's offerin' to come that way to help out if you need him. Otherwise, we've still got two agents embedded already, one keepin' tabs on Amy's house, the other discreetly movin' through town and keepin' an eye on the businesses. You want me to have Z come that way?"

"Tell him to hold off for now. I'll see what I can do, but have your guys check in with me if they see anything suspicious."

"Will do," RT said, then disconnected.

"What's wrong?" Wolfe asked when Rhys tucked his phone away.

He sighed. "They lost sight of Kelly."

Wolfe's eyebrows slowly lifted as he stood to his full height. "Looks like it's time to get this shit done with."

Rhys shook his head. "Don't you dare go renegade on me, cowboy." The mere thought of having to lock Wolfe up for doing something stupid made his gut twist.

"I'm keepin' her safe. No matter the cost."

Exhaling heavily, Rhys moved toward the door. "Don't do nothin' stupid, Wolfe. I'll let you know what I know. For the time bein', I think you should keep her here."

Wolfe nodded.

At least they were in agreement on that front.

For now.

Chapter Twenty-Seven

EVERY SMALL TOWN IN TEXAS SEEMED TO have a Dairy Queen, and Embers Ridge was no different. It wasn't a classy place by any means, but the food was good and the people were friendly, so Lynx was happy when Reagan agreed that it sounded better than the diner. Not that he was all that picky about where he ate, but this was something different.

Plus, it was fast.

Which, ultimately, had been his reason for suggesting it. The sooner they ate, the faster he could get her ... somewhere.

"Did you even taste that burger before you inhaled it?" Reagan asked, staring at him from across the table.

Lynx grinned, then stole a couple of her French fries. "Yeah."

"How do you eat so fast?"

"I'm efficient."

Getting up from his seat, Lynx shifted over to Reagan's side of the booth, forcing her to move over toward the wall.

"What're you doin'?" she asked, suspicion lacing her words.

Lynx put his arm around her shoulder while she continued to hold her burger in her hands.

Leaning in, he placed his mouth close to her ear. "I'm gonna tell you all the dirty things I have in store for you later." He felt the shudder that ran through her. "Maybe then you'll eat faster."

Reagan chuckled.

"First, I'm gonna strip your clothes off," he told her, nipping her earlobe gently.

"Lynx," she whispered.

"Yep, I'm gonna be makin' you scream my name when I slide my tongue into your warm, wet pussy, then I'm gonna—"

Before he could continue, Reagan's hand landed on his mouth. Her eyes were wide, her cheeks flushed.

"I'm finished," she said quickly.

Lynx glanced down at her half-eaten burger. "No, you're not."

"Oh, trust me. I am."

"What the fuck?"

Lynx's head jerked over, his gaze coming to land on Billy Watson standing beside their table.

Son of a bitch.

Rather than get to his feet and confront the asshole, Lynx remained where he was, his body tensing, muscles gearing up for a fight.

To his surprise, Reagan continued eating as though there was nothing out of the ordinary here. No asshole ex-boyfriend standing there, glaring at them.

"What're you doin' with this dickhead?" Billy asked, his eyes imploring Reagan.

She didn't answer.

"This is bullshit," Billy grumbled. "He's fuckin' married, Reagan."

To give the guy a little credit, at least he hadn't verbally attacked Reagan at this point. That was possibly a first.

"*Actually*," Reagan began, wiping her mouth and reaching for her drink, "the divorce is final."

Yep, as of yesterday, he was a free man. Hence the reason he'd spent the majority of yesterday in bed with Reagan. They had agreed to hold off until the divorce was final, and for the most part, he'd held up his end of the deal except for that one little slipup at the warehouse. But most importantly, Lynx was happy that it was no longer an issue between them.

"Is that right?" Billy smirked, his gaze coming to rest on Lynx. "So that means I can go back to fuckin' Tammy and she don't have to get all freaked out afterwards?"

"Have at it, son," Lynx stated, meeting Billy's stare.

The smirk fell from the guy's face. He'd obviously expected to get a rise out of Lynx. It wouldn't work. Not when it came to his ex. Now, if he went after Reagan, that was an entirely different story.

"Y'all are made for each other, Billy," Reagan said, a hint of anger in her voice. "And good luck with makin' that one last."

It didn't surprise Lynx one bit that Billy had been fucking Tammy. And vice versa. Nor did it bother him in the least.

"Fuckin' bitch," Billy grumbled beneath his breath.

Lynx was on his feet in the span of a single heartbeat, coming toe-to-toe with Billy. He glared down at him. "I'll put up with a lotta shit, but you will *not* talk to Reagan like that. Not now, not ever. Are we clear?"

"So defensive," Billy retorted, a gleam of amusement in his eyes.

"You're damn right I am," he confirmed, keeping his voice low, his tone serious. "So from here on out, you keep your fuckin' mouth shut where she's concerned and we won't have any problems. Otherwise…" Lynx knew he didn't need to finish that sentence.

A small hand on his arm had Lynx glancing to the side. To his surprise, Reagan's hand moved down to his, her fingers linking with his. "Come on. We've got things to do."

Lynx met Billy's gaze once more, then nodded.

"Tammy's better'n bed, anyhow," Billy called from behind him.

Reagan tugged on Lynx's hand, keeping him moving forward. That was the only thing saving Billy from a beatdown right here in the DQ.

"I told you already," Reagan said, "he ain't worth it."

That was the truth. However, Reagan *was* worth it. And that was the point Lynx was trying to make.

"Now, I think I recall you promisin' to do some dirty things to me," Reagan teased, smiling at him over her shoulder as they stepped out into the sunshine.

His dick twitched behind his zipper.

"So, what d'ya say we get to that part?"

In less than a minute, he had her back in the truck. He was about to ask her where they were headed as he pulled out of the parking lot, but she beat him to the punch.

"Let's go back to my house," she blurted.

He glanced over at her. "You sure?"

Reagan nodded, not looking quite as sure as she was pretending to be.

Lynx nodded. "I'm good with that. I'm up for christenin' that place, too."

The blush that stole up her cheeks made his dick even harder.

Not to mention, it had his foot heavier on the gas pedal.

No sense wasting time at this point.

REAGAN WAS PRETTY SURE SHE'D PLAYED THAT one off casually. At least she'd tried to.

Part of her had wanted to yell at Billy, to ask him how it was possible that they'd spent all that time together and he didn't even give a shit that her bar had burned to the ground. Why she'd wondered more about that and not about the fact that Billy had been screwing Lynx's ex-wife, she didn't know. Nor did she care.

However, it did have her curious as to how she could've been so stupid for so long.

Granted, Billy didn't matter to her anymore. She didn't care what he did or who he did it with. Sure, it pissed her off to find out that he'd been fucking Tammy, but it didn't surprise her at all. It was just a wonder that she hadn't known.

Glancing over at Lynx, Reagan frowned. "Did you know Billy and Tammy were fuckin'?"

Okay, so maybe she hadn't meant for that to come out quite so bluntly.

His head snapped toward her. "What?"

She cocked an eyebrow. No way was she repeating that.

Lynx shook his head and turned his attention toward the road.

Reagan waited for a response.

"No," he finally said. "Had no idea."

"Does it bother you?"

"Fuck, Reagan," he grumbled. "Nothin' they do bothers me. I don't give a shit."

She stared out the window.

"Does it bother *you*?" he asked.

"Not that they did it, no," she told him truthfully. "The fact that I stuck around knowin' he was steppin' out is what bothers me."

"Why *did* you stick around?"

Reagan could hear the sincere curiosity in his tone. She laughed without mirth. "Because I'm an idiot?"

Lynx grumbled. "You're not an idiot."

"Then what do *you* call it?" Reagan shook her head. "Never mind. I don't even care."

Lynx pulled the truck to a stop in front of her house. He didn't say a word as he climbed out. Before she could get the passenger door open, he came around to her side, opening it for her.

When Reagan turned to hop down, Lynx put his hands on her hips and stilled her.

"I don't care, either," he said, his eyes locking on hers. "Just so we're completely clear on that." Lynx's finger curled beneath her chin, forcing her head back slightly. "They're the past. And that's where they need to stay."

She offered a slight nod.

"I'm serious, Reagan," he said, his tone firm. "The only thing that matters to me is you. That's it."

"Why?" she asked, hating that she sounded so vulnerable.

"Why what?" Lynx frowned.

"Why do I matter?"

He leaned his head down, his forehead touching hers. "Because you do," he said softly. "You always have."

Reagan had no idea how that could possibly be true. However, she didn't know how to argue that point, either.

"You matter, too," she finally admitted.

His smile was both sexy and sweet. It was the sweet side of Lynx that she hadn't yet gotten to know all that well. Aside from their conversations ten years ago, she hadn't spent much time with him. And the bad boy was the only side he tended to show the world. It was interesting to see that beneath all that tough guy exterior, the man had a heart the size of Texas.

"Now, what d'ya say I take you inside and get to work on those dirty things I intend to do to you?"

Reagan's body instantly heated at the thought. It had been a really long time since she'd felt this sort of desire. Hell, maybe she'd never felt it. Not for anyone other than Lynx, that was.

"I like that idea," she admitted.

He didn't even give her a chance to get out of the truck before he had her tossed over his shoulder, his big arm wrapped firmly over the backs of her legs, holding her against him. To keep from feeling as though she would plunge headfirst into the dirt, she grabbed on to his belt loops.

"Lynx Caine! I'm gonna hurt you if you don't put me down!"

"I'm lookin' forward to it, girl. Do your worst."

Oh, she would.

But pain wouldn't be involved.

Not the bad kind anyway.

Chapter Twenty-Eight

ONCE INSIDE, LYNX PAUSED AT THE COUCH momentarily, eyeing it from several different directions.

Nope.

Wouldn't work.

Too damn short.

He glanced at the kitchen, then continued into the bedroom and tossed Reagan unceremoniously onto the bed.

When her back hit the mattress, he saw she was smiling up at him, her long hair spilled out around her. The woman stole his breath. She was as beautiful now as she had been at sixteen back when he'd first noticed her, back when he'd first fallen in love with her.

But this Reagan was definitely not sixteen. She was older, wiser, and undoubtedly sexier.

And when she crooked her finger at him, signaling him to her, he couldn't kick his boots off fast enough. Before he joined her, he did the same to hers, yanking them from her feet before crawling over her.

The instant his mouth met hers, Lynx was lost. Settling in beside her so that he didn't rest his weight on her, Lynx curled one arm around her head and kissed her. Slowly, leisurely. It hadn't been his original intention, but holy hell, the woman made his blood boil with a simple kiss.

Then again, there was nothing simple about kissing Reagan. He'd wanted this for so damn long. Part of him hadn't expected it to live up to his memories from so long ago, but shit. It was so much better. And every single kiss was hotter, more intense.

Yeah, he didn't mind making out like teenagers like this. Hell, he could do it all damn day.

Her soft fingers slipped beneath his T-shirt, moving over his skin, causing his breaths to come more rapidly, his body to heat.

Lynx couldn't resist copping a feel himself. He slid one hand beneath her tank top, his fingertips grazing the smooth, baby-soft skin of her abdomen. The way Reagan sucked in a breath was a bonus. He wrapped his hand around her waist, his thumb grazing her stomach, fingers gently pressing into her back. He jerked her closer, wanting to touch every part of her with every part of him.

"Is that your phone? Or are you that excited to see me?" Reagan muttered.

It took Lynx a second to realize what she said.

He laughed, lifting his head as his phone buzzed in his pocket.

"I'm not complainin'," she said with a giggle. "That might be fun." He nodded toward the side of the bed. "In fact, I've got a drawer full of toys we can ... experiment with."

Toys?

Lord have mercy.

His phone buzzed again.

"Ignore it," he whispered, pressing his lips to hers once more.

Unfortunately, ignoring his phone became impossible when the damn thing wouldn't stop.

Extricating himself from Reagan's arms was a difficult feat, but he managed.

"This better fuckin' be good," he grumbled into the phone.

"We got a problem," Wolfe said, his tone rough.

"Talk to me," Lynx instructed.

"Sounds like RT's boys lost track of the police chief. They think he's headed this way."

"Fuck."

"The bigger issue is Rhys can't say anything to the deputies. Travis is on his way to meet Rhys. You wanna head on over to the shop?"

Not really, no. But he didn't tell his cousin that. Instead, he said, "Of course."

"Thanks. See ya in a few."

With a resigned sigh, Lynx turned back to Reagan. She was sitting up, watching him.

"Wolfe said there's trouble. Need to head over to the shop." He cocked an eyebrow. "You wanna go with me?"

She nodded almost shyly.

For whatever reason, that hit Lynx in a way that had his breath halting in his lungs. This woman...

Reaching for her, he pulled Reagan closer, his lips finding hers. He kept the kiss gentle although it would be so damn easy to strip those little shorts off her and bury himself inside her sweet, warm depths.

Damn, this woman did crazy things to him. He'd never felt anything like this, and Lord knew he'd tried his damnedest to get her out of his head all these years.

It had been impossible and he even knew why.

He loved this girl. Deeply. In that forever sort of way.

And now, if they could get past this crazy shit taking place in their small town, Lynx might just be able to start focusing on the future with her.

That was his plan anyway.

REAGAN COULDN'T DENY THE DISAPPOINTMENT OF HAVING to leave her house when she'd had Lynx right where she wanted him, but she understood it.

Even now, as she sat in one of the wooden chairs at the Cedar Door shop, she got it.

"What I don't get is how they could lose one guy," Lynx groused. "How fuckin' hard is it to keep him in their sights?"

Rhys shrugged. "Shit happens, I guess."

That seemed to appease Lynx, although Reagan could tell he was irritated by all of it. And that she understood, too.

Her gaze shot over to Amy. The woman was tense, clearly worried. Reagan couldn't blame her in the least. This man had wreaked havoc on all their lives, but no one had endured anything compared to the hell Amy had lived. Reagan wanted to take the asshole out herself just to keep her friend safe.

"So, what's the plan?" Wolfe asked, his voice rough. "We can't stay holed up in this place forever."

Before Rhys could respond, the shop door opened and in walked...

Travis Walker.

Well, not only Travis this time. Yes, his husband was right behind him but so were... Damn. The line of men who waltzed in behind him seemed to be endless. Not to mention worthy of being on a calendar or something.

"Well, hot damn!" Lynx bellowed, moving toward the group. "If it ain't trouble times seven."

Travis grinned.

"I'll be right back," Rhys said, reaching for his phone and putting it to his ear as he headed toward the door.

As her brother left, the newcomers shook hands with Lynx and did the bro-hugging thing. Loud slaps on the back and a few rounds of laughter echoed in the cavernous space.

"Come on over here," Lynx stated.

When his eyes landed on hers, Reagan forced a smile and stood from her chair.

"Y'all, this is my girl, Reagan Trevino. She's Rhys's sister." Lynx put his arm around her. "Reagan, you remember Travis and his husband, Gage. These are Travis's brothers. Ethan, Sawyer, Kaleb, Zane, and the twins, Braydon and Brendon."

"Lynx was spoutin' somethin' about havin' a girl back at the Labor Day bonfire," the one Lynx pointed out as Brendon stated. "However, none of us ever saw you, so we thought you didn't really exist."

Chuckling, Reagan shook hands all around, recognizing a couple of faces from the bonfire although she hadn't been introduced at the time. "Nice to meet you."

"Likewise, darlin'," the youngest-looking one said.

With his arm still around her, Lynx led Reagan over to where Amy was now standing with Wolfe.

The brothers greeted Wolfe, then shook hands with Amy after another round of introductions. No way would Reagan remember all those names, even if they repeated them a dozen times.

"This is my husband, Beau," Ethan stated.

The big blond guy moved to the front and shook Reagan's hand, then Amy's.

Unable to help herself, Reagan studied the men briefly. She had to admit, the good looks ran in Lynx's family. Still, there was something about Lynx that stood out from the rest. And it was more than just the tattoos.

"So, to what do we owe the honor?" Wolfe questioned, his attention on Travis.

"Thought it was time we put a plan together," Travis stated.

"Yep," Zane added, "and we're the cavalry."

Lynx chuckled. "Hell, boy, I heard you can't even wrangle your kiddo."

Zane grinned from ear to ear, pride etched over his features. "Maybe not, but that don't stop me from tryin'."

The shop door opened and Reagan's head snapped over to see her brother joining them once again. He looked pissed and more than a little tired. She knew this had to be wearing on him. The fact that he was in love with Amy, wanted to keep her safe although his hands were tied, had to be tearing him apart.

Rhys nodded his head at her in acknowledgment and Reagan smiled in return.

"Sheriff," Wolfe greeted, grinning. "You remember my cousins."

"I do."

Once more, handshakes took place, and Reagan attempted to put names with faces as Wolfe pointed everyone out one more time.

"My cousin Jared's on his way," Travis noted. "He's over at DHR with his wife. Said he wanted to be part of this, too. Offerin' up whatever help he can."

Jesus Christ. How freaking big was this family?

Reagan thought *she* had a big family, but hers didn't hold a candle to this.

Not even close.

However, it did make Reagan want to go visit her mother and grandfather. Even if they tended to fight all the time, she still missed them. And now that she wasn't with Billy anymore, she had to wonder whether her relationship with them could be repaired. One day. She figured her mother would eventually have to realize that Billy hadn't been good for her. Despite her mother's belief that a man and woman should stick together no matter what, there was no denying that she and Billy had been doomed from the start. Then again, Reagan couldn't deny one of the main reasons she'd stayed with Billy was to defy her grandfather. The man didn't like anyone.

Not that it was a *good* reason, but it was a reason nonetheless.

Or it was just another excuse she'd come up with over the years to defend her actions.

Whatever.

The last thing Reagan ever claimed was to be perfect. But as she glanced at Lynx, she had to thank God for second chances.

KELLY DIDN'T KNOW WHO THESE ASSHOLES WERE that seemed to be watching his every move, but it hadn't been easy giving them the slip. Part of him wanted to do some digging, but he figured that was a moot point. They had to be tied to Amy somehow. And if those rednecks thought they had the upper hand, they had another think coming.

He wasn't a fucking amateur and they were sorely underestimating him if they thought he was.

Plus, he was smart enough to know he was running out of time. At some point, everyone got lucky and it was high time Kelly made sure Amy was dealt with. One more visit to that stupid backwoods town would do the trick.

This time, he would make sure she was disposed of once and for all.

And he wouldn't leave until he had hard evidence to back it up.

Chapter Twenty-Nine

FOR THE FIRST TIME IN QUITE SOME time, things were starting to make sense.

At least where this whole fucked-up situation was concerned anyway.

Lynx liked that his cousins had arrived with the intention of doing something to stop this asshole. Having to sit back and wait wasn't his strong suit and now it seemed that was in the past.

In fact, rather than remain on the defensive, waiting, it appeared everyone was on board with going on the offense. That was more Lynx's pace, that was for damn sure.

"I guarantee he's on his way here," Travis repeated for probably the tenth time. "I don't care what anyone says, he's headin' back here."

"Why do you think that?" Rhys asked, leaning against the steel beam.

"Because he's not givin' y'all enough credit. Think about who he is, what he's done," Travis stated. "The guy's arrogant and likely believes himself to be untouchable."

"It's true," Amy chimed in. "He believes he's above everyone else. And Travis is right. He'll think he can get to me no matter who's around."

"He's smart, too," Sawyer added. "Damn smart. He's gotten away with a lot of shit. Not to mention, no dumb ass is gonna make it to the top the way he has."

"I still think he's a dumb ass," Wolfe muttered, making several people smile.

"Well, he is and he isn't," Travis said, his tone still somber. "But he knows what he's doin'. Riggin' that bar to blow took brains and patience."

"Not to mention balls," Lynx grumbled. His gut still churned when he thought about that shit.

"Not gonna argue with you there," Sawyer agreed. "And because of that, I think we'll need to be more vigilant. It's evident this guy thinks he's above authority. If I had to guess, he believes he *is* the authority."

"And that's exactly it," Amy said. "He is the authority, according to him. But more importantly, he believes he's smarter than everyone."

Lynx would agree with that assessment as well, based on what he'd heard and seen. And thus far, Kelly Jackson had been. After all, he had managed to blow up the bar without anyone seeing what he was doing.

However, he hadn't been up against the people who were in this room right now. If this asshole wanted to get close to Amy, he was going to have to go through every damn one of them.

"Good thing 'bout a small town," Ethan said, "he's gonna stand out. He can't hide in plain sight. If people don't recognize him, they'll start talkin'."

True again.

"However," Travis interjected, his gaze darting to Rhys, "we do need to get the town on board."

Before Rhys could argue, Travis held up a hand.

"And I get it, I do. You don't wanna point fingers. And we won't. However, we can tell everyone to be on the lookout."

"On the lookout for what?" Rhys asked, obviously not liking where this was headed.

Travis held Rhys's stare. "It doesn't matter. Just that they need to pay attention. A stranger in town right now needs to be suspicious. I don't care if they claim they're just stoppin' for gas. Someone needs to chat 'em up. Verify their story."

Rhys nodded. "I don't want anyone makin' accusations. Not at this point."

"Agreed," Wolfe added. "So, no names. Just get the word out for people to pay attention."

"I'll take care of that," Reagan offered.

Lynx glanced her way. "I'm with her."

"Good," Travis said, agreeably. "The sooner the better."

Reagan nodded, then reached for Lynx's hand.

"Looks like that's my cue," Lynx said with a grin before allowing Reagan to lead him out of the building.

"Where to?"

"I was thinkin' the diner."

Lynx nodded. "You drive, I'll start callin' around."

Her smile was so damn sweet Lynx was tempted to kiss her. Since they seemed to be in a time crunch and he was not looking forward to stopping once he started, he refrained. Barely.

Less than five minutes later, Lynx was still on the phone, following Reagan inside the diner.

"That's right," he told Ed. "Round 'em up and head on over."

"Will do," Ed confirmed. "Give me ten minutes."

"Sure thing." Lynx cut the connection and dropped into his chair after pulling Reagan's out for her. He started dialing almost instantly.

"What can I get you kids?" Donna asked, stopping at their table.

"Some information," Reagan replied while Lynx waited for Jimmy Don to answer his phone.

Donna's eyebrows shot up and a smile curled her mouth. "Well, you've come to the right place."

"Have you seen any strange people around here lately?" Reagan asked.

Donna's eyes instantly slid over to Lynx.

He laughed, grinning up at her. The woman was something else.

"Besides him," Donna said, jerking her thumb in his direction, "can't say that I have. Not lately."

"Well, we need to get the word out," Reagan explained. "Amy's got some trouble and we suspect the man is gonna reappear at any moment."

Donna frowned. "What kinda trouble?"

Reagan shrugged. "Don't know all the details," she lied easily. "But we know he's probably gonna come lookin' for her."

"This guy have anything to do with your bar bein' blown up?"

Reagan shrugged. "Not sure yet. But it's possible."

"I knew that kid was in trouble," Donna mumbled. "And I'm with you, honey. Whatever you need."

"Good. Do you mind if we hold a town meeting in here?"

"Right now?" Donna looked a little leery.

"If at all possible," Reagan replied.

"All right. But don't expect great service. It's just me here tonight."

"No worries." Reagan smiled. "In the meantime, keep an eye out for anyone suspicious. And make sure you tell everyone you see to do the same."

Lynx disconnected the call with Jimmy Don. "But keep in mind, my cousins are in town," he noted. "They're suspicious, but you can overlook them."

Reagan and Donna both grinned.

"Anyone related to you is suspicious," Donna said. "But I'm sure I'll recognize those boys."

"This guy's older," Reagan informed her. "He'll stand out."

Donna nodded, her eyes darting over to the door when the bells overhead rang.

Yep. The town was already starting to trickle into the diner. Exactly what they wanted right now.

Hopefully, by the time the sun went down, they'd have a few dozen eyes looking out for this asshole. And by tomorrow morning, this shit would all be behind them.

If they were lucky.

"LET'S DO RIGHT BY THIS GIRL," REAGAN continued, speaking directly to all the people with eyes currently trained on her. "She's had a rough time and she's part of this community now." She paused momentarily. "She's family."

Several people mumbled their affirmation of that statement. And it was true. In a small town, it took time for people to be brought into the fold. But it was possible. Reagan knew that these people already considered Amy one of theirs. She was with Wolfe and Rhys, and that alone offered her protection from these people.

"So, keep your eyes open. If you don't recognize the person, find out why they're here. This guy's smart, but he's not gonna keep his cool if people are askin' questions."

"At the same time," Rhys interjected, "don't push too far."

Reagan knew her brother wouldn't be able to sit this one out. As much as he wanted to pretend that he was on the side of justice — innocent until proven guilty — he couldn't deny that what had happened to Amy was a tragedy and this asshole needed to be brought to his knees. And as far as Reagan was concerned, by any means necessary.

"So, what's goin' on with the bar?" someone asked from the back.

Lynx stepped forward. "If you're interested in helpin', come see me. We've got plans drawn up and permits are underway. We're gonna start buildin' soon. And Reagan's will be back in business as soon as we can make that happen."

Reagan felt the blush creep up her neck. She loved this town. Always had. And the people … they were her family, too.

"But before we focus on that," Lynx added, "I want you to confirm that you'll keep your eyes open. If you have any questions on that, come see me, too."

Reagan had to admit that she admired the way these people looked at Lynx. They saw him as family, respected him, even if they were willing to push his buttons from time to time. When all was said and done, they trusted him.

And they had good reason to, she realized. Lynx Caine had never gone back on his word, he'd never broken a promise, and more than once, he had come through for each of them.

The same way he was coming through for her.

The door to the diner opened and Reagan's head automatically turned to see who was joining them. Her stomach twisted when she recognized Billy and Tammy. Together.

Her eyes flew over to Lynx, but he wasn't even looking their way.

"Hey, Donna! Can we get some service over here?" Billy hollered, drawing the attention of everyone in the place.

"Actually, no," Donna called out. "I'm a little busy right now."

Reagan's gaze shot over to Donna to see the older woman glaring at Billy and his ... date.

It was then that Reagan realized the place had gone silent. All the noise had dimmed, the conversations dying off.

"Are you sayin' you're refusin' me service?" Billy countered, his eyes shooting from one person to another.

"That's what I'm sayin'," Donna shouted back.

The door opened and someone walked inside. An older man who looked oddly familiar, but she couldn't place him. The man paused momentarily, his eyes drifting from the group over to Billy and Tammy, who were the only people seated on the far side of the restaurant.

Reagan glanced at Tammy, noticed Lynx's ex-wife looked completely shocked by what was going on around her. For a brief moment, Reagan actually felt sorry for the woman. Then she thought about how Tammy had been fucking Billy while they'd both been in relationships with other people. Her sympathy died quickly.

"That's bullshit!" Billy shouted, getting to his feet.

Fully expecting Lynx or Wolfe to address the situation, Reagan nearly fell over when the older man turned toward Billy.

"I'm a payin' customer," Billy announced. "And you need to do your fuckin' job and—"

The newcomer interrupted, a frown on his face as he took a step closer to Billy. "You and me need to have a word outside, son," he said, his tone hard, his body ramrod straight.

"Who the fuck're you?"

"Name's Curtis Walker," the man stated firmly.

Curtis Walker?

Reagan glanced over at Travis and his brothers. Then she realized why the man looked so familiar. He was a much older version of Travis. Which meant he was … his father?

"I ain't goin' nowhere with you," Billy snapped. "Now if you'll mind your own fuckin' business—"

In a move that Reagan would've expected from a much younger man, Curtis grabbed hold of Billy's shirt and tugged him toward the door. The older man's eyes cut across the room briefly, and then Travis and Sawyer were heading his way.

Lynx and Wolfe followed.

Reagan was about to go with them, but Rhys pulled her up short.

"Let it be," her brother said softly.

"But—"

"I'll go out there, but I get the feelin' this'll be handled civilly."

"How do you figure?" Reagan knew Lynx and Wolfe. They didn't take kindly to outbursts like that. Not when there were women around. And although Tammy wasn't high on Lynx's list, Reagan knew he would intervene if he had to.

Rhys didn't bother to respond before he marched out the door, following close behind the others. Reagan instantly turned to find Amy standing in the corner by herself, her arms wrapped around her middle. She looked so small, so fragile.

Okay, so clearly she had more important things to deal with. Her friend was obviously having a difficult time.

"Hey. You okay?" Reagan asked as she approached Amy, trying to keep her voice down.

Amy's eyes lifted to hers and Reagan recognized the fear there. It had been prominent on Amy's face for so long.

"No," Amy admitted. "I'm really not."

Placing her hands on her friend's shoulders, Reagan waited until Amy looked at her. "It's gonna be all right."

Amy shook her head. "It's not."

"Don't say that," Reagan admonished. "They're gonna catch him and he's gonna be locked away for a long, long time."

Reagan could tell Amy was pretending to believe her. She hated seeing that look, wished she could do something to help, to make Amy's pain go away.

"I… I just need a minute," Amy said, her voice strained. "I'm gonna go to the bathroom."

Reagan dropped her hands and nodded. "I'm here if you wanna talk," she told her.

Amy's smile was clearly forced when she said, "I know. I know you are."

And then Reagan watched as Amy walked away, slipping down the narrow hall to the bathroom.

She couldn't wait for the day that Amy didn't have to look over her shoulder. For the day the woman could finally settle into her new life and be happy.

Reagan had a feeling that day would be coming very soon.

As MUCH AS AMY WANTED TO PRETEND she was fine, she couldn't. That was proven by the way her hands were shaking as she ran cold water over her wrists, attempting to calm the anxiety that filled her like an overinflated balloon.

She peered up in the mirror and winced.

The woman who stared back at her looked more like the fragile, damaged woman she used to be than the woman she'd become. And the truth was, she didn't like it all that much. Every one of these people filling this restaurant where she used to work were looking at her as though she were a delicate flower, ready to blow away in a stiff wind.

She wasn't delicate.

Not anymore.

In the time she'd been here in Embers Ridge, Amy had changed.

As she continued to watch herself in the mirror, she shut off the water and dried her hands, straightening her back. No, she wasn't that girl anymore.

Yes, she was still terrified that Kelly was going to grab her, that he was going to finally finish what he'd started and she would never get to see Wolfe or Rhys again. The man obviously wanted her dead. However, she didn't want to hide behind Wolfe or Rhys or anyone else in this town. Sure, she appreciated the effort they were going to in order to help, but Amy knew it was futile. Kelly never failed.

But if one more person weighed her down with a sympathetic look, she was going to scream. And maybe that was selfish, but she couldn't bring herself to care right now. She wasn't a fragile doll they could wrap in cotton and set high up on the shelf until the danger was gone. She needed to be a part of this, to feel as though she wasn't the one putting everyone else in danger.

"But you are," she told her reflection.

Her face crumpled and the cycle started all over again.

Chapter Thirty

LYNX WATCHED FROM THE SIDELINES AS CURTIS Walker gave Billy a good talking-to.

It was pretty impressive to watch, if he was being honest. The man didn't raise his voice, he didn't talk down to Billy, he merely told him how it was going to be. Apparently, Curtis had a major issue with a man letting his mouth get away from him when there were women present. He was relaying that in lengthy detail to Billy.

"Lynx."

Turning at the sound of his name, Lynx saw Tammy moving toward him. "Can we talk?"

He instantly peered in through the diner window, seeking Reagan. He wasn't even sure why he did it, but he had to know where she was, that she was all right. Not that he thought Tammy would do anything. The woman might've been a shitty wife, but she wasn't a bad person at heart. How she'd gotten mixed up with Billy, he didn't know. Nor did he want to know.

"What?" he asked, keeping his attention divided between Tammy, Curtis, and Reagan.

"I'm..." She sighed. "I'm really sorry for this. I didn't know you'd be here."

He shrugged one shoulder. "Why would that matter?"

"I don't know," she said, her eyes locked with his. "I just thought maybe it..." She shook her head. "I thought maybe it'd bother you to see me with Billy."

"It doesn't," he said honestly. "But why would that even matter to you?" He was sincerely confused. He lowered his voice. "You were screwin' him when we were married, Tammy. You didn't seem worried about it then."

She blushed, her eyes not meeting his. For whatever reason, having Tammy's confirmation didn't help matters. Although he hadn't loved her, it still pissed him off that she would treat him that way. He'd done his best to do right by her from the beginning.

Tammy took a step closer, lifting her head so that she met his eyes. "I really am sorry."

"Don't sweat it," he said, trying to keep his tone neutral.

When he looked up, he saw Reagan watching him through the window. Something that looked a lot like pain flashed in her eyes, and he instantly regretted standing there talking to Tammy. Not that he was doing a damn thing that she should be worried about, but he had to put himself in her shoes. If he saw her talking to Billy, he'd probably be in a jealous rage right about now.

Sure, it would've been an irrational reaction, but Lynx couldn't deny he didn't want her anywhere around that asshole.

"Look," Lynx said, peering down at Tammy once more. "I gotta go."

Tammy nodded.

"And if it's worth anything, you might consider keepin' your distance from Billy. He's not gonna do right by you. No matter what he tells you."

"And you did?" she snapped, her eyebrows darting down.

Lynx's gaze shot to hers. "Yeah. I did. Or I tried anyway."

"If it really mattered, you would've tried harder."

Feeling as though he'd just walked into some sort of twilight zone, Lynx took a step back. He stared down at the woman he'd once been married to and shook his head. Clearly she didn't remember things the way he did.

"On the other hand," he said, hating that he was stooping to her level, "maybe you and Billy will work out."

With that, he spun on his boot heel and headed inside. He knew the Walkers had this situation with Billy under control and he really needed to see Reagan.

Once inside, Lynx glanced around at all the familiar faces, searching for Reagan. He found her sitting in a booth across from Amy.

"Everything okay?"

Reagan peered up at him, her expression cool. "Yeah."

He noticed that Amy didn't look up.

Rather than ask Reagan if she was ready to go, Lynx slid into the booth beside her. He knew she was upset with him, although he didn't know exactly why other than she'd seen him talking to Tammy.

Knowing better than to toss his arm around her and pretend nothing had happened, Lynx rested his elbows on the table and glanced between the two women.

"I'm really okay," Amy finally said, obviously noticing they were both staring at her. "I just hate that this is happening."

"We know," Reagan said reassuringly. "But it'll get better. Soon."

"I agree with Reagan," Lynx added. "Trust Wolfe and Rhys. They won't let anything happen to you."

This time Amy nodded and it appeared she believed that much.

"I just want him to go away. I'm so tired of having to worry about him, thinking he'll pop up any second and steal this life from me."

Lynx didn't bother to tell her that was a real possibility if the man pulled a stunt like he'd pulled at the bar. On the flip side, the guy might be smart, but he wasn't invincible. He would be caught. Eventually.

However, Lynx truly believed that they needed to take care of it sooner rather than later. Before someone else got hurt or, God forbid, killed.

The bells over the doors jangled and Amy's gaze swung over instantly. Lynx twisted to see who was coming inside. He wasn't surprised to see that Billy wasn't with the group. Apparently, Curtis had talked a little sense into the man. How long that would last was anyone's guess.

"I'm gonna go talk to them for a sec," Lynx told Reagan. "Then you ready to head out?"

She nodded but didn't make eye contact.

Forcing himself to his feet, Lynx wandered over to where the others had gathered. He shook Curtis's hand, then said his good-byes to the others, letting them know he'd meet up with them tomorrow.

A strong hand on his shoulder had him turning, coming face-to-face with Wolfe.

"Hey, bro. You good?"

Wolfe shrugged. "Will be. When this is all over."

"Soon," Lynx assured him. "In the meantime, let me know if you guys need anything."

"Yeah. And … thanks. For backin' us up."

"That's what family's for," he said with a smirk.

He got a genuine smile from his cousin in return.

After finishing up with Wolfe, Lynx turned to find Reagan, realizing the table they'd been sitting at was empty.

"You see where Reagan went?" he asked Wolfe.

His cousin glanced around, then shook his head. "No. You see Amy?"

A sense of foreboding took hold of Lynx, his insides going cold as he frantically searched for both women, not seeing either of them anywhere.

"I'm gonna go look outside," Lynx told Wolfe, trying to keep the panic down.

"I'll have Donna check the restroom."

Lynx nodded, then headed toward the front doors.

His heart nearly came out of his throat when he saw Reagan talking to Darrell in the parking lot. Taking a deep breath, he pushed open the door and stepped out into the warm evening air.

Without pausing, he walked right over to Reagan, this time putting his arm around her shoulder. He didn't give a shit if it made him appear possessive. He had to touch her in that moment, his fear subsiding somewhat.

"Thanks," Reagan told Darrell, smiling. "I really appreciate all that you're doin'."

"Thank this guy," Darrell said, nodding to Lynx. "He's definitely lookin' out for you."

Reagan peered up at him and this time she didn't appear angry. A little more tension left his shoulders.

That somewhat easy feeling didn't last long when Wolfe came barreling out of the diner.

"You see Amy?" he yelled.

Lynx looked at Reagan, hoping she had an answer for them.

"She was at the table when I left her," Reagan told Wolfe. "She's not inside?"

"No," Wolfe growled.

A second later, Rhys came storming out the door. "She's not out back."

"Where the fuck is she?" Wolfe hollered, clearly not talking to anyone specific.

And for the first time in his life, Lynx saw true terror on his cousin's face.

REAGAN STEERED THE TRUCK INTO THE PARKING lot of the Cedar Door store.

"Stay here," he ordered. "Lemme grab Cope and then we'll keep lookin'."

Before she could get it in park, Lynx was hopping out of the truck, running toward the side entrance.

As though it would help, Reagan scanned the area, looking for Amy. After another trek through the diner, searching high and low, they hadn't been able to locate her. It was as though she'd vanished and everyone was in a panic.

Reagan wasn't sure she'd ever seen grown men look as terrified as her brother and Wolfe had. Not even the Walkers had tried to console them. Instead, everyone had gone their separate ways, hopping in trucks so they could start scouring the area. No one had bothered to say what everyone was thinking though. If that madman got his hands on Amy…

The door to the truck opened, and Reagan's head snapped over, her heart slamming against her ribs until she realized it was only Lynx and Copenhagen.

"Where to?" she asked, hoping he didn't hear the quiver in her voice. She put the truck in drive and steered out of the lot.

"What did she say when you talked to her?" Lynx asked, his focus obviously still on locating Amy. It was the same question Rhys and Wolfe had asked her at least a dozen times after they realized Amy was gone.

"Nothin'. Seriously. She just said she was worried, hated that this was happenin'."

"Do you think she would've left?" Lynx was watching her. "Maybe she thought disappearin' would help matters."

Reagan shook her head, although she wasn't exactly positive about that. The way Amy had been talking did have her thinking just that. But she couldn't see Amy doing it. Reagan didn't know the woman all that well, but she knew her enough. Enough to know that she loved Wolfe and Rhys, that she wouldn't want to hurt them like that.

"Maybe she went back to your house," Lynx said.

It was a stretch, but they really had nothing to go on, so rather than question his logic, Reagan pulled out onto the main road and put her foot to the floor. She was surprised that Lynx had wanted her to drive. But when he had grabbed his phone, it made sense. He started calling people, asking for their help.

It took a tense twenty minutes to get to her house. They were walking up to the front porch when Lynx's phone rang.

"Yeah?" he barked into the phone.

Reagan turned to look at him and the relief that settled over his features made her realize she'd been holding her breath.

"They found her," Lynx told her, his words coming out in a rush. He turned his attention back to the phone call.

When he looked over again, she asked, "Where?"

"She walked around to the side of the building."

Reagan frowned. The side of the building? And she didn't hear people calling her name? Really?

"Yeah, Wolfe. Thanks. Lemme know if you need anything." He disconnected the call.

Fully expecting him to finish the conversation, to explain what Wolfe had told him, Reagan was surprised when Lynx reached for her, jerking her into his arms. She went willingly, the stress from a few minutes ago leaving her feeling slightly dizzy as she processed everything that was going on.

When Lynx moved over to one of the rocking chairs, pulling her into his lap, Reagan went willingly, snuggling against him, resting her head on his shoulder.

They were both silent for a few minutes, the only sound the rapid thump of her heart as it tried to slow.

"When I couldn't find you earlier," Lynx finally said, his voice barely above a whisper, "I thought I would lose my mind."

Reagan lifted her head and stared at him. "I didn't go anywhere."

"You were outside," he stated. "Talkin' to Darrell. I thought you were inside with Amy. When I couldn't find you…"

It was clear he'd been worried. The hard lines on his face told her he was still reliving that moment. She slid her hand up to his cheek, trying to smooth them away.

Lynx gripped her wrist, pulling her hand to his mouth. He kissed her palm, then pulled her against him, their mouths melding together.

Reagan sighed, the events of the evening dissipating and leaving nothing but the two of them. Here. Alone.

She wasn't thinking about the madman on the loose, not about seeing Billy and Tammy together, or even about watching Lynx talk to his ex-wife. None of it seemed to matter right then.

It all faded away, leaving her with a contentment she hadn't known before.

This.

Being in Lynx's arms.

It was the only thing she wanted.

Now and forever.

Chapter Thirty-One

"YOU SCARED ME OUTTA MY FUCKIN' MIND," Wolfe growled, thrusting his hand through his hair.

Amy watched him closely, hating that she'd put that fear in his eyes. It was true, she had slipped outside, wandered over to the side of the building, and sat on the stone wall that surrounded the air conditioning unit. It was a secluded spot where Donna would sneak out to smoke from time to time. Amy knew no one would see her from the parking lot, so she'd felt safe there, hidden. But she had only gone out there because she had needed a few minutes to herself. With so many people asking her if she was okay, she had felt like her brain was going to explode. It didn't help that everyone seemed to be focused on her, the worry making her feel like an outcast.

"I'm sorry," she whispered. And she was. Truthfully, she hadn't gone far and she definitely hadn't intended to send everyone into a panic. "I didn't realize y'all were lookin' for me. And I couldn't hear you because the air conditioner was so loud."

"I know," Wolfe said softly.

"I really am sorry."

"Don't apologize," Wolfe rumbled. "I'm not blamin' you." He took a step closer, then another until he was close enough to touch her. "I'm just tellin' you how I felt when I couldn't find you."

Amy watched as his eyes locked with hers.

"I can't lose you, Amy," he whispered roughly. "You and Rhys… Y'all are my everything. I want you to understand that."

She did. How could she not? The man's emotions were written on his face. Every time he touched her, kissed her ... Amy could *feel* it.

"I never meant for this to happen," she told him, holding his stare. "Never wanted it."

Wolfe pulled her into his arms. "I know that, darlin'. God, I know. And if I could make it all go away, I would."

Wrapping her arms around him, Amy held on. She felt safe with Wolfe and Rhys. But at the same time, it terrified her that she might lose them. With Kelly out there... She knew what he was capable of. She had lived it. And he had told her that she would not live without him. She knew what that meant.

And any second now, she expected him to make good on that promise.

The worst part ... Amy was terrified something would happen to Wolfe or Rhys. At that point, her life *would* be over.

And she feared Kelly knew that.

Which meant the nightmare would continue until they found him.

Until they stopped him.

LYNX HAD SO MUCH ON HIS MIND, so many things he wanted to say to Reagan, but he couldn't make his voice work. Instead, he had settled on showing her.

Which was the very reason he had carried her inside, never wanting to let go. Even now as he stripped them both, his mouth sliding over her smooth, warm skin, he couldn't seem to break away from her.

"Lynx," she moaned softly when he sucked one nipple into his mouth, pulling her closer as he laid her back on the bed.

"I fuckin' love when you say my name." He would never tire of it, not if he lived to be two hundred.

When he tried to kiss down her body, Reagan's fingers tugged roughly on his hair, pulling a rough groan from his chest, the sensation making his dick throb.

"Inside me," she insisted roughly. "Right. Now."

He grinned, unable to refuse her anything.

Sitting back on his knees, Lynx rolled the condom over his length, watching the sexy woman laid out before him. Her eyes were traveling over his body, leaving heat in their wake.

"Turn over," he commanded, meeting her gaze.

The sexy grin she shot him had electrical sparks igniting beneath his skin.

Reagan Trevino on all fours before him was a sight to behold, there was no doubt about that.

However, he had something else in mind.

Wrapping one arm around her waist and one hand around his dick, he pulled her back so that she was kneeling before him, her back pressed to his chest. He brushed the sensitive head of his cock against her entrance.

"Lynx," she hissed, her hips pushing back against him. "Don't tease me."

He chuckled softly. "Trust me, girl, I ain't teasin'."

Lynx pulled her hips back, the head of his dick pushing inside her as he kept her body as close to his as he could manage. He groaned as the hot sheath of her pussy engulfed him.

Before he could work himself into her slowly, Reagan eased down on him, his cock sliding in deeper.

"Fuck," he groaned, wrapping both arms around her and holding her to him. "You feel so fuckin' good. So goddamn good." He rocked her forward, then pulled her down on him until he was lodged balls deep in her sweet pussy. "Now fuck me, Reagan," he ordered.

She began rocking back against him, the friction of her pussy making his head spin. He ran his lips over her neck, sucking and nipping while she took what she needed. He wasn't in a rush, so he kept her wrapped tightly in his arms, allowing very little movement. It was enough though. It was fucking perfect.

That didn't last long as Reagan writhed, trying to take more of him, seemingly as desperate as he was. When Reagan began rocking faster, Lynx thrust harder, deeper. While their bodies slapped together, Lynx held on, sliding one hand down the smooth, taut skin of her belly, seeking her clit with his thumb.

"Oh, God ... Lynx."

"I'm gonna make you come," he insisted. "Then I'm gonna fuck you some more."

Reagan moaned, long and loud.

"That what you want? Me to fuck you all night? Buried in your sweet pussy?"

"God, yes," she whispered roughly.

Lynx pressed his thumb against her clit, circling the swollen bundle of nerves while Reagan writhed against him.

"Oh, shit…" she cried out. "Lynx … I'm gonna…"

"Come for me, girl."

Her body tensed and Lynx pumped his hips, fucking her with shallow strokes while she rode out her first climax. When she relaxed slightly, he released the tight grip he had on her body and followed her down so that he was kneeling behind her, his cock still buried to the hilt inside her wet heat.

Gripping her hips, he began fucking her deeper, pulling out slowly, then pushing in again. Over and over, he kept a slow, leisurely pace, the friction of her body against his cock the greatest feeling on earth.

"More," she begged. "Harder."

Lynx retreated, then drove in deeper, harder, leaning over her so that his chest was once again pressed against her back, his hips driving forward, back. His pace increased with the urgency of her moans. He sucked the sensitive skin of her neck into his mouth. He didn't give a shit if he marked her. Hell, he wanted that. He wanted the fucking world to know that she belonged to him.

The longer he fucked her, the more tension eased from his body until he was nothing more than one sensation after another. Pure feeling.

"Stop," Reagan insisted.

Lynx's hips stilled instantly, his head spinning. He wasn't sure what was happening.

She tossed her hair back and grinned at him over her shoulder.

"I wanna be on top," she said, that sexy smirk making his cock jerk inside her.

The next thing he knew, Lynx was sitting up against the headboard while Reagan was straddling his hips, taking him inside her body once more.

"Now, kiss me," she demanded, her lips coming over his.

Lynx did. He kissed her, holding her to him while she rode his cock.

She nipped his lower lip and he hissed, his cock jerking.

"Keep that up and I'm gonna come," he informed her.

"That's what I'm hopin' for."

"Yeah?" God, he loved this woman.

"Oh, yeah. I want you to lose control for me," she whispered against his mouth.

"Trust me. You don't want that."

Reagan pulled back, her eyes meeting his. "Yeah. I do."

"You don't know what you're askin' for, girl."

And Lynx knew she really didn't. Because she was right. He had been holding back.

But one day, he would unleash on her.

And at that point, he would make her his in every possible way.

THE ROUGH RASP OF LYNX'S VOICE HAD Reagan watching him closely. She was trying to read between the lines. She knew better than to push him, to ask for things she probably couldn't handle. However, it was what she wanted. She'd been denying herself this for so long. Now that she had him, she never wanted to let him go.

It was the exact thought she'd had when she'd seen him talking to Tammy. She hadn't been jealous that he was talking to his ex. No, that wasn't the exact emotion she'd felt. It was more along the lines of possession. She wanted Lynx to be hers, the same way she was his. It was in that moment that Reagan realized she was going to go at this thing between them with all she had. No holding back.

"I want everything," she told him, her hips dropping down, his cock pushing in deep once again.

He filled her so perfectly.

Lynx shook his head, lifting her off him, then pulling her hips forward and burying himself deep again. "When that happens, I'm gonna claim you in every fuckin' way I can."

She cocked one dark eyebrow, daring him. "And how do you plan to do that?"

Lynx slid one hand down over her ass, his finger sliding between her legs. He brushed his fingertip against her asshole.

Reagan sucked in air, the sensations slamming into her as he teased the hypersensitive flesh. She moaned, her eyes closing.

"You want me to fuck you here?" he asked, his voice rough. "To take your ass? To make you beg for more?"

Reagan's breath rushed in and out of her lungs.

"You ever been fucked here?" he asked, the blunt tip of his finger pushing against her anus.

She shook her head.

"You want me to fuck you here? To claim you the way no one ever has or ever will? No one besides me?"

Somehow she managed to nod. "Yes."

Lynx growled, jerking her forward again, taking control although she was on top of him.

Another orgasm was building, this one stronger than the first. She rocked against him, allowing him to control the motion as much as she could.

"Lynx…" She was so close. "Oh, God."

Crushing her mouth to his, Reagan let herself go. Her orgasm slammed into her in a rush of heat and light. And when he growled into her mouth, his hands tightening on her hips, his body going rigid against her, she knew he was coming, too. In fact, his climax triggered another, and she was coming again, her pussy clenching around him.

His hand cupped the back of her head as he kissed her, the intensity shifting from boil to simmer as his tongue slid against hers.

There was no doubt about it, this man might be looking to claim her body in ways he hadn't yet, but Reagan knew he had claimed her heart.

In ways she'd never thought possible.

"SIR, I'M GONNA NEED YOUR LICENSE AND registration," the officer demanded as he loomed over the driver's-side window.

The guy was big. Impossibly so. Kelly couldn't tell for sure, but he had to be a good six and a half feet tall. Black as night and solid as a fucking brick wall. This guy clearly took his job seriously. No donuts for him.

"Do you even know who I am?" Kelly demanded when the officer continued to stare down at him.

The cop's expression didn't change. "No, sir. But if you'll provide license and registration, I'm sure I can figure it out for myself."

When Kelly had seen the red and blue lights in his rearview mirror about a mile back he'd been pissed. Of all nights to get pulled over... This was the last damn thing he needed.

As it was, he was only a few miles from his destination, and having his name go on record for being this close to Embers Ridge wasn't going to work out for him. It meant that his plan for the night had been shot to hell.

Unless...

Kelly could always state that he was following a lead on the Southern Boy Mafia. He'd had a conversation with his FBI friend, who had informed him that the Adorites were being tracked to central Texas. Apparently they were looking to set up shop down there. Kelly thought it was bullshit, but then his buddy had informed him that they'd trailed one of the sisters to Embers Ridge, of all places. Of course, that had put Kelly on edge at the time. Seriously. What were the odds? But now that he thought about it, that could be the very excuse he needed to be here.

"Sir. License and registration," the cop demanded, his white teeth flashing in his dark face.

Kelly glanced down at the name tag on the man's shirt. SMITH.

"Look, *Officer Smith*," Kelly said, trying to keep his tone firm. "I'm actually in a hurry here. I'm following a lead."

The big man didn't move. He continued to stare him down. "A lead?"

Kelly sighed. "My name is Kelly Jackson."

The man's dark eyebrow lifted. Evidently he didn't recognize his name. Stupid fuck.

"I'm the Houston police chief," he explained.

Still no recognition in the guy's eyes.

If they weren't on a deserted stretch of road in the middle of the damn night, Kelly might've been tempted to get out and make a scene, but as it was, there was a sense of foreboding that continued to dance up and down his spine the longer he sat there.

"Look, Officer, I don't mean to make your job difficult. It's just that this is a hot lead and I have to follow it."

"Once we get this outta the way," the officer said firmly, "then you can do your thing. Now, license and registration. Please."

Okay, this was bullshit.

"You don't mind if I call to confirm your badge number?" Kelly suggested, watching the man closely.

"Do what you need to do," the officer replied.

Before he could get his phone out, another set of headlights appeared behind them, a good mile or so back. Kelly watched, waiting for them to get closer. Perhaps this was the distraction that he needed.

"Actually, Officer..." Kelly pushed the door open as the headlights neared.

The officer took one step back, his dark eyes still focused on every move Kelly made. He paid no attention to the headlights approaching.

Kelly took his time getting out, allowing the vehicle to get even closer. He was armed and ready, knowing in a second he could have this situation turned in his favor. He just needed a few more...

Rather than pass, the car pulled up behind the squad car.

Kelly's eyes darted up to the officer's face. That's when he noticed the man was smiling.

"What the hell is going on here?" Kelly snapped, reaching for his gun.

Before he got the holster released, pain smashed into his face from the big guy's fist.

"Not tonight, you don't," he heard the officer say as the darkness threatened to pull him under. "Kelly Jackson, it's time you pay for your sins. And I'm happy to tell you, the devil's waitin'."

Strong hands released his gun from his holster, then patted him down, relieving him of the backup at his ankle and the knife he kept on the opposite ankle.

He heard the sound of footsteps, his head pounding. Kelly pretended to be out cold, not wanting them to know he was still conscious.

"Mr. Adorite is waiting, Rock," a voice said. "I'll take the car. Dispose of it."

"Better get a move on," the officer said. "Before we get any traffic down this way."

"Understood."

A second later, Kelly felt himself being shifted over onto his stomach. Before he had the sense to fight, his hands were yanked behind his back and something wrapped tightly around them. He jerked quickly, but it did no good. The man's hold was too strong.

"You won't get away with this," Kelly demanded, rage boiling beneath his skin. "I am the goddamn law. No one is above me. I'll hang your ass out to dry."

"Oh, we've already gotten away with it," the man referred to as Rock grumbled, tightening his grip as he shackled his hands behind his back. "This is just the fun part."

"Fuck you," Kelly growled. "I'm the goddamn chief of police."

"No," the man rumbled close to his ear. "You're a fuckin' monster who preys on women. But don't worry, you'll be in hell soon enough."

Before he could yell, the man grabbed his head and slammed it into the concrete.

This time, the darkness won out.

Chapter Thirty-Two

DARKNESS HAD SETTLED THROUGHOUT THE ROOM WHEN Lynx woke a few hours later. He shifted, feeling Reagan's warm weight on top of him, her body sprawled half over him, half off. He slid his hands up the smooth skin of her back, loving that she was right there with him.

"You're awake," she whispered softly. "I was wonderin' if I'd have to wait till mornin'."

Lynx grinned in the dark. "Wait for what?"

She shifted, her lips pressing against his collarbone, sliding lower.

He growled softly.

Her mouth trailed down his stomach, her tongue gliding over his abs.

"If you get to play," he whispered, "then so do I."

He couldn't see her, but he felt her lift up. Lynx took the opportunity to grab her. In one swift move, he turned her around so that she was straddling his face.

Reagan squealed as he pulled her pussy onto his mouth, his arms wrapping around her thighs to hold her in place.

Okay, so this was his new favorite way to be woken up.

"Mmm," he hummed as he pressed his lips to the inside of her thigh.

"Two can play that game," she retorted, giggling.

While he feasted on her pussy, the warmth of her mouth engulfed his dick, making him groan.

Best position in the world.

Granted, it was a little distracting, with her tongue sliding up and down his shaft, but he was nothing if not a multitasker.

Plus, the darkness added an entirely different perspective. Everything seemed to be heightened, the sensations sharper, brighter. His sense of touch and taste were significantly more potent as he ran his hands along her smooth skin, his tongue delighted by her taste as he delved into the slickness of her pussy.

Her hips jerked and he plunged his tongue deep inside her when she started grinding against his mouth.

"Lynx..."

He had to hold on to her thighs to keep her from bucking off him while he worked her with his tongue and lips. He licked, sucked, flicked, wanting to make her as crazy as she was making him. The vibrations of her moans made his cock roar to life. He was so hard he hurt, but her mouth was heaven as she sucked his dick fervently, as though she couldn't get enough of him.

Lynx licked her clit while his finger slid over her asshole. He teased her back entrance until she released his cock entirely, her eager moans echoing in the small space. He wanted to fuck her there. He wanted to take her ass, to claim her in a way she'd never been claimed before.

Fumbling blindly for the nightstand, Lynx felt around in the top drawer, wondering just what he would find. She had mentioned she had toys, but he had yet to catalog them for future use. When his fingers found what appeared to be a pump bottle, he lifted it out.

"I assume this is lube," he said. It was too dark to see anything. Not even a sliver of light shone through the blinds.

Her body jerked. "Probably."

"It's not antibacterial shit, is it?"

Reagan laughed. "God, I hope not. That might hurt."

Lynx chuckled, then pumped some into his hand as Reagan crawled off him.

"On your belly," he commanded, reaching out with one hand on her back to keep her from disappearing.

She dropped onto the mattress as he smoothed the slick liquid between his fingers. Definitely lubricant.

"What is it you use this for?" he asked, getting to his knees.

"A girl's gotta take care of herself sometimes."

Lynx pressed his lips to the middle of her back, his lubed fingers sliding between the smooth, rounded globes of her ass. He pushed one finger inside her anus, slowly, gently.

"Relax for me, girl," he whispered, kissing up her spine, licking her skin, tasting as much of her as he could. He continued to trail over her smooth skin, all the way to the back of her neck.

He lay beside her, half covering her body while he fucked her ass with his finger.

"Feel good?"

"Mmmhmm." She pushed back against the intruding digit.

"Don't wanna hurt you." He leaned down, nipping her earlobe.

"You won't," she replied, lifting her head until he found her lips with his.

Lynx kissed her softly, loving the way her tongue slid into his mouth, dueling, gently at first, then more urgently as he continued to pump his finger inside her ass.

When he added another, Reagan moaned loudly.

"Hurt?"

"Uh-uh." She kissed him harder.

He wasn't intending to take this any farther, wanting to work her for a while, prepare her. However, his intentions changed when she bit his lower lip.

"Fuck me," she demanded, her words raspy, breathless. "Fuck my ass, Lynx. Please."

Pre-cum pooled on the head of his dick, the damn thing throbbing. Her commanding tone did it for him in ways he hadn't expected.

Lynx used two fingers, pushing into her ass, stretching her as gently as he could. She whimpered but then pushed back against his hand, panting roughly.

"Please," she begged.

She was wearing him down quickly.

"Don't wanna hurt you," he repeated, getting to his knees behind her.

"Just fuck me," she insisted, making him chuckle.

"I love when you get all demandin' on me, girl."

He made quick work of rolling on the condom, then generously lubing his dick and her ass. While he stroked himself, he fingered her ass again, waiting until she was up on all fours and slamming back against him before he lined up his cock and pressed the head against her tight hole.

Lynx gripped her hip with one firm hand, stilling her. "Easy, girl." He smacked her ass playfully. "This here is mine and I intend to take it how *I* wanna take it."

The groan of frustration that came from Reagan made him laugh. The sound died instantly when he pushed past the tight resistance, the head of his dick inching inside the blistering-hot depths of her ass.

Reagan hissed.

"Push back against me," he insisted, forcing himself in deeper, deeper still.

He was sweating, his body hard as he tried to take it slow. Her ass was clamped down on his cock painfully hard.

"Lynx…" She whimpered again.

Leaning over her, he put one hand on the mattress, his mouth sliding over her shoulder, her neck. He nipped her skin as he pushed in all the way. Rather than pause, Lynx retreated, not pulling out completely before fucking into her again. He repeated the movement until Reagan was panting again, her fingers linking with his against the mattress, tightening as he fucked her slow and deep.

"God, you feel so fucking good," he whispered against her neck. "Tight, hot."

Her whimper turned into a moan, her body rocking against his.

"Mine," he said softly against her ear. "Mine in every way. From here on out."

He wasn't sure of her response to his words, but he couldn't seem to stop them. He wanted her to know how he felt, that this thing between them was permanent. He had waited what felt a lifetime for this woman, and now she was giving herself to him completely.

"Tell me, Reagan," he growled.

"Yours," she whispered. "Now and always."

God, he fucking loved this woman.

Lynx pumped his hips, still going slowly, not wanting to hurt her as the sensations overwhelmed him. The tight sheath of her body, the warmth of her skin, the throaty moans that came from her.

Reaching beneath her with his free hand, Lynx slid his fingers through her slickness, grazing her clit with his thumb until she was whimpering again, this time more urgently.

"Lynx... Make me come... Please... Make me come."

He thrust his hips forward, retreated, then thrust again, fucking them both into oblivion.

"Mine," he groaned. "All fucking mine."

"Yes!"

When her other hand covered his and she began working her clit with his thumb, Lynx knew he wasn't going to last.

"Fuck, girl... Jesus... Sweet ... Christ!"

He slammed into her, praying he wasn't hurting her. She was pushing him to his tipping point. He couldn't hold back, his need for her driving him higher and higher.

"Lynx! I'm... Oh, God... Oh, fuck!" Reagan's scream echoed in the silence, her body locking down on his dick, dragging his release from him.

He came hard, his cock jerking, twitching, his muscles tightening. He could hardly breathe from the intensity that slammed through him.

And even then, Lynx knew he would want this woman until the end of days. Nothing and no one would ever change that.

REAGAN WAS SLIGHTLY ASTONISHED BY WHAT THEY'D just done. More so that she'd wanted it so badly.

While there had been discomfort, there was something about the action that had been hotter than anything she'd ever known.

And now she was trying to catch her breath, her body wrung out from the powerful orgasm.

"You up for a shower?" Lynx mumbled against her ear as he held her tightly.

"Not sure I can walk," she told him. And it was true. Her legs were noodles.

"I'll hold you up."

When the mattress shifted, she realized he was serious. Considering the lube was a little sticky, Reagan figured a shower wouldn't hurt.

Several minutes later, they were in the shower, the lukewarm water pouring over them. Lynx washed her, lathering his hands and running them over every inch of her body. He didn't miss a single crevice, and while he was being thorough, her body was heating again. Reagan wasn't sure how she could want more after what they'd done tonight, but she did.

In fact, she was beginning to wonder if she would ever get enough of this man.

Once Lynx rinsed her, Reagan took her time returning the favor, soaping him up, her fingers drifting over every hard plane and angle of his body from his neck to his toes. She took her time, watching him as she went along.

He was the most remarkable specimen she'd ever laid eyes on. His body was sheer perfection, all hard muscle and sinew and the beautiful ink that decorated his body.

She was gearing up to take him in her mouth when he took her hand and pulled her to her feet.

"Why is it you always stop me when I'm about to have fun?" she teased.

His eyes locked with hers, his face serious.

Her smile fell from her lips, her belly fluttering from the look in his eyes.

When he cupped her face, leaning in and pressing his lips to hers, Reagan sighed against him, wrapping her arms around him, her fingernails gently digging into his back.

There was something mind-blowing about this kiss. Something deeper, more intense. As though it wasn't merely physical.

"Reagan," he whispered, pulling her against him, one arm banding around her back.

She molded her body to his, their mouths fused together.

And when he reached between them and guided his cock into her slick pussy, she lifted her leg and placed one foot on the side of the tub. She matched his groan with a moan of her own when he pressed against her entrance.

"Need to feel you," he whispered against her mouth. "Can I? No barriers, Reagan."

She nodded, remembering how he'd said he had never had sex without a condom. She hadn't either, but her reasons hadn't been *only* for birth control. Not only had she not been looking to get pregnant, she feared what Billy might give her.

"I've never had sex without a condom," she told him. "I didn't want..." She couldn't finish that sentence, not wanting to bring her past into this. Not when she had Lynx like this.

"Me, neither," he admitted.

"I... I'm not on the pill," she told him, needing him to know the repercussions of his actions. She trusted him implicitly and she ... God, maybe she was crazy, but she wanted this too. She wanted to be one with this man, nothing between them.

Lynx pulled back, his hand still cupping her jaw as he stared down at her. "You're it for me, Reagan. Always have been. I'll take you however I can get you, but I want you to know..."

Reagan felt tears forming as his words trailed off. He didn't even have to say them for her to know how he felt. That was the way Lynx was. There was an undeniable connection between them. She'd felt it all those years ago and she felt it now, stronger than before.

"I love you," she whispered. "I've loved you since I was sixteen years old."

Unable to stop it, a tear slid down her cheek, but she smiled.

Lynx growled softly, then pressed his hips forward, joining their bodies.

Reagan sighed as the pleasure consumed her. He was hot and hard inside her and it felt different, more incredible. Every sensation seemed more powerful. Her hands roamed over his back as they stood there in the cooling water, his body warming her from the inside out.

"I love you," he rasped. "No one else, Reagan. I've never loved anyone else."

How, she wasn't sure, but Reagan knew that to be true.

And she also knew it was true for herself.

This man…

He was it for her, too.

Chapter Thirty-Three

LYNX FUMBLED FOR THE WATER, SHUTTING IT off without leaving the warmth of Reagan's body. He even picked her up and carried her out of the bathroom and back to the bed. They were both dripping wet, but he didn't care about that.

The only thing that mattered to him was making love to this woman right here, right now.

"Reagan," he whispered against her lips as he settled himself between her legs, her thighs cradling his hips as he pushed inside her, skin to skin.

Lynx was overcome by emotion, something he hadn't felt before. It was as though his heart was too big for his chest, threatening to explode.

Burying his face in her neck, Lynx made love to her, as slowly, as perfectly as he could. His hips shifted forward, back, his cock tunneling in and out of her body. The way she cradled his head with one arm, her other hand sliding over his back, had those emotions rioting. He'd never felt as whole as he did right at that moment. Here. With her.

"You're it for me," he repeated, his words muffled by her skin.

"And you're it for me," she replied.

Lifting his head, Lynx met her gaze. "Forever, Reagan. That's what this is. I won't let you go. I can't."

Her smile was so sweet.

He locked his gaze with hers. "And you can be as ornery, as stubborn, as sassy as you wanna be and that won't ever change a thing."

Her eyes glistened with tears.

"From here on out…"

Reagan nodded, her eyes never leaving his.

The mere thought of getting Reagan pregnant was an aphrodisiac like no other. He loved this woman to the depths of his soul. He had always known that his life would never be complete without her. And he'd held out for the most part.

But now that he had her … no way would he ever let her go.

"Love me, Lynx," she whispered, pulling his head down to hers.

He melded his lips to hers as he pumped his hips. His pace increased, his thrusts grew more shallow as he found himself wanting to be as close to her as he could be. Resting on one elbow, Lynx loved her, just like she'd asked. He loved her with everything that he was.

And when he finally brought them to the brink of ecstasy, spilling his seed inside her, he held on as tightly as he could, feeling the last part of himself go.

She owned him.

Heart, body, and soul.

"YOU WON'T GET AWAY WITH THIS," KELLY snarled.

He had no fucking clue where he was or what these assholes were planning to do to him. He vaguely remembered the car ride. He was pretty sure it had taken several hours, but he'd drifted in and out of consciousness.

He'd heard the name Adorite on more than one occasion, but he had yet to see anyone other than the black guy who'd been impersonating a cop and a taller man wearing a suit and a somber expression.

"What the fuck do you want from me?" he snapped, trying to get the attention of the asshole manning the door.

He had already tried to free himself from his bonds, but to no avail. They had him shackled to a chair in this concrete room. There were no windows, just a steel table and a single chair, which he was currently sitting in.

The sound of the lock disengaging had Kelly's eyes darting to the door.

Finally.

Fuck.

The door opened slowly and a man walked in.

Not just any man, either.

Kelly recognized him. Every law enforcement officer in the state would recognize Maximillian Adorite. The guy was the notorious leader of the Southern Boy Mafia. He was ruthless, and his list of crimes was long, yet he'd never been charged with a damn thing. And the FBI had been trying for years to nail the Adorite family with something, anything. Oddly enough, the Adorite patriarch had been killed sometime back, and Max had quickly moved into the role of mob boss, taking over for his father.

If he played his cards right, Kelly figured he could probably get on this guy's good side. At this point, he was willing to do just about anything. Hell, he had more money than he knew what to do with. The life insurance policies he'd had on his wives had padded his bank accounts nicely.

Kelly knew every man had his price, and he was more than willing to pay whatever he needed to in order to get out of this fucking dungeon.

"Mr. Jackson," Max greeted, his tone flat, his brown eyes cold.

"Why am I here?" Kelly demanded.

A small smile tilted the corner of Max's mouth. "I find it amusing that you'd even ask that."

"I have no beef with you," Kelly retorted. "So I'm sure we can get this misunderstanding cleared up and I can be on my way."

"To where?" Max asked. "Embers Ridge?"

Kelly frowned. "I have no idea what you're talking about."

"No?" Max watched him closely. "That wasn't you who blew up that little bar?"

"Bar?" Kelly feigned ignorance. "What are you talking about? I'm the goddamn chief of police. In Houston. Why the hell would I—"

"Oh, cut the shit," Max sneered, his eyes locking on Kelly's face. "I've heard that girl's story. And let me tell you, once was more than enough."

"What story? What girl?"

"Does the name Amy Manning ring a bell?"

"No," he lied easily.

"Really?" Max chuckled, but there was no humor in it. "Maybe you know her as Jane Doe."

Kelly was working hard to conceal his reaction, but he got the feeling Max could see right through him. Knowing this would move along faster if he would just own up to whatever it was Max thought he knew, Kelly decided to change the direction of the questioning.

"What does she have to do with you?"

"Everything," Max stated easily. "Every *goddamn* thing."

There was a knock on the door and Max pivoted around to open it. Someone passed something to him and then he was turning back toward Kelly holding … a pen and paper, plus a cell phone.

Okay, so the latter gave him hope.

Max laid the items on the table in front of him. "I'm gonna give you two options here."

Kelly sat back, prepared to argue, but Max held up a hand.

"Let me finish."

Kelly nodded.

"Your first option is to make a list of your transgressions, including the kidnapping and torture of Amy Manning, as well as your part in the deaths of your first wife, your second wife, Amy Manning's aunt and uncle, as well as Detective Tannenbaum. Oh, and while you're at it, you can confess to the attempted murder of Amy Manning."

"Fuck you," Kelly spat.

Max continued as though Kelly had said nothing. "Once that's done, I'll need you to sign and date the suicide note, as well."

"The *what?*" Kelly sat up straight, fear lancing through his bones. Okay, drastic times called for drastic measures. "Wait. I've got money. I can pay you. Then you can let me go and no one'll be the wiser."

"Pay me, huh?"

Yeah, Kelly knew money would appeal to a man like Max. "Absolutely."

"That's somethin' to consider."

Kelly nodded toward the cell phone. "I can wire the money to your account right now."

Max seemed to consider this for a moment. "I'm listening."

"One hundred thousand dollars," Kelly offered.

One dark eyebrow lifted, signaling Max wasn't impressed. Shit.

"One hundred fifty," Kelly said.

"Five hundred thousand," Max countered.

"Fine."

Before he knew what was happening, Max touched the screen on the phone, bringing it to life, then typed in the numbers.

"How do you know my account?" Kelly asked, a sense of dread filling him.

Max's smile was what Kelly would've envisioned on the devil. "I know everything about you, Mr. Jackson."

Glancing down at the phone again, Kelly watched as Max hit more buttons and then the screen showed "Transfer Successful."

"So you'll let me go, now?" Kelly asked, hating how hopeful he sounded.

"No."

Kelly jerked, trying to break his arms free, but nothing happened.

"You finished yet?" Max asked, his patience seemingly never-ending.

"While you're still considering your first option," Max continued, "maybe you should hear your second."

Kelly narrowed his eyes. "I fucking paid you."

"You did. And I thank you for that. Amy Manning will thank you for that." Max crossed his arms over his chest and regarded Kelly once more. "If your first option's not to your liking, then I'll invite my friend Ace in, and he can take care of things the easy way."

"The easy way?"

"Yes," Max stated firmly. "It's damn sure easier on me because I have shit to do and" — he motioned his hand toward the paper — "waiting for you to write all that shit down is gonna take time. I'd much prefer to be on my way."

"Easy on *you*?" Kelly asked. "Not *me*?"

Max shook his head and a sardonic smile turned up the corners of his mouth. The man leaned over and stared Kelly directly in the eye.

"Nothin's *ever* gonna be easy for you again, Mr. Jackson. The nightmare you put those women through… Let's just say hell's a good resting place for you."

When Max stood to his full height again, Kelly jumped when Max shifted the table to the side, revealing…

Kelly's eyes went wide when he saw the drain in the floor.

His gaze slid up to the ceiling, noticing for the first time the chains that hung there. His heart pounded in his chest as the fear sliced through him.

"I'll take the first option," Kelly blurted. Eating a bullet was a hell of a lot easier than … whatever this man had in store for him.

Max rubbed his chin and Kelly could feel him assessing him.

"You know what?" Max said thoughtfully. "I think I'll have to rescind my first option."

When Max turned toward the door, Kelly shouted his name, but he didn't turn back around.

And when the door opened and a tall, bald man stepped inside, his eyes as cold as the steel blades in his hands, Kelly swallowed hard.

"Thanks for comin' down, Ace."

"Max!" Kelly yelled.

"My pleasure, boss."

"Max!"

"I'll leave you to it, then."

"Son of a bitch," Kelly screamed.

Ace nodded and Max stepped out of the room.

Max's head appeared around the door once more. "Sucks, don't it?"

"What?" Kelly asked, his voice trembling.

"Not having any options."

Kelly frowned.

Max's smile was menacing. "Now you know how *they* felt."

And with that, Max was gone.

The bald man moved around behind him and Kelly jerked against the chains holding him down.

"Don't worry. No one can hear you, so feel free to scream," the scratchy voice said from behind him. Ace's head appeared beside Kelly's face. "I like it when they scream."

Chapter Thirty-Four

"YOU WANNA GO OUT?" REAGAN ASKED COPENHAGEN when she forced her tired body out of the bed at first light. She grabbed Lynx's T-shirt and pulled it on.

Lynx was still asleep, his breaths even, the hard lines that had been around his eyes last night gone.

Smiling, Reagan pulled the door closed, hoping he could sleep a little while longer. They hadn't slept much last night, but for some reason, that didn't seem to matter to her. She felt lighter this morning and she knew why. It was her heart. It was no longer heavy.

"Come on, boy," Reagan urged Copenhagen, leading him to the front door.

She stepped outside onto the porch, her gaze straying to the rocking chairs sitting there. Reagan moved to the closest chair and sat down while Copenhagen sniffed around. Pulling her legs up, she tugged the shirt over her knees, covering herself completely.

The cool morning breeze caressed her skin and she heard the cows in the distance. A rooster crowed from somewhere down the road.

Reagan sighed, enjoying the moment.

This was what contentment felt like.

It wasn't something that she was used to. Not in this capacity anyway.

Sure, she'd been happy from time to time. She loved her bar, loved her family, but she had never felt as though she truly belonged.

With Lynx, she felt that.

In fact, she felt everything with that man. Safe, loved, cherished even.

Copenhagen found his way back to the porch, curling up beside her chair as they sat there in the quiet of the morning.

Reagan had no idea how long she'd been out there when she heard the screen door squeak behind her. She glanced over to see Lynx leaning against the doorjamb, his eyes on her. Without his shirt, the man looked like the bad boy everyone knew him to be. But Reagan knew a side of him they didn't know. The sweet, kind, gentle man who … loved her.

"Mornin'," she said with a smile.

"Mornin'." He still looked tired.

"You okay?"

He nodded. "Please tell me you have coffee."

The way he said it sounded like a plea. As though he wasn't going to make it through the next few minutes without it.

"I actually don't."

His eyes widened and she couldn't help but laugh.

Launching out of the chair, she skipped over to him, going on tiptoe to kiss his mouth. "But we can change that right fast. Just let me get dressed and we can go to the diner."

Lynx glanced down at his watch, then back up at her. He smiled. "Sounds like a plan."

Reagan went to move past him, but he grabbed her around the waist and spun her back around.

"Although, I might have a little time to spare." Lynx pulled her into him, burying his face in her neck. "Because Lord have mercy, woman, seein' you in my shirt…"

She laughed, unable to help herself.

"Later," she said, playfully pushing him away. "First coffee. Then work. *Then…*"

"So mean," he grumbled, laughing into her neck.

Yeah, so Reagan could totally get used to this.

Turning to head to her bedroom, she was pulled up short when Lynx reached for her hand. Once again, she was pivoting around to face him.

"I'm never gonna get dressed if you don't—"

"I love you," he rasped.

Her heart turned over in her chest. A full flip, which stirred the butterflies in her belly.

"I love you, too," she whispered back.

"Makin' sure you know I meant what I said last night," he clarified.

Reagan nodded. "I know." She did. Again, she wasn't sure why that was, but she believed him.

"Good." Lynx released her wrist. "Now go get dressed so I can get my coffee, girl."

Laughing, Reagan raced to the bedroom to find clothes.

Half an hour later, after they had taken Copenhagen over to the store, Reagan and Lynx were sitting in the diner when Amy and Wolfe walked in.

"Well, if wonders never cease." Wolfe's smirk said as much as his statement.

He was giving Lynx a hard time already.

Wolfe pulled the chair out for Amy, and Reagan greeted the other woman, noticing she was as pale as she had been the night before.

"Everything okay?" Reagan asked, keeping her voice low.

Amy nodded.

Concerned, Reagan shot a look at Wolfe. He shook his head slightly, as though telling her he couldn't fix the problem. And she could only assume he had tried.

"The usual?" Donna asked them as a group, passing over a cup of coffee to Lynx with a grin.

"The usual," they all said at the same time.

The woman disappeared. Reagan had to wonder if Donna would ever stop asking, simply bring them the usual. One day, she figured, it was bound to happen.

"What's goin' on?" Lynx asked, leaning back in his chair, his booted foot resting against Reagan's.

She liked that he wanted to touch her. It was a comfort she hadn't known before.

"Not a whole helluva lot," Wolfe answered.

Reagan could see the tension in Wolfe's shoulders. It was clear he was trying to look more relaxed than he was.

"Is there a problem?" Lynx asked, sitting up. Obviously he'd picked up on it, too.

Wolfe shrugged. "Not sure. Travis asked us to meet him over here. Thought he'd be here by now."

That got everyone's attention and all eyes narrowed on Wolfe.

"Seriously. He didn't say what he wanted to talk about, just wanted us to be here. He asked me to keep Rhys away though."

Reagan frowned. "What? Why?"

Wolfe shot her a look, but Reagan couldn't quite decipher it.

"Because he's the sheriff," Lynx added softly.

Her eyes widened.

If they didn't want her brother here because he was the sheriff...

The bells over the door jingled and all eyes swung over to the door.

Looked as though she wasn't going to have to speculate anymore.

The man of the hour had just arrived.

"TRAV," LYNX GREETED AS HIS COUSIN PULLED a chair over to their table.

Lynx was surprised to see that he was solo this morning. At the very least, his husband was usually by his side. And the lack of his significant others had Lynx on edge before the guy even got his ass in the chair.

As everyone waited for Travis to sit, the tension in the small space ratcheted up a few notches. The conversations around them continued, but they seemed to be a million miles away as the four of them focused solely on the big man joining them.

"Is there somethin' wrong?" Amy asked, her voice low, brittle.

"Actually…" Travis said, glancing around as though he was making sure no one was close enough to hear. When he turned back, his expression was somewhat somber. "I got some news this mornin'."

"News?" Lynx wasn't sure he liked the sound of that.

Travis placed his arms on the table and regarded each of them. He took a deep breath, exhaled slowly. "I'm only gonna say this one time, and then no one is to ever talk about the subject again. Understood?"

Lynx nodded along with Wolfe. He noticed Amy and Reagan were just staring at the man.

Travis's eyes cut to Amy. "There is no longer a situation that you have to worry about."

Her eyes widened.

Travis continued. "From this moment on, you are free to live your life, to never have to look over your shoulder."

"What happened?" Amy inquired, her eyes wide, her face pale.

Travis shook his head. "I don't know and I don't wanna know. Neither do you. But the source I received it from is legitimate." Travis reached out and touched Amy's hand. "No matter what you hear or read, I want you to understand one thing. If you hear nothin' else I've said, I want you to understand this."

Amy nodded, her eyes wide as she waited for him to continue.

"You're safe," Travis said firmly. "Completely and totally safe."

Lynx watched, his heart breaking when Amy dissolved into tears. Wolfe instantly wrapped his arms around her, holding her close, brushing his hand down her hair.

Reagan reached over and took Lynx's hand, as though she needed to touch him. He linked his fingers with hers and squeezed gently.

Travis sat back, glanced over at Lynx, then Reagan. "Someone's makin' an anonymous donation to the rebuilding of your bar. Don't ask questions, just move forward as you were." Travis jerked his chin toward Amy. "And any extra money, I suggest you donate to a college fund when these kids decide to have a baby. It doesn't make up for ... what happened, but it's somethin'."

Lynx nodded. He got it.

He might be a redneck, but he damn sure wasn't a dumb ass.

"And tell Rhys I'm sorry I had to exclude him. I think he'll understand."

He would. Even Lynx knew that much.

"Now, if you don't mind," Travis said as he got to his feet, "I'm gonna get outta your hair so you can have breakfast."

As though she heard his suggestion, Donna appeared with four plates of food, setting them down before scuttling off to another table.

Travis reached down and stole a piece of bacon off Lynx's plate.

"Hey! Them's fightin' words, cuz."

Travis laughed, slapping Lynx on the shoulder.

Amy lifted her head, wiping her eyes and laughing when she noticed what had happened.

"So, we good here?" Travis asked after tucking the chair back at the vacant table.

Lynx met Wolfe's gaze and they both nodded.

There was no need for questions.

The answer was all they needed.

RHYS PEERED UP FROM HIS COMPUTER AT the knock on his office door.

Leaning back in his chair, he motioned Reagan to come inside.

"What's up?" he asked, trying to hide his curiosity at seeing his sister in his office. He couldn't even recall the last time she'd come to see him.

"I just wanted to drop by," she said sweetly, easing into the chair across from him. "Wanted to see how you're doin'."

Rhys chuckled. "You wanted to see how *I* was doin'?"

"Yes," she said haughtily. "Is that a crime?"

"Not the last time I checked, no."

"Good."

Her eyes instantly dropped to her lap and Rhys knew she had something on her mind. She wouldn't have come to see him otherwise.

"Spill it, Reagan."

When she lifted her gaze, there was a smile on her face.

He wasn't sure when the last time was that he'd seen a genuine smile on her face. He liked it there.

"I wanted to let you know that me and Lynx are..."

Rhys lifted an eyebrow. "You and Lynx are *what?*"

She shrugged. "Honestly, I don't know what we are right this minute, but we're somethin'."

Reagan laughed and the sound was enough to erase the fake scowl he'd plastered there a second ago. He leaned forward, resting his arms on his desk as he regarded her.

"Are you happy?" he asked.

"More than I've ever been."

"Then that's all that matters."

"Hey, that's my line."

"It's a good one," he agreed.

"True. It is." Her smile brightened even more. "I'm not sure why I wanted to tell you, but I thought..."

Once again, Rhys waited for her to continue. When she didn't, he filled in for her. "Don't worry about Mom. She's always gonna be the way she is. She never liked Billy when y'all were together."

"No, but she always insisted I stay with him."

"Yeah, well. She's not all there when it comes to relationships, Reagan. You know that. But deep down, she wants you to be happy."

"I'm not so sure about that."

"She does. We all do." Rhys sat up straight. "And you know what? We've all known that Lynx had a thing for you all these years." Before she could say anything, he waved her off. "The past is the past. Your mistakes and his. Those are all behind you. The only thing that matters is movin' forward."

"Did you know he's helpin' to rebuild my bar?"

"I did." Rhys leaned back in his chair again. "He came to me the mornin' after the explosion. Told me what he wanted to do." Taking a deep breath, Rhys resigned himself to admitting the truth. "Lynx is a good guy, Reagan. Sure, he's rough around the edges, and he gets on my last damn nerve with all the fightin', but he's a good guy. Y'all are good for each other."

He noticed tears welling in his sister's eyes.

"I love him."

"I know that." Rhys had always known that. Yes, she might've fought her feelings tooth and nail, but to anyone with eyes, it had been obvious.

"Okay, Mr. Know-It-All. Then I'm not sure why I even came to see you," she said, laughing.

When Reagan stood, Rhys stood.

"Because I'm your brother and you love me."

"I do not," she countered. "I tolerate you."

That made him laugh.

"Okay, well, I've taken up enough of your time, Sheriff."

"That you have. I've got shit to do."

"Yeah?" She peered around his office. "Like what? Play solitaire on your computer?"

Rhys jerked his eyes back to his computer screen. No way could she see it.

Reagan laughed loudly. "Oh, shit. I was kiddin'. But you are, aren't you?"

Rhys pointed toward the door. "Get outta my office, woman. Before I lock you up for bein' a pain in my ass."

Still laughing, Reagan threw her arms around him, hugging him tightly. "I'm happy for you, too," she said softly. "And as long as you're happy, that's all that matters."

Yeah, he had to agree on that one.

Poking her in her side, Rhys laughed. "Now get outta my office."

"Okay, okay." Reagan backed up. "I'll go."

"Hey, Reagan," he called after her when she stepped into the hallway.

"Huh?"

"Be good."

"I've been good my whole life," she retorted. "Now that I've got Lynx, I'm thinkin' I wanna be bad for a while."

Rhys jerked his finger toward the door. "Go away."

Reagan laughed, then spun on her heel and waved over her head.

He couldn't help but smile. Rhys truly was happy for his sister. Lynx Caine was a pain in Rhys's ass, there was no doubt about that, but when it came down to it, Rhys knew the man would take care of Reagan the way she deserved.

And she definitely deserved it.

Chapter Thirty-Five

Two days later

"THIS THE NEWS REPORT YOU MENTIONED?" GAGE asked.

Travis peered up at his husband as he stepped into Travis's office. "Yeah. Looks like Max has been a busy man."

Leaning back in his chair, Travis hit the button to turn up the volume. Gage came around to stand behind him, his hand warm on Travis's shoulder.

Stay tuned for a breaking news report...

We're following up on the disappearance of Houston police chief Kelly Jackson. As we previously reported, Chief Jackson has been missing for at least two days, and there are still no leads on his whereabouts.

The Houston police chief seems to have vanished into thin air. Our sources tell us that during a well-check visit to Chief Jackson's home on Thursday morning, some disturbing things were uncovered. While investigators were searching for evidence of possible foul play, they found some items that have raised some questions as to what is really going on here.

Our sources have told us that there were detailed journals found on the man's home computer, outlining in horrific detail a sordid history of abuse to Jackson's two deceased wives. Although investigators aren't sure exactly where Jackson is, they are working with the families of both women to have the bodies exhumed and autopsies performed to determine whether or not foul play was involved.

It has also been stated that there are questions regarding embezzlement of city funds by Jackson. When we have more details on this, we will pass them along. And the Houston Police Department is asking that if you have any information regarding the whereabouts of Chief Jackson, please contact the non-emergency hotline. Any and all leads will be followed. We have also been advised that, until further investigations prove otherwise, Chief Jackson is to be considered armed and dangerous.

"Journals?" Gage asked, coming around and leaning against Travis's desk. "The man really kept journals?"

Gage's disbelief rang as loudly as Travis's had when he first heard the story.

Travis stared up at the man. "I'm sure that's Max's doing."

"Ah, well. That makes sense. Especially considering there was no mention of..."

Amy.

"Nope. And there won't be," Travis assured him.

Ensuring there was nothing that tied Amy back to Kelly Jackson probably hadn't been easy. However, Travis didn't question how Max had taken care of business. He didn't want to know.

"Like I said before," Gage stated, smiling, "I'm not sure how I feel about you havin' mob ties. But if that man wants to play superhero and save the girl, then who am I to argue?"

Travis got to his feet. "I'm sure that's not the first time Max has played superhero." He leaned over and kissed Gage. "And I seriously doubt it'll be the last."

Gage hooked his fingers in Travis's belt loops. "Probably not. But what d'ya say we sit the next one out?"

Travis chuckled, then leaned in and kissed his husband once more. "I'll do my best. But I'm not makin' any promises."

Epilogue

"COME ON! CUT THE RIBBON, WOULD YA?" Wolfe shouted, needling Reagan as she stood on the front porch of the new bar. "We've been waitin' a long damn time for this."

Reagan laughed, as Wolfe had expected her to.

Beside her, his cousin watched Reagan closely. The man was so far gone it was amusing. Or rather it would've been if Wolfe didn't know exactly how the man felt.

These past few months had been … well, amazing was one way to put it. Although that was probably an understatement.

"Y'all ready for this?" Reagan asked the crowd that had gathered in the parking lot.

Wolfe was pretty sure half the town was there despite the fact that it was unusually cold for winter in Texas.

A chorus of cheers erupted.

"You sure?" Reagan asked, cocking her head to the side.

Lynx laughed, then moved closer to his woman.

Wolfe waited along with everyone else.

Finally, Reagan leaned down and snipped the ribbon that was tied between two cedar posts that supported the overhang covering the wraparound porch. Lynx had mentioned that Reagan had always wanted a wraparound porch, so it had been added at the last minute. Wolfe knew his cousin would go to any lengths to make that woman happy.

Lynx gave a whistle and everyone cheered.

It had taken them three months to get the bar built, and the day had finally come to open the place. Granted, it probably would've been built even sooner than that had his cousin not decided that he wanted to start building his own damn house *while* they were in the process of erecting the damn bar.

It seemed to have worked out for everyone though.

Well, maybe not everyone.

There were still a couple of pissy people, but as Lynx said, you couldn't please everyone all the time. Wolfe had to agree. Truth was, it didn't fucking matter if everyone else was happy. Decisions were made, lives were changed, and people were smiling. All was right in their world and those who didn't like it could fuck off.

Glancing around, Wolfe set his sights on the two people he'd been waiting for.

While the rest of the crowd stood patiently waiting for the doors to open, Wolfe wound his way around the horde to the spot where Rhys and Amy were standing beside Rhys's truck.

"You're seriously workin' tonight?" Wolfe grumbled.

"Someone's gotta keep you crazy-ass Caines in line."

True.

Rhys tugged Amy close and kissed the top of her head. "You don't let our boy get in any trouble tonight."

Wolfe laughed.

Amy chuckled. "I'll try. But I can't make any promises."

Not caring who was standing around watching, Wolfe closed the distance between him and Rhys. He stood there, toe-to-toe with the man he loved, while the woman they loved smiled up at them.

"So, sheriff," Wolfe said, keeping his voice low. "You gonna kiss me or what?"

The blush that stole over Rhys's face had Wolfe's dick twitching. God, he fucking loved this man.

Wolfe glanced down at Amy. "That was the agreement, right?"

"Technically," Rhys said, clearing his throat. "I agreed to kiss you in public when Lynx announced—"

Wolfe interrupted him. "Wait for it."

"Oh!" Lynx's booming voice sounded from behind them. "And one more thing! We've got some celebratin' to do tonight."

Wolfe cocked an eyebrow, never looking away from Rhys.

"My girl said yes, y'all! Reagan's gonna be my wife!"

And the cheers shot to a deafening level.

Wolfe merely grinned, waiting.

Rhys shook his head and Amy laughed.

"Come on," Wolfe goaded. "What've you got to lose?"

Surprising him, Rhys leaned forward. Wolfe's breath halted in his lungs when the sexy sheriff grabbed his shirt and jerked him closer, crushing his mouth to Wolfe's.

Hot damn.

He fought the urge to take the kiss further, but it wasn't easy.

More cheers sounded.

Amy giggled and Rhys pulled back, both of them glancing down at her.

"I think they're happy for you," she said sweetly.

"For us," Wolfe clarified, wrapping his arms around her and lifting her off her feet. He pressed his lips to hers and grinned against her mouth when she wrapped her arms around his neck.

Yeah. It was safe to say, they were holding things together just fine.

LYNX SHOOK SOME HANDS AS PEOPLE PASSED by him into the bar. He kept one arm wrapped around Reagan, not wanting to let her get too far. They had been counting down to this night for so long it was almost hard to believe that it was finally here.

Granted, three months wasn't a terribly long time, but when it came to getting the bar opened up, it seemed like an eternity.

"Congratulations!" Darrell Jameson said, smacking Lynx on the arm.

"Thanks, man. Go on in, grab a beer. You and your lady're drinkin' free tonight. This place wouldn't be here if it weren't for you."

Darrell nodded, then took his wife's hand as they slipped inside.

A couple more people passed by, congratulating them both before heading inside to see the new place.

Lynx tried not to look obvious as he glanced around, scanning the area for one specific person. He wasn't sure how well he was doing, especially when he caught Reagan watching him.

"What're you up to?" she asked, pinching his side.

Lynx laughed, trying to pull back but still refusing to let her go. "What makes you think I'm up to—"

"Congratulations." The deep, raspy voice had them both turning.

And though he had known this was going to happen, Lynx felt the emotion slam through him. He couldn't help it. His eyes teared up and his lungs stopped working momentarily.

"Oh, my God," Reagan choked out. "Oh, my God!"

Lynx met his father's eyes, trying to remain steady on his feet as the man he loved more than life stood there in front of them. It was the first time Cooter had ventured out of the house since...

"You think I'd miss this, honey?" Cooter asked, smiling at Reagan. "Not a chance."

Reagan threw her arms around Cooter, and Lynx's old man held on to her for a minute, probably giving her a little privacy to cry. Hell, Lynx was still hovering on the edge of tears himself.

"Thanks, Dad," he mouthed.

Cooter nodded, then released Reagan when she pulled back. He leaned down and looked into her eyes. "You good, honey?"

Reagan laughed. It was a watery sound, but it was a laugh nonetheless. "I'm good. I'm so glad you're here."

She squeezed Cooter's hand, then stepped back.

Lynx wrapped one arm around her shoulders and tugged her into his side. "Go on in," he told his father. "Have a beer. Calvin's in there somewhere."

Cooter nodded and their gazes held for a second longer. Lynx was so proud of his father. So fucking proud.

Being in love with Reagan, Lynx knew the kind of love his father had felt for his mother. He didn't want to ever imagine the pain Cooter had gone through, but he understood exactly what had driven the man to lock himself up in his house all this time. That sort of loss... It was unbearable.

Reagan turned her face into his chest when Cooter headed inside. Lynx hugged her tightly.

Someone cleared their throat and Reagan pulled back.

Lynx found himself looking down at Billy Watson. Two steps away, Tammy stood by his side. Neither was smiling, which he didn't find surprising. Considering Tammy was four months pregnant and the pair had endured what might've been called a shotgun wedding at the hands of her father, Lynx didn't imagine they had much to smile about. He had heard that Billy had attempted to pay Tammy off to get her to claim the baby wasn't his, which had sent her into a fit of rage. Couldn't blame her for that.

Needless to say, Tammy's father hadn't been happy about any of it, but they had come to the decision to keep the baby and to get married. The best part was, Billy and Tammy were living with Tammy's parents in Austin. Looked as though date night had brought them back to town.

"Congrats," Billy said, his tone defeated.

"Thanks," Reagan quipped, leaning in closer to Lynx.

"I promise," Tammy said, looking directly at Reagan, "he won't be causin' any trouble tonight."

No, Lynx didn't figure he would.

The pair moved into the building and Lynx turned to Reagan. "You ready to get this party underway?"

She nodded, then shot him a sexy smirk. "I'm lookin' forward to midnight."

"Midnight?" That was closing time. He cocked his head, trying to decipher her meaning.

"Keep thinkin' on that one," she said sweetly. "And get back to me when you figure it out."

With that, the sexiest woman on the planet spun around and headed into the bar.

Damn. He hated to see her leave, but he fucking *loved* to watch her go.

Midnight

"You 'bout done in here?" Lynx asked, watching Reagan as she pushed in one of the chairs before flipping off the overhead light.

"Not quite," she told him as she moved toward the bar. "I need help with somethin'."

"What's up?" he asked, following her around behind the bar.

She turned to face him, that sexy smirk from earlier back on her face. "Thought maybe we could christen this place tonight."

The impact those words had was like a punch to the gut, stealing his breath. However, this wasn't a bad feeling. Not by a long shot.

Gripping her waist, he hefted her up onto the bar, coming to stand between her legs.

"I like where your head's at," he told her, sliding his hand beneath her hair and pulling her in for a kiss.

The thunk of her boots hitting the ground had him chuckling as he pulled back. He noticed she was already unbuttoning her jeans.

"Hot damn, girl," he rasped. "Lemme help with that."

A few minutes later, he had her naked, her bare butt planted on the bar top, tits beckoning him. She took his Stetson from his head and propped it on her own.

The woman didn't know how fucking hot she looked just like that. Hell, Lynx wasn't sure he could look away long enough to do this moment justice.

"I'm not sure this is what Wolfe had in mind when he designed this bar," Lynx said, his hands cupping her breasts as he lifted one to his mouth. He laved her nipple with his tongue, watching her face as he did.

"Not sure if the health inspector would be too happy about it, either," Reagan said, her eyes bright as she watched him.

Lynx released her nipple. "What he don't know won't hurt him."

"True."

"Now, where was I?"

Reagan lifted her breast toward his mouth. "Right here."

Damn, this woman knew how to drive him absolutely crazy.

Leaning in, Lynx grazed her nipple with his teeth, then sucked her into his mouth.

Her moan echoed in the empty room.

He fucking loved that.

When her fingers slid into his hair, holding him to her, Lynx gave her his full attention. His hand slipped between her thighs; his thumb trailed between her smooth, slick lips.

He released her breast from his mouth, then hooked her knees over his forearms. "You're wet for me."

"I am," she agreed. "I always am."

He met her eyes for a second before dipping his head down and sliding his tongue through her slit. Reagan leaned back, propping herself up with her hands, which practically offered her pussy to his eager mouth. He didn't waste time.

"Lynx... Oh, God..."

Listening to her sexy moans, Lynx ate her like a starving man, working her close to the edge and then backing off until she was practically bucking against him.

"Quit teasin' me," she demanded.

Grinning to himself, Lynx went full throttle, lapping at her pussy, then sucking her clit until she was screaming his name.

She was breathing hard when he stood up.

"So, how 'bout we try that again?" he suggested.

"Try what?" she asked, her chest heaving.

Lynx helped her down from the bar and spun her around.

"Stand right there," he told her. "On that step."

Reagan did as he instructed.

"Now put your hands across the bar," he insisted, helping her to curl her fingers around the outer edge. "And don't move."

"Okay, but what are we gonna try again?"

Lynx freed his cock from his jeans, then lined up behind her. He ran the sensitive head of his dick through her slickness, then pushed inside her.

"Fuck..." he hissed, the pleasure almost too much to bear.

When she started to push back against him, Lynx stilled her with his hands on her hips.

"Hold on, girl," he whispered against her ear. "This time, when you scream my name, I'm gonna make it fuckin' count."

Reagan giggled, but that died off quickly when he thrust into her.

He fucked her right there in the bar until they were both out of breath.

And when she screamed his name *that* time...

Fuck yeah!

ACKNOWLEDGMENTS

Sometimes a story simply comes. And just like the first book in this 2-book series, Lynx and Reagan's story was just there. I knew going into Hard to Hold that I was absolutely crazy in love with Lynx and he had to have his own book. However, I knew that he would play a big role in the underlying story that was set up in Wolfe's book. And for that, I want to thank everyone who took a chance on me and endured the wait for the continuation. Now, I need to thank all the people who help me to make these releases successful.

First and always, I have to thank my wonderfully patient husband who puts up with me every single day. If it wasn't for him and his belief that I could (and can) do this, I wouldn't be writing this today. He has been my backbone, my rock, the very reason I continue to believe in myself. We spent the majority of our time packing and moving while I was writing this book. It wasn't easy for him on the days I had to sit at my computer and get the characters out of my head, but like always, he endured. I love you for that, babe.

Chancy Powley – If you don't like something, you tell me. And sometimes I see your rational. Sometimes I don't, but the fact that you stick with me no matter what is the reason I consider you my best friend. So, thank you for that. And thank you for keeping me going.

Allison Holzapfel – Girl, you might've made my head spin a little with your feedback on this one, but I appreciate your dedication and your willingness to tell me how you really feel. It's one of the reasons I think you're awesome!

Amber Willis – As always, you were there for me, getting in your feedback while juggling all the other things in your life. Thank you for allowing me to be a part of your life. It means a lot.

Karen DiGaetano – I definitely like the suggestions. Keep them coming because that's what makes a great beta reader.

Wander Aguiar and Andrey Bahia – You two are class acts in every way. Thank you SO much for giving my characters life. Working with you is a true pleasure and I look forward to what the future has in store for us.

Jonny James - YOU are the man. I've had the honor of working with you and I've got the pleasure of calling you friend. You're going all the way to the top! I know it. Keep being you!

Thank you to my proofreaders. Jenna Underwood, Annette Elens,

Theresa Martin, and Sara Gross. Not only do you catch my blunders, you are my friends and it is an honor to call you that.

I also have to thank my street team – Naughty (and nice) Girls – Your unwavering support is something I will never take for granted. So, thank you Traci Hyland, Maureen Ames, Erin Lewis, Jackie Wright, Chris Geier, Kara Hildebrand, Shannon Thompson, Tracy Barbour, Nadine Hunter, Toni Thompson, and Rachelle Newham.

I can't forget my copyeditor, Amy at Blue Otter Editing. Thank goodness I've got you to catch all my punctuation, grammar, and tense errors.

Nicole Nation 2.0 for the constant support and love. You've been there for me from almost the beginning. This group of ladies has kept me going for so long, I'm not sure I'd know what to do without them.

And, of course, YOU, the reader. Your emails, messages, posts, comments, tweets... they mean more to me than you can imagine. I thrive on hearing from you, knowing that my characters and my stories have touched you in some way keeps me going. I've been known to shed a tear or two when reading an email because you simply bring so much joy to my life with your support. I thank you for that.

About Nicole Edwards

New York Times and *USA Today* bestselling author Nicole Edwards lives in the suburbs of Austin, Texas with her husband and their youngest of three children. The two older ones have flown the coup, while the youngest is in high school. When Nicole is not writing about sexy alpha males and sassy, independent women, she can often be found with a book in hand or attempting to keep the dogs happy. You can find her hanging out on social media and interacting with her readers - even when she's supposed to be writing.

Want to know what's coming next? Or how about see some fun stuff related to Nicole's books? You can find these, as well as tons of other stuff on Nicole's website. You can also find A Day in the Life blog posts, which are short stories about your favorite characters, as well as exclusive contests by joining Nicole Nation on Nicole's website. To join, simply click **Log In | Register** in the menu. ,

If you're interested in keeping up to date on any new releases and preorders, you can sign up for Nicole's notification newsletter. This only goes out when she's got important information to share.

Want a simple, fast way to get updates on new releases? Sign up for text messaging. If you are in the U.S. simply text NICOLE to 64600 or sign up on her website. She promises not to spam your phone. This is just her way of letting you know what's happening because Nicole knows you're busy, but if you're anything like her, you always have your phone on you.

Connect with Nicole

Website: NicoleEdwardsAuthor.com

Facebook: /Author.Nicole.Edwards

Instagram: NicoleEdwardsAuthor

Twitter: @NicoleEAuthor

DEAD HEAT RANCH
Boots Optional
Betting on Grace
Overnight Love

DEVIL'S BEND
Chasing Dreams
Vanishing Dreams

MISPLACED HALOS
Protected in Darkness
Salvation in Darkness
Bound in Darkness

OFFICE INTRIGUE
Office Intrigue
Intrigued Out of the Office
Their Rebellious Submissive
Their Famous Dominant
Their Ruthless Sadist
Their Naughty Student
Their Fairy Princess

PIER 70
Reckless
Fearless
Speechless
Harmless
Clueless

SNIPER 1 SECURITY
Wait for Morning
Never Say Never
Tomorrow's Too Late

SOUTHERN BOY MAFIA / DEVIL'S PLAYGROUND
Beautifully Brutal
Without Regret
Beautifully Loyal
Without Restraint

Made in the USA
Coppell, TX
11 April 2021